Treasure & Treachery in the Amazon

BROTHERS at ARMS

JOHN J. HORN

THE MEN OF GRIT SERIES

Brothers At Arms: Treasure & Treachery in the Amazon

The Boy Colonel: A Soldier Without a Name

Secret of the Lost Settlement: The Duty of Warriors

ISBN 978-1-930133-46-4

Cover Design and Photography by Daniel R. Prislovsky

To my brother by blood, who has
always been there for me.

To my brother by marriage, for the
adventures the future holds.

To my brothers by friendship, for the
many memories shared.

Table of Contents

Chapter 1

I grasped the cold pistol handle and squinted at the target. The little wooden sparrow swung in the wind, a cord looped round its neck and tied to the old oak above. It looked very volatile, dangling there, and very small.

"Do you want first or second shot?" asked my brother, Chester.

"I don't want any shot at all, Chester. You know how little accustomed I am to firearms."

Chester chuckled. "Yes, I know, that's why I loaded for you. But you must learn sometime. What if some gent insults your favorite philosopher? At any rate, I'll take first shot to show you how it's done."

I gladly stepped aside. He looked the sportsman, as he cocked the hammer, and leveled the barrel at that swinging bird, but he was still a boy. Only two days before he had come to me to ask how many eggs were in four dozen.

"Two points for a head shot, one for a body, and none if you miss," he said.

I knew the shot was coming, but I still jumped at that unnerving crack. The smoke cleared quickly, but the string was empty, and the headless bird lay at the foot of the old door that Chester had propped against the hillside. A 'bullet-catcher,' he called the door.

"That would be two points." Chester grinned at me as he looped the string round a new carving. "Your turn."

I gulped. The pistol I must use lay on a table, alongside the powder, bullets, oily rags, and other assorted paraphernalia.

The moment I leveled the pistol it became illogically heavy. The barrel simply would not point straight, and the moment I thought I had it reasonably centered, that ridiculous bird would swing away. I thought about measuring the trajectory, but the effect would have been nullified by the target's incalculable swinging.

A pebble was under my right boot. I nudged it away and planted both feet firmly in the wet grass.

I closed my eyes, tried to close my eardrums, and pulled the trigger.

Crack. The acrid sulfur smell attacked my nostrils.

Chester coughed. "That would be none."

I opened my eyes. The sparrow was still swinging.

Chester strode to the door and scraped his knife-blade over the scarred planks. "Lawrence, these are all old. You missed the whole double-door!"

I pressed the pistol back into its case and fished for my handkerchief. "I suppose there is a reason I don't come out here very often."

Chester snorted. "There isn't a reason for that, that *is* a reason, the reason you can't hit a double-door at ten paces! Why, you couldn't have done worse if you had closed your eyes and fired blind!"

I stiffened. "Well, I suppose you might say that in a way, I did." I found the handkerchief in my waist-coat pocket and used it to wipe stray powder grains from my hands.

"What are you talking about?" Chester asked.

"I had my eyes closed."

Chester's expression resembled that of a fellow who is having an elephant stuffed down his throat.

"But—but—you can't do that!" he spluttered.

"I just did."

"But—but—you can't!"

"Chester, I both can, and did."

He scowled at me as he stroked his pistol with an oil-blotched rag.

Our home's chimney stacks poked over the gentle hill behind us, beckoning to my cozy, mahogany-paneled room and the open book laying on my desk. Chester was still scowling and muttering. Perhaps I could spare a moment to give him a lesson.

"Look here, Chester."

He scowled.

"Now, in the eighteen years of my life, I can remember firing a pistol no more than five times. You shoot every day. If you want a comparable competition, I will be happy to take any test you like in mathematics, history, philosophy, theology, or science."

"You can take the test for both of us." Chester dropped the pistol into its case and slammed the cover. "You go back inside and stick with your school books, and become some stuck-up philosopher professor. I intend to have adventures, not walk around in black robes and wish for the days of Socrates."

The world has greatly advanced since the days of Socrates, but I didn't bother to say so. It was the same old argument, and Chester showed no signs of succumbing to logic. Still, one might hope.

"Good pistol-shooting and fencing won't make you a famous man, Chester. Look at Alfred the Great, or even Alexander, who you like so much—he had an adventurous life, but he also knew geography, mathematics, necessary sciences—"

"Oh, bother. I don't want to be Alexander the Great. I want to be Chester the Great." He leaned on the pistol case and stared at me, eyes wide. "You be patient, Law, old boy, and perhaps, when I've tired of astounding the world and exploring new places, I'll send you some real birds to shoot at from Africa."

"You?" I shook my head. "Stop deluding yourself. You have no self-control, no concept of the deeper things of life, and no interest in aught but exercise and foolish novels."

"No self-control?" He clenched his fists and slammed the table. "How dare you?"

His outburst surprised me. He rarely paid attention to my words.

Chester stepped closer. "Do you think rising at six each morning to ride, and standing still for hours to perfect my shooting stance, and fencing till I vomit, requires no self-control?"

He swept up the pistol-case and tucked it beneath his arm. "Can't make a name for myself, eh? You wait, Professor. Some day you'll hear the name Stoning and know that you've something to live up to."

"Indeed?" I yawned. "Do let me know when the day arrives."

"It'll be sooner than you think."

Chapter 2

The next day, I stood in the hall outside my father's study. I summoned my courage, eased the door open, and peered inside. The late-afternoon sunlight penetrated the window in the wall on the right and lit the room in a dying glow. Slanting columns of dust particles floated in the sunbeams. My father sat at the far end of the table in his usual red velvet chair, pen in hand. Jagged stacks of books coated the polished mahogany, which flashed little stabs of light at me.

I cleared my throat. "I'm afraid that I have some bad news for you, Father."

I stepped to the near end of his table and clasped my right wrist with my left hand.

He blinked at me. "Oh—Lawrence—how are you? Please, shut the door, it disturbs my concentration. Much better. What were you saying?"

"I have bad news, Father."

"Bad news?" He set down the pen and folded his hands. The room smelled of sherry and sweet ink. "A philosopher must be prepared for any possibility, whether he finds it to be advantageous or disadvantageous to himself. What is your news?"

"Chester has run away."

"Run away? Do you mean that he is exercising, or do you mean that he has left this place of abode with no intention of returning?"

"The latter, sir."

My father raked thick fingers through his oily hair and wiped an inky sleeve over his forehead. "Hmm. I hadn't thought much of it before, but now that you mention it, he has been somewhat restless recently."

He pulled a five-inch stack of papers out of the top right-hand drawer and scratched a line of words on the top sheet. He mumbled something, then began the next line.

I coughed.

He glanced up. "Ah, you're still here. What reasons did Chester give for departing?"

"He didn't honor me with his confidence, sir, but if I may conjecture, I expect it has something to do with last night's altercation."

"Altercation? Oh, that." He frowned at me. "Lawrence, I have told you that altercations are unworthy of philosophers."

"You have, Father, but as Chester is not a philosopher, I believe that he is quite capable of altercations."

His wrinkled forehead contracted farther. "Chester is a hot-headed, impetuous boy." He thrust a pinch of snuff into his left nostril and sneezed. "He kept asking me about adventure, or some such nonsense, and he had the impudence to scorn the immortal phrase of Socrates—'I know that I am intelligent, because I know that I know nothing,' when I offered it during our philosophical disagreement."

I could easily imagine Chester's reaction to the oft-repeated quote.

"Most likely, Father. At any rate, he left on the early coach this morning for Liverpool. He placed a note on his dresser, stating that he intends to join the British Auxiliary Legion, which is forming there."

"A soldier!" My father struggled to his feet. "War!" He reached stiffly for his glass of sherry and drained half of it. The glass shook as he put it down.

"A soldier. But—that cannot be. He! A soldier." He eased back into his chair and looked at me over the book-stacks. "Lawrence—he can't be a soldier."

I shook my head. "Not to dispute the point, Father, but I believe that he can. He's eighteen, old enough to join, and he shoots, and fences, and boxes all day, so he should be physically acceptable."

My father's hands played with his books mechanically, but his eyes were looking at me—or rather through me. I switched to clasping my left wrist. "Father?"

His eyes focused. "Oh, yes, Lawrence, you're here. You said—you said that Chester is a soldier?"

I narrowed my eyebrows. Surely, this wasn't my philosophic father, always calm, never ruffled. "Yes, sir, he intends to be one."

"Oh, but you must stop him."

"Sir?"

He waved his arms. "You must stop him! He cannot be a soldier. The army has destroyed our family."

I frowned. "But—no one from our family has been in the army."

"No, no, my brother is in the army. He could have done so much with his life, and instead he joined the army. He was a corporal—he still is, I'm told, in Siberia."

"Oh. I didn't know."

"And my sister. She married a soldier, a colonel." He sighed. "She died, and I'm told that her husband went mad. He was a respected man, and grew up with our family."

"I'm sorry, Father. You never told me this."

He shook himself, as if waking from a dream. "Have I not? No, I suppose not. Little human tragedies should not affect a philosopher."

He clasped his hands behind his back and paced the far end of the study. "Socrates said that 'wars and revolutions, and battles, are due simply and solely to the body and its desires.' Socrates was a great man. No good can come from fighting."

"Then why did you let Chester fence, and box, and shoot?" I asked.

"Because he wanted to, of course. It is all for the experiment, my son, a generational experiment." That scientific gleam entered his eye. He fingered the stack of papers. "I have told you many times, Lawrence, that you are an experiment. So was I. I was raised strictly, and my brother William was allowed to do as he liked. What he liked was to become a soldier, and he has since done nothing for the good of mankind."

I nodded. "Yes, sir. That's why you've raised me strictly, and let Chester do as he liked. But, is not letting Chester go to war a part of the experiment?"

He fumbled with his cigar-box, lit a cigar, puffed, and tossed it absentmindedly onto the carpet. I extinguished the burning end with my boot. He would probably burn the house down some day.

"No." His voice was firm. "He must not follow his uncle's path. You must bring him back."

My spirits fell. "Bring him back, sir?"

"Yes, bring him back. Lawrence, this will be an excellent occasion to prove your responsibility and intelligence. I commission you to follow your brother and bring him home safely. Do not return without him, and ensure that he comes to no harm. If you should experience any troubles, write me immediately, so that I may make record of them."

I unclasped my wrist. "Yes, sir."

The usual dreamy, absent look slowly settled back on his face, and he waved me away.

"Go now, Lawrence, and have the butler bring in my lunch."

"I'm sorry, sir, but it's supper-time."

"Is it? Very well, then have him bring supper."

I hesitated. "Don't you think, Father, that it might be beneficial to let him seek adventure, and realize the realities of the world?"

"The butler?"

"No, Chester."

"Oh, Chester again." He shook his head decidedly. "No, I don't. He shall not be a soldier."

I retired. I expected to be sent after Chester, but it was very inconvenient, as

I was deeply engaged with Gibbon's *Decline and Fall of the Roman Empire.* Chester always picked the worst times for his adventures.

I found our servant, James, and ordered him to saddle my horse.

"Yes, sir." He bowed respectfully. "Do you wish me to notify your mother?"

"Where is she?"

"Visiting the new occupants of the Halmond estate, sir."

"No, there's no need. Even if she returns before us, I doubt that she will notice our absence."

We waited on the highroad for the Liverpool coach until twilight. A gusty wind blew, flecked with droplets of rain. Thunder rumbled in distant counties. Finally, the rumbling was varied by rattling, and the coach appeared.

James took my horse's bridle, and I paid the fare and entered the coach. Sweat and tobacco fumes thickened the air, sharpened by a tangy odor. A rotund gentleman in a tight waistcoat sat with his back to the rear wall, clutching a leather bag between ample calves. He looked to be a professed patron of the pastry maker's, and as there was hardly room to spare on his seat, I chose the opposite bench, half-occupied by a lean foreigner.

"Be careful for the peels." The foreigner nodded at a pile of orange-peels on the vacant seat.

I brushed the soggy mess off and turned to sit down. The rotund man stared at me through a thick monocle.

His voice was high. "You're not a robber, are you?"

I paused, half-sitting, half-standing. "Excuse me, sir?"

Crack. The driver's whip cut through a thunder-roll and the floor slipped away from my feet. I clutched empty air and bowled head first into the fat gentleman's stomach.

"Help! Help!" he squeaked, clawing my face. "Robber! He's got me!"

The lean man snorted, and I hastily clambered back to my seat.

"Don't touch me!" the fat fellow cried. "I'm armed!" He thrust his arm into his bag and struggled with some lengthy object inside, while his monocle bounced around in his eye-socket but somehow managed to stay attached. After a few minutes of rooting, his arm emerged holding a rusty pistol and presented it at my face, two of his fleshy fingers trembling around the trigger.

The lean man snatched it away.

"What are you doing, fool?" His voice was shrill.

The pastry-patron stuffed himself into the corner and pointed at me. "He assaulted me! Did you not see his brutal assault?"

"The carriage jolted, and he was thrown onto you. I feel very much like myself throwing on you!"

The fat gentleman blinked. "Doing what?"

"Oh, I apologize." The foreigner laid the pistol down and performed a sitting bow. "I sometimes reverse my words. My meaning was that I would not mind to throw myself on you."

The fat gentleman coughed. "I—I'm sorry, but I am rather nervous. You see, I've been reading of the highway-men and their methods of robbing unsuspecting victims." He tried to smile at me. "Please accept my apologies, young man."

I was heartily tired of the whole affair, so I accepted his apology and arranged the lumpy cushions as best I could. The headrest was slick with a generation of hair oil.

The next hours passed quietly inside, though the thunderstorm quickly broke and the elements raged outside. Lightning flashes sporadically lit the interior, usually showing the fat gentleman occupying himself with a black flask.

The foreigner offered me an orange.

"Thank you." I peeled it and bit into the juicy fruit. "Very fresh. Pardon me for being inquisitive, but I interpret your accent as originating in Spain. What part of the country are you from?"

He smiled. "Basque country. I am an archeologist, I travel the world, but Spain is my home. Men call me Sabas, because I love old things."

Another lightning-flash lighted his face. It was sharp, centered by a somewhat beakish nose, and his cheeks looked pinched and unhealthy, but he appeared to be in good spirits. I judged that he was between thirty and thirty-five, though his back hunched like an older man's.

"Your language is beautiful, and in my opinion is superior even to French and Italian. It is quick and passionate, but also regal."

"You know my language?" Sabas raised his eyebrows, showing a pair of piercing dark eyes. "You surprise me. What is your name?"

"Lawrence Stoning."

"Ah! This gentleman was just speaking of that name."

The fat gentleman rapidly tucked the bottle behind his back. "Oh, yes, why, I was but repeating the common talk." He coughed. "Your—your father has *quite* a name, young man."

His words had a deeper meaning, but I pretended not to notice. "I suppose you mean as a philosopher?" I asked coldly.

"Oh, yes, of course, and, as a man with—er, unique tastes." He tapped his nose.

I frowned. "I doubt my father would wish for his tastes to be discussed in such a public manner."

"Oh," Sabas interrupted, "I am sure he meant no harm, he simply was making—what is the word? conversation, on this lonely road."

"Lonely?" Fabric rustled, as if the fat gentleman was scooting on his seat. "Yes, it is lonely. And dark." He thrust his head out the window and tried to screw his neck upwards, but his thick jowls hindered the move. "Do you think the guard above is trustworthy?" he asked, pulling his head back in.

Sabas shrugged his bony shoulders. "How should I know? Do you have money with you, that you are afraid so—so afraid, I mean?"

"Money?" I couldn't see his face, but his voice sounded pale. "No, no, I have no particular money with me, why do you ask?"

Sabas shrugged again. "Oh, no reason, but you seem to be so fearful of robbers."

The gentleman coughed and laid a pudgy hand on my knee. "If—if there were to be any—any problems, young sir, would you be capable of defending this coach with a pistol?"

I thought about the shooting match. "I can pull a trigger, but I have very little experience with firearms."

"Then—you don't have a pistol in your bag?"

"No. Much better, I have Gibbon's *Decline and Fall of the Roman Empire*." I stroked the book's smooth leather binding. I should be at my desk, annotating the volume.

Someone shouted outside the window. There was a sharp crack and a flash of light, less bright than lightning, and something heavy thudded on the roof. I groped for the window sash, but a horse neighed and the carriage scraped to a halt, catapulting the fat gentleman into me. Something wet poured down my face. *Blood*?

I licked the corner of my lip. *Rum*. That explained the black flask.

The door flung open and a lantern thrust inside.

"Oot!" barked a rough voice. The light blinded me for a moment, but I caught glimpses of a fellow with a dirty rag tied beneath his eyes. "Oot o' the coach, all of ye, if ye want to see the light o' day again!"

A pincer-like hand gripped my forearm and wrenched me out the door. I threw up my left arm to protect my head and plowed thick mud. Slime filled my nostrils. A boot struck my side and I rolled over, pain shooting through my ribs. I was in shock. *God, help me!*

I raised my face from the mud and looked desperately around for a way of escape. All was black save for the lantern's flickering circle of light.

Sabas stepped out calmly, but the fat gentleman blubbered over his bag and stuffed himself into the coach's farthest corner. Our driver, pale and trembling, leaned against the coach with another masked man standing next to him, pistol in hand. A groan from the roof explained the first shot, and the guard's absence.

"Git oot!" shouted the first robber. The fat gentleman whimpered. The robber leaned inside and stuck his pistol barrel an inch from his victim's nose. "Ye know what it's loike to 'ave 'ot lead rip through ye skin?" The fat gentleman clutched his bag and cowered deeper into the corner. "Ye're about to if ye don't git oot right now!"

The fat gentleman sniffled and crawled toward the door. With a brutal laugh, the robber grasped his collar and heaved him into the mud.

"I says, Bill, slim pickin's tonight," the second robber growled as he peered into the empty coach.

"No names, ye fool." The first ruffian scowled at me and jerked his thumb up. I struggled to my feet, grasping my side to subdue the fire within.

The robber grinned at our fat friend and pulled him up. "This gent ain't slim. Drop the bag, guv'nor."

"No—no—no! This is a dream! Robberies don't happen anymore!"

"Don't they, now?" The other ruffian laughed. "Then this niver happened neither. Drop the bag." He grabbed a corner of the satchel and tore it from the gentleman's hands. A stream of guineas splatted in the mud.

"That's more like it!" The first robber scooped them up, his fingers trembling with eagerness. "Check the next 'un."

Sabas glared at them. "*Esto es una indignidad!*" he said angrily, arching his back to his full height.

"I says, Bill, he's a foreigner." The robber grabbed Sabas's watch chain and swung it beneath the lantern until the light sparkled on the polished gold.

"I said no names, fool. Check his pockets. Gold is gold, foreign or no."

Sabas spouted a string of Spanish protestations, but the robbers paid no heed. I ground my canine teeth and prepared for the coming indignity. *Wait! What's that Sabas is saying?* He wasn't simply arguing with the robbers, he was talking to me!

"*Derribe al hombre.*" Brilliant! He was telling me to knock down the robber closest to me. I cautiously swiveled my head. Both robbers were focused on Sabas. I looked at him, and he returned my gaze, then shut his eyes.

What should I do? If I remained still, they would probably rob me and let me go in peace. If I fought back—*where's Chester the one time he would be helpful?* I sucked a mouthful of air to soothe my aching ribs. I wanted to strike the villain, but something kept me from doing it. My heart was hammering. A deeper fear grasped me. Was I a coward?

They finished rifling Sabas. Hot vapor, almost tears, clouded my vision. I felt so impotent. What to do? The robber next to me turned. *I mustn't be a coward.* I squeezed my eyelids shut and tried to lash out with my right arm, but my blood seemed to freeze, and I toppled into him instead with my arms round his neck. We fell.

Crack. Lightning and a pistol flashed together. The robber cursed and dug his elbow into my stomach. My ribs contracted, fighting for air, and he wrenched free from my grasp. A moment later he collapsed onto me, this time without a quiver. Sabas grabbed my hand and pulled me up.

"You think quick, boy, but you fight much more slow. I said knock, not grab. Next time, hit your man." He flashed a smile at me and wiped his muddy hands on the robber's trousers.

I shook my whirling head. "I—I suppose I'm not much accustomed to knocking men down. Thank you for rescuing me."

Raindrops dripped down my nose. My coat was filthy, wet with mud and falling rain. Somehow, it all seemed far away, a slight inconvenience, compared to what I had just survived.

"How were you so calm?" I asked.

Sabas smiled again. "I am from Spain. Many are the robbers there. This was a practice for good—good practice, I mean, for I am traveling home now. Perhaps I will meet more robbers soon?"

The driver was already petting and soothing his horses, and our fat friend had crawled back into the coach with his torn satchel clutched to his stomach. The first robber lay in the road, blood oozing from a hole in his forehead.

My stomach churned. "Was it really necessary to kill the fellow? Couldn't you have simply disabled him?"

Sabas shrugged. "What is one more dead robber?"

The dirty rag had fallen from the man's face. He was young, clean-shaven, with wisps of blond hair curling out beneath his cap. I shuddered.

"Once again, thank you. If I may return the favor at any time, it will be my pleasure."

"Thank you, but I think that cannot be. I have a long job in Spain. Unless you would like to come there, I do not think I can use you."

"Then I'm afraid that you won't be able to use me. I'm searching for a prodigal, and the moment I return him, I must make up for lost time with my books."

Chapter 3

Liverpool. My ribs still ached as I stepped from the coach, and the muscles in my back felt as flexible as frozen sticks. I twisted my lower back until it began popping like firecrackers on Guy Fawkes Day.

I was a boy when last at Liverpool, stuffed into my Sunday best to be displayed to some of my mother's aristocratic friends. That was the last time she took me visiting. I think I grew too old, thus making her seem older in comparison.

My memory of Liverpool was that of an enormous, bustling world full of danger and excitement. It didn't look as big to me now, but it was moving just as fast as I remembered. Cabs raced past with barking dogs at the horses' heels and sweepers scrambling out of the way. Businessmen strutted down the muddy sidewalks with confident gait, while dirty ne'er-do-wells slouched against walls and eyed prospective pockets.

I meditated for a moment on the sidewalk. Should I change my muddy clothing or eat first? Dignity prompted the former, but my growling stomach prompted the latter. Being robbed apparently generates an abnormally insistent appetite. I threaded the early-morning crowds and located a clean corner tavern.

The waiter was less clean than the establishment, carrying a healthy supply of grease and sour beer on his shirt, but my stomach was too insistent to be picky.

"Glass o' beer?" he inquired.

I shook my head and sank into a chair. "Tea, and make it strong."

He cocked an eye at my clothes, shrugged, and entered the kitchen, returning in a few moments with a cup of tea and a tray of steaming biscuits. "From the country, eh?"

"Yes." I demolished a biscuit and washed the last orange bits out of my teeth with the tea.

"No beer, and from the country, eh?" The waiter folded his arms. "You a temperance man?"

I frowned. "What does it matter to you?"

"I don't like 'em. Too stuck-up and priggy."

"Then don't associate with them. Do you have a paper?"

He pulled a greasy *London Times* out of his shirt and plopped it on my table.

"There's a good murder on page four. Reporter's got flare."

I scanned through the greasy pages, trying to keep my fingers away from the previous reader's oily thumbprints. *Grisly Murder, Butcher Suspected, full story from Alexander Somerset*. I turned the page. If I wanted to disgust myself I'd buy a penny dreadful.

A bold heading on the next page attracted me.

British Legion Completing Last Preparations—Men ready to take a crack at the Dons.

I flipped to the front. It was that day's paper, 3 July, 1835. I must find Chester quickly before his impetuous nature got him in trouble. At least the paper didn't mention him assaulting the night-watch or burning down the city. I dropped a coin on the table and snapped my fingers at the waiter.

"Do you know where they are recruiting for the British Legion?" I asked.

"I might."

"You might?"

"That's right." He coughed, and glanced at the coin. "Information don't come cheap in Liverpool."

So that was his game. "You expect me to pay for an answer to my question?"

"I ain't forcin' you to do nothin'."

My ribs twinged at the thought of force. He rubbed his palms together and coughed again. I wasn't about to pay good money for such a slight bit of information, but I didn't mind a mental exercise. Everyone has a chink in his armor, and I would find his. I rubbed my chin and tried to look innocent.

"Surely, I'm not the first country lad with the same question?"

"That's the truth." The fellow snatched my cup and wiped the rim with his shirt. "I'm tired of you glory-hunters, and I ain't ashamed to say it."

I rubbed my lip. "And yet, they must have brought some good money into these quiet lanes?"

He snorted. "They should 'ave, but the wharf-rat taverners won't let 'em come. Keeps all the business to 'emselves."

"Indeed." His armor was more than chinked—it was rust-eaten. "Surely, though, the recruiters must be steadier fellows, who know better than to consort with the common herd at the wharves."

"I haven't seen one for a week. It's all those wharf-rat taverners' doing."

I rose calmly and nodded good-day. "I must be going now, but thank you for your information."

He blinked. "Information? What information?"

"Why, for telling me that the recruiters are stationed on the wharves, of course."

I smiled a quiet, victorious smile, and strode away to the river. Now, to find Chester.

The docks were teeming with life, and the morning fog hung heavy with the smell of tar, hemp, and rotten fish. I was looking for a recruiter, but one found me first.

"Hello, Stoning, you're here earlier than I expected."

I spun around. A tall, uniformed man with a massive mustache and honest gray eyes was smiling at me.

"I beg your pardon, sir, but how do you know my name?"

He frowned and pushed his garrison cap higher on his head. "Why, Chester, you haven't forgotten me already? You just signed the papers at my station less than—well, less than eighteen hours ago."

"I'm sorry, sir, but I believe that you have mistaken me for my brother, Chester. I am Lawrence Stoning."

He stared at me. "But—that's impossible! You're the spitting image of young Chester Stoning who signed his papers and joined the British Legion just yesterday!"

So he had already joined. "Actually, sir, I rarely indulge in spitting, and I am certainly not made in his image. The mistake is easy enough. We are twins, Chester and I, and it is also nearly impossible for a stranger to discriminate between our voices."

"Twins!" The sergeant shrugged and pressed his cap back down. "Well, that's a new one. I say, you could play some devilish pranks in the regiment, if you had the mind. What do you say? Would you like to follow in your brother's footsteps?"

"To be perfectly honest, I try to keep as far away from his footsteps as possible. At the moment, however, I *am* looking for him. Would you happen to know where he is?"

"No, but he'll probably be along in an hour or so. We sail in a few days."

He seemed a reasonable fellow, so I decided to immediately begin the process of rescuing Chester from himself.

"I'm sorry to say that Chester has run away from home without my father's permission, so I'll need to unsign him, or do whatever is required. Is there a fee?"

"You want to get him out of the Legion?" The sergeant frowned at me. "Young fellow, you've no idea how hard it is to get good men these days." He hesitated a moment, then motioned me toward a barrel covered in papers.

"Chester is but a boy, Sergeant—"

"Reynard's the name." Sergeant Reynard sat down and folded his arms. "I thought you were the same age. If you call him a boy, wouldn't you think of yourself as the same?"

Well-reasoned, according to the geometrical proof. "No sir, I don't, but Chester has always been the younger type, if you understand my meaning. How hard will it be to get him out?"

Sergeant Reynard pulled the ends of his mustache. "Well, you'll need my signature, and his. I suppose you can have mine, if you say your guv'nor's hard up against it, but I'm not so sure you'll get his."

"I'm quite confident on that score, thank you, Sergeant."

Chester finally arrived, swaggering through the fog with some ridiculous object on his head. He jumped at sight of me and the swagger melted into one of the many puddles.

"Hullo, old chap," he said, scanning me from toe to head. "You're worthy of a painting. Have you been studying mud?"

I looked down at my coat and realized that I had forgotten to change. Of course, Chester didn't have the decency to keep a closed mouth about it.

I shook hands coldly. "It's good to see you as well, Chester. I've come to take you home."

"Take me home?" He snorted. "Law, old boy, I've joined the British Legion. Taken the King's shilling, and all that rot. I've an appointment with the Dons in Spain. Go home? Impossible."

"Chester, Father is quite adamant that you come home."

"Adamant?"

"A type of rock, synonymous with firm, determined, and in this case, insistent. Look, Chester, I've wasted precious time and a great deal of personal comfort to follow Father's orders to bring you home, and I intend to do it. Sign the sergeant's paper, and we'll be going."

Chester looked at the sergeant, then at the paper on the table, and then at me.

"Now, Law, I've three things to say. Two, actually, but that's just as important. One, you've no authority over me, two, I'm awfully sorry that Father doesn't like me going, but I need to do more with my life than rot on our little estate, and three, I'm not going home." He snapped his fingers. "I say, that was three after all."

Was my brain interpreting his words correctly? Chester was defying both me and our father, and there was no way to get him home without his agreement.

"Chester, I have Father's definite orders to bring you home safely. I'm not going home without you."

He shrugged. "Then it may be some time before you see that mahogany writing desk again. I'm going to Spain."

I wanted to stamp my foot. What could I do? He was stubborn as a mule, though not as stable. If he said he wasn't coming home, then he wasn't coming home. Father's orders were clear. Bring him back safely. I saw only one way to do so.

"Very well, then I'm coming with you." I picked up a pen. "Where do I sign, Sergeant?"

Chester's jaw distended vertically. "You! Join the army! Why, you crazy chap, you'd have the Dons dying of laughter! You, the professor, trudging through knee-high mud with a knapsack on your back and a musket in your arms! You can't hit a door, let alone a Don."

His words galled me. Certainly, I was not exactly built from soldierly material, but I wasn't the fool he was painting me as. I tapped the table impatiently. "That's nonsense, Chester. Officers don't slog through mud with muskets in their arms."

He exploded in laughter. "Do you really think," he managed to get out, "that you can become an officer by signing a recruiter's paper? Oh, Law, I nearly think I should bring you along, if only for laughs round the campfire."

I stared at him. "But—you're an officer, aren't you?"

"Not a bit of it. I'm a private."

"A private! A Stoning, as a private?"

Sergeant Reynard coughed. "A private's an honorable post, young gentleman. I started there myself."

"Perhaps it is, but not for a Stoning. Chester, if you're honestly bent upon this Spanish war, you must go as an officer."

He shrugged. "How?"

I searched my brain. I remembered reading that commissions were bought—that was it, they were bought by people with influence.

"Mother has influence. I'll write Father, and she'll pull strings. You know Mother; she couldn't stand a Stoning being in the common ranks."

"I didn't think she'd worry about me either way." Chester tossed his head. "Fine, you get me a commission, and I'll take it. Just don't blame me when you get killed over there."

He flicked his boat, or hat, or whatever he had on his head, and stalked away. I sighed.

Chapter 4

Chester's lodgings were small and smelled of the previous lodger's tobacco, but the blazing fire he had stuffed into the tiny hearth dispelled the physical shadows.

I rested my notebook on the scarred table and opened to a blank page. This wouldn't be an easy letter to word. Not only must I explain that we were not returning, but I must ask for two commissions in the British Auxiliary Legion. That would require some significant string-pulling, and in a very short space of time.

Screech—scrape—scratch. A cacophony of discordant notes attacked my ears.

I jammed my thumbs into my ear canals and turned on Chester. "What *are* you doing?"

He was puffing into something cupped between his hands, but he stopped and raised his eyebrows at me. "Making music. What's your problem?"

"What is that?"

"A harmonica." It resumed screeching.

I clenched my teeth and tried to focus on the blank paper before me. *My dear father, it is my unpleasant duty—what deaf man invented the harmonica?—to inform you that Chester has declined—the fellow's friends must also have been deaf—to come home according to your direction—*

I dropped my pen. "Stop, Chester, I can't concentrate."

He growled, but desisted. I returned to my letter in peace.

After four minutes my pen nib broke and I had to select a new one from my satchel. Chester was whittling a piece of kindling half the size of his knife.

"Chester, do you think it's possible to get two commissions at this short notice?"

"No idea, I'm sure." He licked his knife blade and squinted at the reflection. "Mother knows a number of big wigs, but it's an awful lot to ask. By the by, do you really think you could command soldiers?"

I found the right nib and fitted it to my pen.

"I would certainly do my best," I replied, after some deliberation. "I hope you understand, Chester, that I'm coming from no desire of my own. The only reason I *am* coming is to follow Father's order to bring you back safely."

"Your sentiment is heartwarming," he said dryly, "but I don't see how you'll do even that. You'll have your own men to take care of, and your own missions."

"What's that?" *My own missions*? I hadn't thought of that. But that would mean— "won't I be with you?"

Chester laughed. "A few meals a week, perhaps. Law, if you go as an officer, you're wherever they assign you."

I blinked. It made sense, now that I thought of it, but it was a horrid, dastardly sense. *Whoever invented armies in the first place*? I twined my fingers and gazed into the fire. That was that. If I couldn't do my duty as an officer, I must sip a more bitter brew.

"Very well, then I must go as a soldier."

He looked up from his knife and squinted at me. "I thought you said that Stonings were above the rank and file?"

"I did, but duty is duty. Father told me to remain with you, so that's what I must do."

He shook his head. "Law, you never cease to amaze. Still, that won't put you much closer. They can put you wherever they want. It's highly unlikely you'd even be put under my command."

"What?"

"You heard me. Honestly, Law, the only way you could stick with me as you want, would be to be my servant."

His servant? My mouth nearly dropped open. *Travel to Spain, be a servant, to Chester!*

"Obviously," Chester continued, oblivious to my staring eyes, "you aren't going as my servant, so I really don't see how you can do what you want."

My throat felt dry and raspy. *A servant. For Chester.* My duty was clear, but the path to that duty was as cloudy as a ten-year-old's blotting paper. I forced words over my dry tongue.

"Are servants soldiers or civilians?" I croaked.

"Servants?" He shrugged. "Civilians, why?"

"They can't be transferred to other places, or other masters?"

"Well, not that I know of, unless they start robbing chicken-coops, or some such nonsense. Why?"

I looked down at the half-written letter. *Two commissions.* I poised my pen, bit my lip—and struck out 'two.'

"I'll do it."

"Do what?"

"I'll be your servant."

I'm not certain whether it was entirely astonishment, or a combination of astonishment and exaggeration, but at any rate, Chester's seat fell backwards and he followed. A moment more and he was up and at my side.

"A servant? Did you say, a servant?"

"Are you deaf, Chester? I said I'll be your servant."

"But—but—" he wandered back to his chair, picked it up, and slowly sat down. "Lawrence, I can only have one servant. A servant would wash my clothes, cook my meals, pitch my tent—you can't be my servant. You're my brother!"

"I'm well aware of that last fact, thank you." I steeled my nerves and finished the rest of the letter. I could visualize my father sitting in his chair, slicing the seal, and staring at my words. A groan, probably, a sip of sherry, then two notes in our records.

We waited two days. Chester fidgeted about the docks and bought his kit while I explored the Liverpool bookshops and tried to uncover what the war in Spain was actually about. At last, the letter came, and with it an official document proclaiming Chester to be an officer in the British Auxiliary Legion. If this had been a governmental expedition, the paperwork never would have arrived in time. Even so, Mother must have some high connections.

My father's letter was simple, but also somewhat surprising.

> *Lawrence,*
>
> *I received your letter of the 3rd instant. I am very sorry. Chester disappoints me. He has not turned out as I had hoped at the beginning of this noble experiment. Your mother was regrettably emotional last night, when your letter informed us that you intend to travel as Chester's servant. I attempted to console her, but, as doubtless you have observed, she is not of a philosophical temperament. She has used her influence to procure a commission for your brother, however, which I enclose. Bring the boy back safely.*
>
> *Your obedient servant,*
> *Adam Socrates Stoning*

I say surprising because some of his sentences were short. And, he didn't even mention Socrates. He must have been more shaken than I expected. At any rate, my path was clear—and Chester's boots needed shining.

Chapter 5

"I welcome you on the behalf of Señor de la Castillo."

Chester gave his invitation to the servant and handed me his hat.

"Don't lose that, Professor."

"Yes, sir." I clacked my boot-heels together and bowed a few degrees. Three weeks of servanthood and it was just as irksome as the first day.

This was Chester's first social engagement since arriving in San Sebastian, Spain, and he was bubbling. This particular de la Castillo was a wealthy Spaniard, very friendly to the English, and thus friendly to our officers. His villa was massive, carpeted in red rugs, with paneled walls and faux silver statues of Spanish heroes. They must have done intense digging to find enough heroes for all those statues. Classical paintings framed by gold-enameled woodwork decorated the walls.

A wide ballroom floor shone under a glitter of chandeliers. This was already occupied by a flitting crowd of dandied Dons and mantilla-flapping girls. Little clumps of our officers moved among them, jesting with the men and flirting with the girls.

Chester entered the ballroom while I wandered up a flight of steps on the right into a gallery where a line of servants waited until their services were required. By the time that the last comer had arrived, most of the off-duty Legion officers were scattered over the ballroom floor.

A little knot of Spaniards and their daughters stood directly beneath me. Chester was in their midst, making some loud comments which seemed to delight the girls. I sighed, folded my arms, and leaned on the bannister. This would be a long night.

I was deep in thought-land when I felt a presence next to me. He was a little uniformed man with a red mustache that curled upwards on both ends.

"Which one's yer master?"

I tensed. "Master?"

"Right. Your officer."

"Oh." The group below had broken up. "The gentleman I serve stands there, speaking with the Spaniard by those casement windows." I pointed to the far wall.

The little fellow stared at me. "Yer a funny talker."

I stiffened. "I am a gentleman."

"Wot?" He stepped back and scanned my clothing. "That's no officer uniform. And yer carryin' two hats."

I was wearing a uniform which Chester had rummaged, saying that it made me look more like a man and less like a walking inkstand. The fabric was as abrasive as a bucket of nails, the boots were a half-inch too small, and now this impertinent servant was acting as if I was wearing leopard skins.

I stared coldly at him. "I'm a servant."

"Yer a liar."

I curled my fingers into fists, but kept them pressed to my sides. "How dare you call me a liar?"

"You just said yer a genn'lman, now you say yer a servant."

"They're not mutually exclusive. I am a gentleman, and temporarily a servant. Why does it matter to you?"

He shrugged. "Doesn't, I suppose." He twirled his mustache and stared at me for around forty-five seconds, then settled down on the bannister. "Do you dance?"

"I do not."

"Your master does."

The floor was covered with a whirling mass of dancers who spun, and twirled, and bobbed like a box-full of tops. Chester was with a group of young officers and Spanish girls, grinning. I wondered where he learned to dance.

"What do they call that?" I asked.

"They calls it a quadrille. Four sets o' partners moving together. Guess our officers are introducin' the Dons to it. Yer master's good."

"Please stop calling him my master."

He shrugged. "Have it your way."

The dance looked quite foolish to me. If you want to talk to someone, then talk to them. Pigeon-strutting round a room with a person doesn't facilitate conversation.

I thought I had made clear that I was not interested in conversation, but this little fellow was annoyingly persistent.

"Do you know," he said, "that there are prob'ly five or six staunch Carlists down there?"

A Carlist is a supporter of Don Carlos, who is trying to become King of Spain, and as the British Legion was here to fight Don Carlos, this information was surprising. I tried not to show it.

"Why do you say that?" I asked, trying to sound careless.

"Oh, common knowledge. He's got supporters everywhere, plenty here in San Sebastian. See that Don with the stub nose?" He pointed.

I swallowed my disgust at having to consort with men who pointed and discussed the physical features of others. "I see him."

"He's a wealthy merchantman. Cheerful chap, though a bit ruthless with the dollars, they say. I hear he was suspected of supportin' Carl."

"*Was* suspected?"

"That's right. Some real Carlists believed the rumors, so they came to him, and he turned 'em in."

"I see."

"See that servant?" He pointed to an old man far down the gallery, who stood back from the bannister, looking down.

"What of him?"

The little man winked. "Wouldn't surprise me if he's a spy, government or Carlist. He's been watchin' that merchant all evenin'."

I looked closer. He did seem to be watching the man through the railing. "Then shouldn't you do something about it?" I asked.

"Me?" He shook his head. "I don't care about the Don."

I snapped. "If you don't care about him, then why should I care about your opinions regarding him and his supposed watcher?"

He frowned. "What's wrong with you? Can't you stand a jolly bit of gossip?"

"It's not my habit, no."

He snorted and stalked away. Exactly the course of action I desired. I would do my duty as a servant, but my duty didn't include bearing with fellows like that.

I was heartily glad when the evening finished.

Chester was still bubbling as we strolled through the quiet streets. "You missed a wonderful time, Law. Too bad you couldn't mix with the rest of us."

"If I must make a fool of myself, I prefer to do so in private locations."

"Eh?" He cocked his head. "Oh, you think dancing's for fools. Suit yourself. I'll enjoy myself while you mope."

I had not 'moped.' I had exercised my brain on various subjects, such as calculating the amount of ground which the collective dancers tread each hour, and how much hot air was being exhaled by the collective company. My own feet were in a sorry state from tramping the rough cobblestones in those horribly tight boots. Short as my time in the army was, I realized that the entire point of military life is to make the soldier as mad as possible, then tell him to go fight the enemy. It's no surprise that we English generally win.

I woke from my thoughts to Chester oozing about the quaint homes, the balmy night air, his partners, and the relaxing town sounds. As he made this last observation a decidedly unrelaxing sound startled us. "*Venganza!*"

The black mouth of an alley yawned on our left, and this was where the cry came from. Chester bristled.

"Someone needs help!" he cried, grasping his sword-hilt.

I grabbed his arm. "Wait, Chester, it's probably some drunken soldiers quarreling. There are too many soldiers and too much wine in this town."

"*Auxilio!*"

Chester wrenched his arm away from me. "Someone needs help, and I'm going to help them." Another moment and he was dashing down the alley.

What could I do? The whole reason for my being in Spain was to keep him safe, and here he was, dashing into the first fight he could find. I sighed, flexed my aching feet, and took off after him. Footsteps ahead of us echoed in the close alleyway. Whoever needed help wasn't waiting to greet it.

The alley spilled into a lighted street. Chester leaped into the air, and I immediately discovered why by plunging through a pile of soggy rubbish. As I regained my footing I glimpsed two figures darting into the opposite alley. The nearest man was waving a foot-long knife.

Chester was panting, but gaining ground. The center of the alley was nearly pitch-black, barely lightened by a sliver of moon. Someone snarled, answered by a gasp. The knife-man was also gaining ground. A fire burned in my right side, and Chester's breathing sounded as thick as old ink, but I kept my pinched feet moving. I would bring Chester home alive.

At last, the fugitive turned to grapple with his pursuer, and we sped over the last few yards. I saw a knife in the air descending toward the exhausted fugitive. Chester tensed beside me, and I knew the moment had come. I must protect Chester, but how? I forced my last bit of energy into those cobblestones and leaped.

I don't know if I hit him, or if he hit me, but we collided and slammed into the stones. Something struck my right arm, then footsteps clattered away down the alley. I lay prone, sucking the foul alley air, and wondering why my right arm hurt.

"I say, are you alive?" Chester grabbed my collar and lifted me.

"I believe so," I managed to reply. I felt my legs, and they seemed sound. Something was wrong with my right arm, though. "Chester, can you see my arm?"

"We should leave the alley and find more light," said a soft Spanish voice.

"What did the fellow say?" Chester asked.

"He's suggesting that we move into the street so we have light." I should mention that the only Spanish words Chester knows are *amor* and *pistola*, and he can't even pronounce those properly. I translated for him, but for your sake, I'll render most Spanish into English from now on, always trying to keep as much as possible of the natural dignity of speech.

"Excellent idea." Chester hooked my left arm around his neck and helped me toward the lighted street. "I say," he exclaimed, as we came into the light, "you're bleeding!"

He was right. An ugly black stain was oozing through a gash in my right sleeve.

"Of course, the bumbler gets the glory," he mumbled. He tapped the Spaniard on the shoulder and pointed at me.

"Hospital? Rags? Hot water? You—bandage—him?"

"I need my arm bandaged," I translated.

"Of course!" The Spaniard seized my left hand and wrung it. "You are both so brave, to interfere in a fight that was not your own! I will reward you and thank you a thousand times! Come, you must come to my home, my servants will bandage you and clean the wound."

"What's he saying?" Chester asked impatiently.

I translated.

"Oh. Then let's get going." He reached for my arm, but paused. "I say," he said, squinting at the Spaniard, "why was that fellow after you?"

The Spaniard, a small fellow with a stub nose and friendly eyes, frowned. "I do not know for certain," he said in fluent English, "but I suspect that he is a suitor for my wife's sister who I turned away."

Chester grunted. "Oh. You speak excellent English. Remind me not to reject any suitors while I'm over here. Come, Law, give me your arm."

I felt weak by the time we reached the Spaniard's villa. The only benefit was that my throbbing arm had usurped the pain in my feet. A woman opened the door, looked at us for one moment, and fell back in hysterics. I was no stranger to this female affliction, so I took the most curative course, completely ignored her, and sank onto the closest sofa.

"Atalya!" the Spaniard exclaimed. "Be sensible, woman, stop your tears. You must thank these brave English soldiers for saving my life."

"Oh Garcia!"

I let her bathe my hands in tears for a few moments, then nodded at Chester, to remind him that I needed warm water for my arm as well. My brother had shut the door behind us, and was now staring over my head at something across the room. I followed his gaze. My arm throbbed.

There stood a Spanish girl, probably about our age, looking at us in surprise. She was a medium height for a girl, with dark eyes, long brown hair, and a determined chin. She was dressed in black from head to toe. Quick as a pen-stroke, the entire situation flashed upon my mind. Chester had just helped save this cheerful Spaniard's life, and now he meets his wife's sister as he is fresh from victory, and looking very manly with his tousled hair and disordered uniform. If those two fell in love, there would be no getting Chester home safely.

"Chester," I growled, "this arm isn't healing itself."

Atalya gathered herself for a fresh outburst. She wouldn't be much help.

The Spanish girl gestured me to wait and faded into the room she had just exited, returning in a few seconds with a steaming teapot and a rag. She knelt beside me and tore the sleeve away from my arm.

"Stay calm, and I will wash it," she said quietly, in good English. My wound smarted as she dabbed it with the hot rag.

Chester cleared his throat. "I say, we should probably have some proper introductions here."

"Of course!" Garcia bustled out of a corner with a bottle of wine and three glasses. "You must think I am a poor host, but I have been much excited this evening. Please, drink." He poured me a glass, but I motioned him to Chester.

"My name is Garcia Dedoras, and I am a shipping merchant. I was attending a ball, at the villa of one of my friends, when I was attacked."

His nose was stubby. *Stub-nosed. Where had I heard that before?* Why, this was the merchantman who had been wrongly suspected of being a Carlist. And who was supposedly being watched at the ball. How interesting.

He sipped his wine and gestured at the woman who opened the door. She was still young, and quite pretty, though her eyes were red from hysterical weeping.

"This," he said, "is my dear wife. This," he pointed to the girl, "is my wife's sister, Señorita Pacarina Garnica."

Chester snatched off his garrison cap and bowed. "It is a pleasure to meet you, Señor and Señora Dedoras, and Señorita Garnica."

Garcia waved his hands. "No, please, you are the saviors of my life, you must not be so formal. I am Garcia, my wife is Atalya, and her sister, my ward, is Pacarina."

Chester shrugged and took a chair. "Very well then, Señor Garcia, it's nice to meet you. My name is Chester Stoning, and that's my brother, Lawrence."

Garcia beamed. "I knew that you must be brothers, for you are almost mirrors of each other."

"We should be, seeing that we're twins."

"Ah?" The girl, Pacarina, I suppose I should call her, looked up from her task. "I knew you must be. Which of you is older?"

I coughed. "I am, Señorita."

Chester snorted. "You know that's not true, Law."

"Of course it is. In what other way could you explain our personalities?"

"A few come to mind." Chester looked at our hosts, who appeared rather bewildered, and laughed. "My apologies, Señor Garcia, I suppose I should explain ourselves a bit."

Garcia brought some seats into the parlor, and Pacarina began bandaging my arm with some clean linen strips.

"We come from England," Chester began, "and we're the only children in our family. Our father is a philosopher, and my brother's quite close."

"I'm not a philosopher," I clarified, "only a thinker."

"At any rate, we're twins, but we're also opposites. I suppose part of that is by nature, and part by training. You see, my father being a philosopher, he decided to make us an experiment. Lawrence nearly drowned in a pile of books when he was three, and he's been swimming ever since. If you have a question about mathematics, science, languages, or anything else that's dull, he's the fellow to ask."

Pacarina laughed. "It sounds that you do not think much of his studies, Señor Stoning."

He smiled. "I don't, and I'm Chester, by the way." He sipped his wine. "Good stuff. Where was I? Oh, right, so I don't like studies, and I wasn't made to study. I was left to myself, and had a splendid outdoor education—boxing, riding, shooting, fencing. Our father is keeping records of how each of us turn out, to determine which educational method is best."

Pacarina abruptly stopped wrapping my arm. "What is this?" she asked.

"Mmm?" I squinted at my arm. She pointed to a dark mark, slightly below the elbow crook. "Oh, that's just a birthmark."

Garcia stepped to my side and examined it. "How odd. It has the appearance of a snake."

"Really?" I looked at it again. He was right; it did look a bit like a coiled snake with his head sticking out of the middle. Strange that I had never thought of it before. "Yes, I suppose so," I said. "It's been there from birth, but it's just a mark under the skin."

"Very interesting." He touched it lightly, as if to make sure that it really was natural. "Snakes are creatures for which I have very little fondness."

"I would agree with you there."

Pacarina pulled the last strip tight and tucked it into a previous fold. "So you do not know which of you is older?"

"Not precisely," I replied. "Our father didn't want the knowledge to affect us in any way, on the chance that it would spoil the experiment, so he never told us. It may sound self-conceited, but I'm quite certain that it was me."

"And I'm just as certain the other way." Chester finished his wine and set the glass on a side table. "At any rate, here we are. I'm an officer in the British Legion, and Lawrence is my servant, for very complicated reasons that aren't necessary to explain at the moment."

"Yes," Garcia said, "and I have you to thank for my life. If you had been a few moments later, I would now lie cold upon the cobblestones."

"The saints be praised," Pacarina whispered.

Chester coughed. "Thank God, if you want, Señorita, but I didn't see Peter or Paul around when we—when Lawrence jumped."

Her forehead crinkled, and she looked earnestly at Chester. "I do thank God, and the Holy Mother, and the saints, for your blessed timing."

Chester shrugged. I stiffly slid my legs off the couch and assumed a sitting position. "I'm afraid that we don't have the same religious views, Señorita, as we are Protestants, and you are, no doubt, a Catholic, but you are quite welcome for anything we were able to do tonight."

Garcia rose. "Once again, I fail as a host. I would give you more thanks, but you are tired. Please, you must go home and rest, and return tomorrow night, when we may talk longer."

Chester agreed before I could open my mouth. This servanthood was becoming increasingly irksome. I never like thanks, and I didn't want Chester to get any romantic notions in his brain, but the decision wasn't mine to make.

"What time would you like us to come?" Chester asked.

"Oh, come—" Garcia paused. "I had forgotten, I have a business engagement earlier." He switched to Spanish. "Atalya, will nine o'clock be a good time?"

She nodded.

"Nine o'clock, then."

"We'll be here."

"Wonderful. Please, be not a moment late, we have much still to talk of." He led us to the door. "Farewell, until tomorrow. Ah, but one more question. You are sure that you are English?"

I cocked an eyebrow.

"Rather," Chester said.

"I knew it." Garcia beamed. "All the English are such gentlemen. *Adios!*"

Chapter 6

"I thought you had duties tonight, Chester."

"I had Gibson take them."

"He must be an obliging fellow."

"Nonsense. I paid him five pounds."

We were strolling through San Sebastian toward the Dedoras' villa. My arm was stiff, and throbbed if I flexed it suddenly, but the cut wasn't deep. Chester was strangely quiet, almost moody, and I feared that he was thinking of the Spanish girl. I needed to get his thoughts on a safer subject.

"What do you think of army life, Chester?"

"Eh? Oh. Drill. The only excitement I've had since we arrived was last night, and even then you had to cut in front and get the glory. I thought you weren't here for glory." He frowned, and kicked the cobblestones.

"I didn't do it for the glory, I did it to keep you safe. Besides, if you had panted less and run more you would have been first."

He turned on me, almost savagely. "I wasn't panting. I was hot, and breathing heavily. Understood?"

I shrugged. "Call it what you will."

We passed the taverns, which spilled light and noise into the quiet street, and entered the wealthier quarter.

"Where do you think the Señorita's parents were?"

I cocked an eyebrow. "Señorita?"

"Señorita Pacarina."

I was afraid of that. He was thinking about her. "Dead, I suppose, as Señor Garcia referenced her as his ward."

"What do you think of Garcia?"

"He seems very cheerful, and grateful of course. I hear that he's a very successful merchant."

"Yes, his house looked rather nice. The Señorita had a pearl cross, probably worth a few hundred pounds."

I stopped walking and put my left hand on his shoulder. "Chester, look at me."

He raised his eyebrows, but stopped and looked at me squarely.

"I'm here to get you home safely, and that means unattached. No doubt she's a nice girl, but I forbid you to fall in love with her."

His eyebrows leaped toward his hairline. "Fall in love? Ridiculous!" He snorted. "It's nice to read about in the novels, but I don't have a bit of interest in the romance line of business. I'm a gentleman, a knight. I rescue damsels in distress, collect gauges, and ride off into sunsets." He pushed my hand away. "I must say, though, you do have a fertile imagination."

He sounded convincing. Hopefully he wouldn't change his mind.

Garcia's villa fronted on a quiet, respectable street, but Chester decided to cut around the back to save time. *Bong! Bong!* The church bells sounded the time, one stroke for each hour. We were halfway round the house when a strange sound joined the bells.

"What's that?" I asked, stopping.

"Breaking glass." Chester scanned the shadows.

"Where?"

"There." He pointed to the far end of the villa, sixteen yards away. A ring of broken glass littered the street. Above this was a window through which two legs stuck out, soon followed by the rest of a man's body. Another man flitted out of the shadows from across the street to his side. They were pulling something through the window—a woman with blazing eyes, streaming brown hair, and a gag stuffed in her mouth.

"My turn!" Chester shouted. He rushed toward them.

My brain reeled as I staggered after him. An attempted murder one night, now kidnappers? My arm throbbed at the thought. The men faced Chester. One pulled a knife. I pounded the cobblestones harder, trying to catch up, but Chester reached them first.

His sword whirled and the knife-wielder melted into the shadows with a shriek. The second man jumped on Chester just as I reached them. A flurry of blows, a reek of tobacco and fruit, and he was gone. His footsteps echoed faintly in the distance.

Chester grinned as wide as—as something very wide, and slapped my shoulder. My wounded shoulder, of course. I didn't grin back. These bodyguard duties would put me early in a coffin.

"I say," Chester said, "that was a quick bit of work. Hello, who have we here? Why, it's the Señorita!"

Sure enough, Pacarina's head and torso were extended through the window. We pulled her out, untied her arms, and removed the gag from her mouth. She leaped to her feet and stared at us, eyes wide, chin set.

I coughed. "A fine evening, Señorita."

"What happened?" she demanded.

"A very excusable question." Chester rubbed his chin. "Either one of your guests forgot where your door was, or you were nearly kidnapped. I should say it was the latter. Do you Dons always live such exciting lives?"

She laughed nervously, and quickly pulled her hair away from her face. "Do you English always have such timing?"

Chester coughed. "Well, some of the English. Now, do you mind if we go around the front and enter in the normal way?"

She tilted her head. Her eyes narrowed. "How did you know I was in danger?"

"We didn't. We were asked to come back this evening, and that's the only reason we came, I promise."

She shook her head slowly. "It is very strange, in two nights, that you should thus save Garcia and myself."

"Strange, but our pleasure. May we go in now, or would you like us to bring those other two fellows back for similar questioning?"

She smiled. "You English speak frankly. I like it. I do so myself, more than is good for me. Come, we will go in."

Atalya apparently liked opening her own door. At any rate, she answered Pacarina's knock and greeted us with a blank stare.

"Pacarina!" she exclaimed in Spanish. "You are in your room!"

"Please, Atalya, be quiet and get some water." Pacarina sat on the couch and pulled back the last stray strands of hair. "I was nearly kidnapped. A strange man burst into my room, tied my arms, thrust a filthy gag in my mouth, and dragged me to one of the back windows. These gentlemen were only just in time."

Atalya gasped and stared with mouth distended. She obviously was of no use, so I peeped into the next room and found a pitcher of water on a table. Neat stacks of fabric lay on the same table, and the walls were hung with pieces of embroidery, bright quilts, and blankets. Pacarina must be a busy girl.

I naturally assumed that she wanted the water, but when I offered her a cup, she pointed to Atalya. A newcomer would have thought that it was the trembling Atalya who had just survived kidnapping, and that her sister was comforting her. Chester and I weren't the only siblings with differences.

Once I was certain that Pacarina was truly composed, I asked for a change of bandages. Chester's wallop had been hearty.

The corner clock pointed to fifteen past nine when Garcia rushed into the parlor, panting. "I am so sorry, young gentlemen, but one of my ships arrived today, and I was held late at my office."

His wife fell sobbing into his arms.

"What is wrong?" he gasped.

Pacarina explained concisely, and consternation captured his features. "What! First they attack me, now they try to steal you away!"

Chester located last night's bottle of wine and poured a glass. "Yes, Señor, some very curious coincidences. Don't you think you have something to explain?"

Garcia took the glass and sank into a chair. "*San Pablo*, I do." He glanced at Pacarina. "I did not mean to tell you of it, but now it appears that I must. I know of few enemies who would wish me dead, and none but one who would also desire to abduct you."

She frowned. "Who?"

He hesitated. "Last week, a man—a young man—asked me a question, and I refused. He—he asked for your hand."

Pacarina stopped bandaging my arm. "Who was this man?"

"You do not know him, and I know him but little. He lives loosely, and does not deserve you." He shook his head. "He must be more desperate and villainous than I thought."

Chester nodded. "It appears so. At any rate, you evidently have a bad apple among your servants. That villain, or suitor, or whatever he was, went out the window, but he didn't come in that way."

"You are right. Some of the servants must be helping him." Garcia grasped his head with both hands. "What am I to do?"

We were all quiet. He really was in a challenging situation. At least one person in his employ was a traitor, and even if he discharged the entire household and hired new help, he could not be sure that the new servants were all honest. Even with an honest household, this mysterious force could track him in the city, and the next time it found him, we would probably not be there to save him.

I motioned Pacarina to continue bandaging and made a suggestion.

"As you can no longer trust your servants, Señor, I recommend that you dismiss them and hire a bodyguard. It might also be advisable to travel to a distant place for a time, if your business would allow."

"But whom could I trust?"

"I am afraid that I cannot help you there." I smiled. "The only trustworthy servant I know is myself."

He stared at me. "You! Of course! Yes, you can be my bodyguard, and we can travel to my old home, Peru, for a time."

Chester fell off his chair. I would have fallen, but Pacarina was sitting next to me and had a foot of linen around my arm.

"Me? No! That is to say, I thank you for the invitation, but I can't leave my brother. The only reason I left England was to keep him safe, and that's still my duty."

Garcia puckered his forehead. "I admire your brotherly affection, young sir, but please, I do not know who to trust, and you have already shown your valor."

My valor? If jumping a few feet equals valor, then there must be some very brave men around. I smiled, but declined again, and turned to Chester for affirmation. That was when I saw the gleam in his eye.

"I think it's a splendid idea." Chester took a long sip, and nodded. "Yes, splendid."

My stomach somersaulted.

Garcia's brow cleared. "Then you will send him?" he asked eagerly.

"Oh, no, he's as stubborn as a prizefighter, and he won't leave me. I mean to say that I'll go."

"You!" Garcia and I spoke in unison.

"Certainly." Chester grinned. "Why not? Sounds just my cup of tea. I'll sell my commission and be ready tomorrow."

"Chester—"

"Will you take me, Señor?"

Garcia beamed and grasped his hand. "Of course! And your brother will come with you?"

I was dazed. "Er—I go where Chester goes."

"Then you will both come with me and be my bodyguards! *Grácias, mis amigos, grácias!*"

Chester bowed. "*Merci.*"

Pacarina looked at me with wide eyes, and I returned the look. At least there would be one other solid person on this trip. If she were a Protestant and didn't stand as an impediment to our safe return to England, then I would have no problem with Chester marrying her. As it was, my work was cut out.

Chapter 7

Sails flapped, gulls screamed, and the distant hills looked like scaled models of the mountains of luggage I was superintending. My back ached from lifting, but I was thankful that my arm had healed during the last two weeks.

Boots clomped up the gangplank behind me. Only Chester could walk like that.

"There you are, Law, I've been looking for you."

I grunted and handed an armload of bags to a sailor. "I've been looking for you too."

"Sorry, I've been finishing a few details. How do I look?"

"Charming, no doubt." I directed two of the sailors to the last trunk and led them to the Dedoras' stateroom. There was hardly floorspace left to walk on, so I had them take the trunk into Pacarina's room, and turned to exit. That was when I saw him.

He grinned. "Well, how do I look?"

I stared. He was as pointy as one of my tutor's lectures. First came a positive eyesore, a massive straw hat, cocked so as to cover the left side of his neck and leave the right exposed. A labyrinth of wide leather belts hung round his neck and shoulders. He had a rifle strapped over his right shoulder, a saber hanging from his left hip, and two pistols stuck in a crimson sash round his middle. He winked and turned to reveal a giant 'X' made by two short swords strapped to his back.

"Do you think I have enough?"

I cleared my throat. "Chester, words cannot express the utter ridiculousness which you currently represent."

He stopped grinning. "Ridiculous? I'm prepared, Law, and that's more than you. Do you think that cutthroats walk around like gentlemen, and ask you to measure swords before attacking?"

"I assure you, I wouldn't know. I have always sought to limit my association with cutthroats."

At this moment our new employers arrived. They looked like a cheerful Spanish family, stepping off the gangplank and eagerly heading for their stateroom. Then they saw the eyesore standing next to me. Garcia stopped short, Atalya stared blankly at Chester, and Pacarina turned away to hide a smile.

"You—you are ready," Garcia stammered.

"Ready and primed, Señor. Do you think I have enough?"

"Ah—yes, I think so."

"Splendid. This is more of a parade dress, you see. I'll probably drop a few for close jungle work, if you take any picnics."

"I see." Garcia rubbed his chin. "Señor Lawrence, thank you for taking care of our luggage."

"Only my duty, Señor."

Garcia invited us into his cramped stateroom. A bed took up most of the floorspace, while the majority of their accessible luggage—the half-dozen or so trunks that couldn't go into the hold—was stowed in Pacarina's room.

Garcia lit a cigar. "You must remember, señors, that although you have agreed to act as our bodyguards and servants for a time, we are in debt to you, and you are our friends, not our servants."

I rested my weary bones on a trunk. Pacarina undid her hat, or bonnet, or whatever they call those things, and hung it on the wall.

"Señor Lawrence, you do not seem to have taken the same—the same precautions, as your brother."

I bowed. "I have a sword with my luggage, Señorita Pacarina, but it only got in my way while supervising the arrival of your luggage. It is true that I cannot boast to have the same number of weapons as my brother, but that does not particularly sorrow me."

She smiled. "You speak very formally, Señor Lawrence. Is it an English habit?"

"Er—no, Señorita, we do not always speak so."

Chester smiled. "You see, Señorita, this here is no ordinary Englishman. This is Lawrence Stoning, philosopher, mathematician, and future professor of sciences and English in some moldy school or other."

I tried to ignore him. "I'm sure, Señor Garcia, that you would like to settle into your cabins. Chester and I will be in our quarters below, should you need us."

"What's that?" Chester exclaimed.

I glared at him. "Move." His rifle stuck in the doorway. He stooped to free this, and his scabbard caught. He twisted to free this, and the swords on his back caught the rifle and jammed. It took two minutes to pry him loose, and I hurried him away the moment he was free.

"Chester, I want a private word with you."

"Ironic, I was just about to say the same to you."

We had a nook below deck for our hammocks, and I let him hang his and get comfortable before I began.

"Chester, I will not have you embarrassing me."

He sat up and glared at me. "Me embarrass you? That's a fine thing for the moldy Professor to say."

"If you so desperately want to be a gentleman, then you need to act and look like one. Currently you look like one of those American porcupines."

"And you look like a spineless ramrod. Outside you're cold and as ungallant as can be, and inside you have a geometry book for a heart."

"I am not here to trade insults, Chester. You must not sully the Stoning name."

He smiled sarcastically. "I suppose you're a sterling silver example of our good name?"

I tried to keep my temper even. "I've done my best to keep it unsullied."

He rolled his eyes. "Oh, I'm sure, you do your best in everything. Just remember, men have muscles for reasons—we aren't just walking brains."

"And what do you mean by that?"

"I mean, Professor, that you need to be a man."

He went on deck and left me to my thoughts.

Chapter 8

Sleep came late, but I was reasonably refreshed when I woke in the morning. Chester's hammock was empty. I found him clambering through the rigging, a leather pistol-holster dangling from each hip. He waved his hat at me and shouted to come up. I waved back and shook my head. I was not a sailor, a monkey, or Chester, so I had no reason to unsettle my stomach in their terrain.

The ship was named *Miriam*, captained by a gruff old sailor named Mathers. It wasn't one of Garcia's ships, but most of its cargo was from Garcia's storehouses. We were the only passengers.

I eyed the crew suspiciously. A suitor determined enough to kidnap a girl was certainly capable of corrupting one or two sailors to act as spies or assassins. The crew was largely Spanish, with a few Italians, Peruvians, and Englishmen mixed in.

I strolled about deck, dodging ropes and wash-buckets. The men were scrubbing the earthy planks and growled when I got in their way. One Spaniard, though, didn't growl—indeed, he moved closer to the bulwark to give me room to stand. His thin hands flicked the holystone along the rough grains.

"Have you sailed long?" I asked in Spanish.

He looked up. "Yes Señor. Since a boy." He swiveled his head, as if ensuring that none of his comrades were listening. "Señor, please, may I speak with you tonight?"

"What?"

"I must speak with you. May I come to your hammock when I am off watch-duty?"

He looked nervous, shifty. Those thin hands could probably use a knife.

"Please, Señor, it is important."

"Er—very well. Come when your watch is off. I will be awaiting you."

I faked nonchalance, clasped my hands behind my back, and strolled to the bow. Could this be a ploy? A ruse to get me alone and stick a knife in my ribs? I could keep my pistol ready—no, that would be more dangerous for me than him. Of course, my weapon-bristling brother would be there. Perhaps he could prove himself useful.

That night, I lay in my hammock and sweated.

"Are you warm, Chester?"

"Not particularly." Only his teeth and the whites of his eyes showed in the below-deck gloom. "Why, are your palms sweating?"

"My palms are dry, but my opisthenars are oozing sweat."

He sat up. "Your what?"

"Er—the backs of my hands."

"Oh." He lay back down. "Remember, I don't speak Greek."

"It's only derived from the Greek, but it's in English medical dictionaries."

"As I said, I don't speak Greek. What's that?"

I tensed. Feet were padding toward us.

Click. Chester extended his arm toward the newcomer. "I'd stand still, my dear fellow. I've just cocked this pistol, and my hand is on the trigger. Please, don't jerk—these fleas have rattled my nerves."

"Please, please, do not shoot, it is I, Señor, Antonio, who you spoke to on deck this morning."

"What did he say, Law?"

"It's the man. You can lower your pistol, but keep it ready."

He rested the barrel on his hip, still pointing toward the stranger.

"What do you have to tell me, Antonio?" I asked.

His silhouette emerged from the gloom. "An old man paid me to give you a message, Señor. It is written." He held a letter toward me.

The paper crinkled in my hands, but it was too dark to read.

"Chester, strike one of those Congreve matches."

The quavery light added an eerie depth to the already sinister words. I looked over the paper at the sailor.

"Have you read this?"

"No, Señor, I cannot read."

"Thank you. Here is another coin. You may go."

I folded the paper and worked it into my pocket.

"Well, what's it all about?" Chester demanded.

I clasped my hands behind my head and swung gently on the hammock. "It's an excellent example of brevity. It simply reads: *Leave Garcia in Peru or you fall with him.* A signature is lacking."

Chester grunted. "These Spanish suitors are persistent."

Chapter 9

Pacarina was the only member of the family on deck next morning. Garcia was busy reviewing accounts and writing business letters to send back to Spain by the first ship we sighted. I did not see Atalya, but a series of gut-wrenching noises was issuing from her cabin. I do not think the sea agreed with her stomach.

Chester collected three deckchairs, and we sat in the stern, watching the wave-tops dazzle in the fierce sunlight. Pacarina was knitting socks. Chester was reading an American novel. I was trying to calculate how deep the little groups of silver-scaled fish were swimming, taking into account our height from the water and the refraction.

I found myself pondering our situation. What did we know of Garcia? He was a successful merchant with a cheerful personality and a proven loyalty to Queen Isabella. And he had spent his childhood in Peru. That was all. Atalya? She was Garcia's wife, and reminded me of my mother. Pacarina was cheerful and rather blunt, but wore mourning.

I made a decision. *If I'm to spend my foreseeable future with these people, then I want to know who they are.*

"Señorita, may I ask you some questions?"

"Of course." She smiled, and her needles click-clacked merrily.

"You wear mourning. I assume that your parents are dead?"

Her needles stopped.

Chester looked up from his book and glared at me. "Please excuse my brother, Señorita. You don't need to talk about it if it pains you."

She looked out to sea, her hands resting idly in her lap. I almost regretted asking. At last, she spoke.

"No, it would be good to talk. I haven't talked of it with anyone. Atalya and I are so different—and Garcia is kind, but I hardly knew him until it happened." She brushed her eyes with the back of her hand.

Chester looked at me reproachfully, as if he had never seen a girl cry before.

"It was but a month ago, Señors, when my parents died. They were traveling home at night from across the mountains. The next morning they were found at the foot of a valley, inside their coach, crushed. I was told that many loose boulders surrounded their coach, and that these must have slid, and swept them off the path above."

"I'm—I'm very sorry," I said.

"So am I." She wiped away the tears and smiled sadly at us. "Don't mind me, Señors. I am only a sad, silly girl. I pity this strange man who wants me as a wife."

"I don't," Chester said hotly. "I think he's quite understandable, though I'll trounce him the moment we meet." He stopped abruptly and blushed.

"Do you have friends still in Spain?" I asked.

She shook her head. "No real friends. I knew some girls, but we were never close. I loved my parents, and I was their all after my sister married Garcia. But it was God's will."

She made the sign of the cross and kissed the little pearl symbol on her necklace.

We stayed silent for ten minutes, each no doubt sunk in his or her own thoughts. If it was my lot to trot round the world as someone's bodyguard, I was glad to have such a sturdy, sensible girl as the object of my protection.

Chester finally closed his novel and turned to Pacarina.

"What's it like to have loving parents?"

"It is nearly the best thing you can wish." She smiled. "Mother taught me everything I know—to sew, to care for animals, to cook, to keep house. She was wonderful. Father would take me riding in the hills, and he taught me to shoot. They both taught me to love and honor God."

"And the Virgin Mary?"

"Of course. You are Protestants, you would not understand."

All my studies in theology and the history of religion flooded my brain.

I shifted my chair closer. "You're right, Señorita, I don't understand. Why do you worship the Virgin and the rest of the supposed saints?"

A religious light sparkled through the remaining tears. "It is our duty, we are commanded to."

"By whom?"

She paused. "Why, by the pope."

"I see. And why do you follow his commands?"

Her eyes widened. "Because he is the representative of God on earth."

"According to whom?"

She frowned. "What do you mean?"

I leaned forward. Chester chewed his hat.

"Who says that the pope is the representative of God on earth?"

She puckered her forehead. "I don't understand."

"Does the Bible say so?"

"I suppose so. I have not read the Bible, but that is what the priests say."

"Hmph. Well, I've read the Bible, and it doesn't say that. If you believe the pope just because he tells you to believe him, then your pope is your God."

She shook her head firmly. "That cannot be true."

"It's actually quite logical. Would you like to read the Bible for yourself?"

She gasped. "I couldn't! It's not allowed."

"That's ridiculous. It's God's Word, and it's meant for everyone. I have one in my satchel, and you may read it."

She crossed herself. "No, please, I can't."

Chester spoke. "Did your priests ever say you couldn't listen to it?"

"N-no."

"Fine then. Professor, you'll just have to read aloud."

I sat back in consternation. "What? Me? Oh, no, I've never read aloud to anyone."

Chester grunted. "It's simple. Any fool can do it. It will be good practice for your sonorous lecturer's voice."

His green eyes were sarcastic. Pacarina's brown eyes were a little uncertain, but they also laughed at my hesitancy.

I sighed. "Very well. I'll read aloud."

Chapter 10

Eight days into our voyage I went on deck and found Chester next to Pacarina. He was grinning at me. That meant trouble.

"Here you are, Professor." He handed me a pistol.

I held it by the muzzle. "Pardon me?"

"We're going to shoot."

I eyed him warily. "Shoot what?"

"A target."

He pointed forward. A piece of cloth with four painted circles was nailed to a small keg, which in turn was tied to the starboard bulwark.

"I've been telling the Señorita that you don't know how to shoot. Since we're her bodyguards now, it's necessary that we can defend her."

I frowned. "I know very well how to shoot. You pull the trigger and the gun fires a projectile."

"Actually, no." He grasped the hammer with his left hand and pulled it until it clicked. "First you cock it, *then* you pull the trigger."

"Oh. Right. Er—of course, that's what I meant."

He leveled the pistol and fired.

"Second circle. Not terrible, though it's hard to compensate for the swell."

The sailors shouted their approbation. Pacarina smiled at me. I gulped.

Pull the hammer back. Click. Raise. Level. Cover the target, wait for the swell to go down, pull—crack!

The sailors shouted. *I must have hit it!* I smiled triumphantly at Chester.

"I told you that I can shoot."

He rubbed his chin. "Yes—you can shoot. But, er—we're shooting at that keg."

My spirits fell. The sailors weren't applauding—they were shaking their fists at me. Antonio pointed to a bullet mark in the mast above his head.

"Perhaps it was the swell," Pacarina suggested.

Chester reloaded the pistol. "Try again."

"I have no desire to try again."

"You need to know how to shoot."

I growled. "Very well. Put that beastly hat on the keg, and I'll shoot again."

He hesitated a moment, then shrugged and removed the hat—the 'Eyesore'—from his head. "I suppose there's not much risk of its getting hit."

I aimed again. The deck was suddenly empty. Where was everyone? *A little to the right, high to counteract the swell—crack!*

Heads popped up, then the crew slowly rose from the deck. Chester cupped his hand over his eyes. "I think that one went into the rigging."

I exhaled. "You use the pistol, I'll use the pen. We'll see who history remembers more."

I didn't meet Pacarina's eye.

"There's still a way to redeem yourself, Professor." Chester pointed up.

Hope glimmered. "You want to shoot the sun with a sextant, then calculate longitude?"

"No. We'll climb to the top and back."

Tops are basically round ledges on masts below the topmast. They're high, small, and swing out over the bulwarks when the swell is heavy. Like today.

I clenched my wrist. Why take such a risk? Why venture my life to a tangle of rope and a stick of wood? To live up to Chester's standards, standards that I refuse to accept as binding?

"No."

Chester's eyebrows narrowed. "Are you scared, Law?"

I looked at Pacarina. "Do you see any reason for me to do this, Señorita?"

She hesitated. "Nothing forces you to, Señor. But it would—" she paused. She didn't need to say more.

I leapt into the rigging. The ratlines caught at my boot heels and stretched low under my weight, but I kept climbing. I'd had enough. Chester may be my physical superior, but I'm still a man. Higher and higher, foot above foot, I climbed. I paused to inflate my lungs and looked down—bad idea. My stomach churned. Higher. There were the smaller shrouds just below the top. I grabbed a taut rope—*no!*

I was swinging, swinging, nothing below but the angry blue sea. My heart pounded, my hands, feet, and knees clung to the rope like closed oyster shells. Back now, a jungle of rope below, scared faces looking up—and Chester!

"Hold on!"

I was holding. The rope jerked and I spun round like a child's top.
"Chester, help!"

Hands grasped my waist. My boot-heels caught on taut ropes. I dropped the rope and clutched the shrouds convulsively.

Chester let me go and wiped his sleeve over his forehead. "I think we know where that last bullet went. You'll have to pay Captain Mathers for a new rope."

The deck never felt so good to my feet before. I realized to my chagrin that I was not impervious to human passions—Pacarina's eyes had shown disappointment, and I wanted to prove myself. I'd often noted how much power girls have over usually sane men, but it wasn't until then that I'd felt the power exerted over me. A look, a hesitation in the voice—and I was acting more impetuously than Chester.

Chapter 11

We were starting Genesis again when we sighted the Peruvian coast. It was low, brown, and sandy. Callao was a few days sail to the north.

The new scenery gave me a respite from Pacarina's questions. Day after day I read, and day after day she asked. Was Peter the first pope? What does it mean to 'call no man your father upon the earth'? Where did purgatory come from?

To change someone's mind, you must first make them question their fundamental beliefs. If they continue to question these, and there are no satisfactory answers, then they will change their minds, unless God allows them to continue in irrational faith. It was my duty to make her ask questions. The rest was in far more capable Hands than mine. Strange how life is. I was working to remove the one insurmountable barrier blocking a serious connection between Chester and Pacarina.

I didn't know the answers to many of her questions, and had to search for them, beginning to realize how little I actually knew of the Bible. What I was learning was making me feel less and less comfortable with the person I was.

Even the high waves and low temperatures round Cape Horn couldn't quell her questions. The sailors said that the seas were exceptionally calm. From what I've read about the Horn, they were probably right, but it didn't feel right at the time. The pounding waves often kept us cabin-bound, giving plenty of opportunity for reading and conversation. At any rate, we rounded the cape successfully, and were now almost at our objective.

Two days after sighting the coast, we three and Garcia were grouped in the stern, watching the land slowly slide by, when Captain Mathers approached.

Garcia bowed. "A few days more, Captain Mathers, and we shall bid you farewell."

"I can't say as that sorrows me." He brushed his nest of unkempt hair farther beneath his hat.

Garcia laughed. "That is a blunt way of putting it, Captain."

"I doan't like passengers, an' I said so from the start. Ye're not as bad as the general lot of 'em, barrin' yer bits o' shootin'—" he frowned at me, "—but all I wants is a full crew of sturdy Jacks."

"Not a—ah, what is the English word—a *gaggle* of females and landsmen, you mean?" Garcia winked at me and slid a cigar out of his brown traveling case. "I do thank you, Captain, for making this special exception."

"You can thank your purse. Most of my cargo is from your stores."

"That is true." Garcia puffed a smoke-swirl at the horizon. "I suppose, Captain, that you did not seek me out to exchange pleasantries?"

"I didn't. I doan't like the look of those clouds." He poked a callused forefinger at a haze on the southern horizon. "I've ordered double-reefs, which is the same as that fool behind us should have done."

"Fool?" Garcia removed his cigar. "What fool?"

A ship under full sail was bearing down on us. It almost seemed as if the evil sky was caught in her wake.

"Perhaps she does not find the weather to be concerning?" Garcia suggested.

"If her captain's a seaman, he do."

Twenty minutes later the strange ship was nearer—so much nearer, that it became fairly certain that she actually was heading for us.

"I doan't like strange ships in strange waters," Captain Mathers muttered. He shouted to the helmsman. "Shift course a point to port."

Our bow turned until we edged slightly away from the coast. The other ship did the same. Our double-reefed sails were no match for her billowing canvas, and she was soon close enough for us to make out figures on her deck.

"No flag." Captain Mathers spat. "Up with the Union Jack. If she doan't reply, we've danger behind."

The crosses of Andrew, Patrick, and George flapped at the masthead.

Chester squinted. "They're doing something."

A long, dark object poked out of the ship's bulwark. "Is that a cannon, Chester?"

"Bow chaser." He grabbed my elbow. "That fellow has a match!"

Smoke spouted from their bow, followed by a muffled roar, and something whistled through the mainsail's bottom right corner.

"I say, they're shooting at us!" Chester exclaimed.

Something pattered against the bulwark, like hailstones. *Whiz.* Wind brushed my left ear, and something plumped into the mast behind me.

"Small arms fire!" Chester shouted. "Down!"

I stared in stunned silence. Sailors shouted and leaped from the rigging. Captain Mathers threw his hat at the enemy and ran for the arms locker.

"Cutlasses!" he bellowed. "All hands to repel boarders!"

"This is why we're here!" Chester shouted. "Quick—I've got Garcia—get Pacarina."

I stared at him. The coach-robbery flashed to mind. "Wh-what?" I stammered.

His eyes blazed. "Get Pacarina!" He grasped my arm and spun me away. The deck slid from my feet and I reached for the bulwark. I found Pacarina instead, and we slammed into the deck. Bullets whistled and whined, and the cannon crashed again.

"What is happening?" Pacarina grabbed my shoulder, her hair cascading all around.

I shook my head and kept between her and the bulwark. "I think your suitor has very serious anger problems."

"Lawrence, get off the deck and fight back!"

Chester tossed a rifle to me and screamed at the enemy. I swallowed my heart and popped up long enough to point the barrel and pull the trigger. The rifle butt slammed into my shoulder like a load of books, and I hit the deck again.

"I—don't know how to load," I gasped.

"I will—Father taught me how." She dumped powder down the barrel and reached for the ramrod. I grabbed my pistol from my belt and peeked over the bulwark. A few paces to my left, Chester fired his rifle. A man dived off the enemy ship, a speck of white water marking the place where he fell. The haze was close. Gray clouds scudded over us.

"They're getting too close." I grabbed the girl's hand and pulled her to her knees. "Quick, farther in!" We crawled for the hatch, wood splintering above our heads. Garcia and his wife were nowhere—*I hope they're below deck*. Sailors were grabbing cutlasses and lining the bulwark. One body lay unattended on the planks with a pool of blood by its head. *Antonio*.

A shock threw us to the deck, three feet from the open hatch. Wood ripped and steel clanged—full battle was joined, ship to ship and man to man.

"A Stoning! A Stoning!"

I whirled toward the action. Chester's hat disappeared into a swirl of brown men on the enemy's deck.

If he dies, I fail! I left Pacarina and dashed for the bulwark. *Miriam*'s sailors were shoulder to shoulder, slashing at a crowd of swarthy boarders.

"Chester, come back here!"

One of our men tripped, opening a momentary gap. I threw my pistol at it and leaped into a jungle of arms and legs.

Another shock and the deck slanted down till the water splashed within a yard of my boots. Up, up we rolled, little brown men clinging to me like dogs on a lion. Dogs on a mouse, perhaps.

Sinewy hands pressed my arms and legs into the planks. I looked up, helpless. Chester's back was to the mast, his cutlass whirling at the crowd of enemies in front. Other men were in the rigging, but they were pulling at ropes, their muscles bulging. The *Miriam*'s masts sped away at the head of the gale.

"Just brilliant, Professor!"

Somehow Chester was above me, striking right and left like a reincarnated Henry V. He went down. My head exploded in pain. The world turned to mist, then night.

Chapter 12

O*h my head.* The whole weight of my head was crushing the bridge of my nose into solid wood. *Did I fall asleep studying?* I lifted my head and little darts of pain collided behind my eyes. *Am I sick?* I tried to spread my hands apart to push against the deck, but they wouldn't spread. Cords cut into my wrists and my under-circulated fingers tingled.

I opened my eyelids. It was too dark to see, but I definitely wasn't sitting at a desk. I lay full-length on rough planks. The bridge of my nose probably had a deep red impression of the wood's grain.

"Are you alive?" Chester's voice was close but I couldn't see him.

I groaned. "Must be. This isn't heaven."

His hands grasped mine and cold steel chilled my flesh. *Stisp.* The cords were loose. I spread my hands apart, slowly pulling the cord out of the grooves it had worked into my flesh.

"Where are we?" I asked.

"In a cabin on the enemy ship. Prisoners, obviously."

The floor heaved, and the whole ship was creaking and groaning. Wind roared outside. I wished that some of it would come inside and sweep away the stench of tobacco and sweet fruit. My eyes were adjusting to the gloom, and I made out Chester's silhouette. He was holding something long.

"What is that?" I asked.

"A knife."

"A knife? It's long enough to be a sword."

He fingered the blade. "No, more of a *gladius*. Those little brown imps took three of my knives, but they missed this one. I had it strapped to my back beneath the shirt."

Chester was illogical and unpredictable—or, rather, annoyingly predictable—but he was helpful to have around in these sorts of situations.

"Do you think these are pirates?" I asked.

"Don't know." He squatted next to me with the knife-sword across his knees. "The ocean is usually boring these days—very little piracy left. I only saw natives, but it's not a native craft. European built, I'm sure."

"In light of our situation, I can't see that this attack is coincidental. When I promised our father to bring you back, I didn't anticipate Spanish suitors."

"Suitors? Law, you don't honestly think that this is a disgruntled suitor?"

"Then what else could it be?"

He leaned closer. "Let's consider." He ticked points with his fingers. "First, we have Garcia attacked in San Sebastian. Second, we have some odorous villain trying to take Pacarina for a walk. Third, we have an entire ship chase us down—with only two cannonballs and very concentrated small arms fire, as if they didn't want to hit something or someone valuable. Next, we'll probably see Attila the Hun raiding Peru in search of us." He shook his head and stood up. "Law, there's much more to this than some love-blind suitor."

His logic was surprisingly well-ordered and concise. But then who else was after Garcia and Pacarina? And why did that warning, or threat, say to leave Garcia when we got to Peru, when the plan was to attack us *before* we reached Peru?

My aching head was unequal to the task. "Do you think Garcia lied?"

"I intend to ask him."

The cabin was eight feet squared, and probably seven high. The door scarcely budged when Chester slammed into it with his shoulder.

"Bolts." He pointed to the wall next to the door-crack. "More over here." He touched the wall next to the hinges. "They probably have two metal brackets outside with a plank resting on them. They were prepared for a prisoner."

"Do you have a plan?" I asked.

He picked absentmindedly at the wood with his knife-point. "Yes. The first three blackguards who come through this door will only leave as corpses."

"I mean a plan for our survival."

He scratched his chin. "Well, we might make a club from that keg in the corner, so that you could finish one or two more imps."

"Chester! Stop thinking about killing and think more about living."

He sighed. "I suppose I can cut the wood away from these bolts. It'll be noisy when the plank falls, but the storm may cover it."

I rose stiffly and examined the bolts. The wood was hard, but not impervious. *I think he can do it.* "Very well, begin."

He forced the blade into the wall and half-scraped, half-sawed a shallow circle round the bolt head.

"It will take some time."

I blew the sawdust out of the cut. "We've nothing else to do."

He scraped, I blew. I also spit all the saliva I could generate into the deepening groove to soften the wood. It was strange, working together.

"It would have been a tale for the history-books." Chester paused to wipe his forehead. "Two Englishmen defend their prison against a crew-full of bloodthirsty blackguards. The dead pile high, sprinkled with the blood of the faithful defenders. The illustration would be a black background with two swirly white shapes slashing at a crowd of swarthy natives."

"History will only mention you if I write it, Chester. Remember, the pen is mightier than the sword."

"Quite likely, but the pistol has them both beat."

He resumed sawing. One bolt finished, three left.

Sweat drops rolled down Chester's forehead and cheeks. "Well, Professor—

Socrates said to 'beware the barrenness of a busy life.' Are you feeling barren?"

"Just exhausted."

"And *you're* only spitting."

A great gust of wind pounded the ship and the floor tilted down, down, down, to port.

"We're sinking!" I cried.

Chester kicked savagely at the weakened wood—it splintered, but another splintering sound drowned it out. A man shrieked, something cracked, and the tilting floor plunged back up. We must have lost a mast.

"The sailors will be distracted!" Chester hacked at the plank on the right, each blow sticking deep in the wood.

"Calm, Chester, calm. Efficiency."

I worked more saliva into my dry mouth and we labored together, cutting and spitting toward freedom. My tutor would be horrified.

Another three minutes and two deep rings circled the bolts. Chester kicked. It splintered, but held. Another kick. His foot burst through the wood and the whole contraption outside clattered to the deck.

"Free!" Chester shouted, hopping backward to free his foot. "Stay close to me and don't shoot anything unless I'm behind you."

The deck was in gloomy twilight, maybe because of the time of day, maybe because of the black storm clouds overhead. The first mast was overboard, and a crowd of natives were hacking at the debris. Each appeared intent on his own duty—no one noticed us as we crawled toward the captain's gig, which lay bottom up behind the rear mast.

"Grab the boat while I cut its ropes!" Chester shouted above the roaring.

I squatted next to an oarlock, wondering how the two of us could ever move the heavy boat. God had different plans. The mast was weighing down our bow, and at each plunge we shipped a load of water. As Chester sliced the last rope, a fresh gust of wind tore out of the south and drove us deep into a wave.

Many tons of water coursed the deck and swept the boat and us before them. Rough deck planks shredded my clothing and dug into my arms and legs. My hands touched a plank—one of the boat seats—I wrapped my arms round it and clung for my life. A rope slipped over my shoulders and tightened round my ribs.

The gig's stern smashed through the bulwark and I hung in space, frothing rollers beneath and glowering clouds above. *Crash.* Churning water engulfed me, and I fainted.

Chapter 13

Sunbeams peeped through my half-open eyelids, reminding me of a picnic nap on a warm summer's afternoon. Only I was lying on rock, not grass, and my exposed skin was being slow-broiled. The last time I woke, my head was aching just as badly, but I was in darkness then—now I craved darkness.

Something screeched. That was what woke me. A creaking, scraping, scratching sound. I opened my eyes and blinked up at a clear blue sky.

"Water," I croaked.

The noise stopped and footsteps crunched nearby. "'Water, water, everywhere, and not a drop to drink,' eh?"

"Chester, is that you?"

"The same." A shadow fell over me, and I looked up into Chester's face. His hair was matted over his forehead, his coat was missing, and his shirt was shredded. I scanned his limbs for blood but saw only a few cuts and some nasty blue bruising.

He stuck his harmonica in his pocket and squatted beside me. "I wasn't entirely sure that you were coming back to the land of the living."

"Where are we?"

"Peru, I believe."

I struggled to a sitting posture and looked around. To my right was the blue ocean, fringed by white foam dashing against a low, rocky coast. I lay on a fragment of one of these rocks, an island surrounded by sand. Not a tree, not a shrub—sand. To my left, far away in the distance, towered an enormous mountain range.

Chester scooped a handful of sand and let it sift between his fingers. "Funny, I always thought of Peru as being green."

"It is, inland." My tongue was swelled with thirst, and I gazed longingly at the ocean. "I read that streams come from the mountains. They form oases."

"Then, if you feel able, we'd best be marching. My tongue feels like an anteater's after dinner."

He lifted me to my feet. As I rose, I touched my forehead, and felt a strip of cloth. "What happened to my head?"

"You cut it somehow on the boat. It's a good thing that rope I tied round you held, or you'd be lecturing the fishes right now."

My head filled with rushing blood and the world spun. "Let me sit."

He helped me down and stood back, his arms crossed.

I gazed stupidly at the sand, my eyes unfocused, my brain trying to sort a hundred stimuli. I think sequentially, and with sequences of memory gone, it was hard to construct an analysis of my present situation.

"What happened?" I asked.

"A wave swept us off the pirate, or whatever she was, and we landed near the captain's gig. I pulled you on, and then we had a little competition with the waves and the wind and ended up here."

"How here? How safely?"

He shrugged. "Here, because I steered for a low spot. Safely, because I stopped us from capsizing twenty or thirty times."

"Thank God."

"I have."

The long voyage had darkened my skin, but even so I felt the moisture draining from my pores. *We must walk. So tired. Weary. A little more rest.* My head drooped on my chest.

"Did Socrates say anything about sand?" Chester asked. I stared at the crashing waves. Chester continued. "He probably compared it to men. Dense when gathered in mobs, light, fleeting, transient when alone."

What? Chester philosophizing? His usually laughing eyes were grave.

"I think she's safe, Chester."

"I hope so. If not—" he balled his hands into fists. "Since I saved our brains from decorating those rocks, I recommend that we use them and start marching before we die of thirst."

"I'm ready." He helped me up again and I stood unsupported, though wobbly. I felt that I could walk. I must.

"Which way?" Chester asked.

"We were sailing for Callao, which is up the coast, so we need to go north."

Chester nodded. "Splendid. So, which way?"

I stared at him. "I said north."

"I didn't ask you the points of the compass, Law, I said which way—left or right?"

I blinked. "Chester, assuredly you know which way north is."

"Do I look like a compass?" He frowned. "We're wasting time, Professor."

I couldn't believe my ears—he didn't know how to tell direction! "Chester, hasn't anyone taught you how to tell direction by the sun?"

He chewed on his bottom lip. "The sun? No. Who would have? Do you think Father did?"

"Well, no, of course not."

"Did you?"

"No."

"Then who would have?"

I shrugged. "I—don't know. My tutor taught me."

"The only time I exchanged more than twenty words at a time with your tutor was when I convinced him to ride old Betsy, and then put a thorn under her saddle." He smiled. "That was quite a ride. Now, will you tell me which way to walk?"

I pointed to the sun. "The sun rises in the east and sets in the west. It's morning, and it's coming from the direction of the mountains, so the mountains are to the east. East is always to the right of north, so when we turn, and put it on our right, we face the north." I did so, and he sighed gratefully.

"Good. I was preparing for a lecture on the solar system. Let's be off." We left the rock and began trudging through the hot sand, my left arm draped around his neck. He glanced up at the sun and muttered something. It sounded like 'brilliant.'

That walk became a blazing nightmare. Heat sandwiched us, and for a long time I watched the half-dozen clouds, hoping that one would drift between us and the sun. None did. Eventually my neck wearied and my focus narrowed. The clouds could take care of themselves. I just needed to put one foot forward. Then the next. And the next.

We didn't talk. There wasn't anything to discuss, and if there had been, it would have been a waste of precious saliva. I longed for the juices I had expended to soften the wood during our escape. My thick tongue stuck to my sandy teeth. The salt smell of the sea to our left didn't help, and my jaw flexed every time the waves came in and hundreds of tons of useless water splashed within twenty yards of us.

At one point, the land jutted into the ocean, but we continued straight, as skirting the coast would take longer, and it was imperative that we reach an oasis soon.

The sun was beginning to droop over the ocean when Chester grasped my shoulder.

"Look!" he croaked.

I tore my eyes away from the foot of sand before me and looked at the horizon. A dark line—a green fringe which meant only one thing: water!

We pushed forward, strengthened by hope. As we staggered closer the fringe took the shape of trees, and beneath their shade something sparkled in the dying sunlight.

We groped past thick tree-trunks. A clear stream, probably five yards wide, flowed beneath the foliage. Might there be diseases in the water? I didn't care. My knees hit grass, then water engulfed my face and I sucked a long, delicious mouthful. My throat opened, my tongue shrank, and my head cleared. I drank until the water sloshed in my stomach, then laid back on the grass and gazed at the green leaves above.

We slept.

Chapter 14

I awoke with a settled head and new energy. Chester must have also, as it was his harmonica's screeching which woke me up.

"Do you have no sense of pitch?" I asked, rolling over.

He paused in his puffing. "I'm trying to draw some natives to us."

"They're probably cowering behind trees with their thumbs firmly inserted into their ears."

"Fine then." He put the instrument into his pocket and folded his half-clothed arms. "What do you propose?"

I studied our surroundings. "This stream obviously descends from the mountain, and its only exit could be the ocean. Humans are always drawn to oases, so I would conjecture that there is a native village somewhere along this stream."

He snapped his fingers. "And there'll be fishers. We'll hire a boat and go looking for that pirate."

"Hire? With what?"

He looked puzzled. "Money, of course."

"Do you have money?"

He slapped his pockets. “No, it all washed away.”

“The same with me.”

He stared. “You’re dry?”

I have always been the big brother, the guardian angel, as they say, in financial affairs. Chester has little concept of the value of money, and not much desire to learn. This was the first time in our lives that I had ever lacked the necessary coins when he asked.

“In that case,” he said, “I’ll have to charm us a boat.”

We set off downstream, very ragged and footsore. The stream was usually one or two feet deep, though occasionally some boulders constricted the flow and deepened it to waist-height. Flocks of birds crowded the trees, and nature seemed at peace with itself. The salt smell was gone, replaced or overpowered by exotic scents which I could not identify.

After a few hundred yards we came upon a trampled path. Pigs grunted close by.

Chester tapped my left arm. “Hold a moment.” He tore one of the last few strips of cloth from his shirt, soaked it in the stream, and tied it round his head. “Now we look identical. You go into the first hut we see. I’ll stay outside on guard duty.”

Something in his eyes said that more than guard duty was on his mind, but I was silent.

A low hut peeped out of the trees on our side of the stream, a hole in the wall serving as door, window, and chimney. Three pigs and two children squatted in the mud where the doorstep should be.

“Hello there, boys,” Chester called.

Pigs and children squealed and dived into the hut.

“I don’t think they speak English,” I said.

Chester shrugged. “It’s the gesture that counts.”

“They may not speak Spanish, either. Remember, this is Peru, and there are many native dialects.”

“Quite so, quite so,” he muttered, obviously not listening to me. “See here, you go in first, and talk to them. I'll be the reinforcements, and make a grand entrance at the right point."

I ducked to enter. As my eyes adjusted to the darkness, I found an old woman squatted in the corner, a piece of cloth in her hands. The children and pigs cowered behind her skirt. A young woman, twenty at the most, stepped out of the shadows and half-bowed, half-curtseyed.

I tried to forget the disgraceful state of my shirt and bowed back. "Do you speak Spanish?"

She replied respectfully, in the same language. I explained that we were shipwrecked sailors and needed a boat. She said there was a village close by, with several fishermen. Indeed, the air smelled like rotten fish. One of these men, she said, was her husband, but he had been taken.

"Do you mean that he is out fishing?" I asked.

"No. Taken." She pushed the air as if she were prodding a prisoner. "A ship stop here, a Spaniard take him. He did not want to go."

"Do you mean that your husband was forced to go?"

She hesitated. "Before he marry me, he work for this man. My husband is an interpreter, knows Spanish, and Quechua, and more. He meet me while traveling and bring me back."

The old woman gurgled.

"She say he very bad man, Spaniard. She is my husband's mother."

I rubbed my chin. "What did the crew of this Spaniard look like?"

"Many natives. Many Quechua, some from other tribes."

So our pirate-suitor had been here. I sent her to tell some other fishermen of our plight, in the hopes that they would offer us a passage, and settled down to study the old woman's physiognomy. It differed strikingly from the young woman's, but before I could begin classifying her features, the young woman returned. Her chest heaved, and her mouth and eyes were fully distended. She pointed a trembling finger at me, then out the door.

So that was the meaning of Chester's 'grand entrance' and the strip of cloth on his forehead.

"Brothers," I said quickly, "twins."

"But—you are the same!" she faltered.

"No, no, not exactly. Come." I took her shaking hand and led her out to Chester, who was rocking on his heels and grinning.

"Stop grinning and hold out your arm," I commanded.

"Eh?"

"Do it." He cocked an eyebrow but held out his arm.

Our sleeves were already torn to shreds, so both of our right elbows were bare.

"There," I said, pointing to the birthmark below my elbow crook. "My skin is marked, his is not. We are not the same, only twins."

Instead of calming, she trembled even more, and her eyeballs threatened to fall from their sockets.

"The snake," she hissed.

Chester shifted his weight to his left foot. "I don't know what she said, Law, but I doubt that's the response you wanted."

The young woman backed against the wall and gazed at us in horror. I scratched my head. What was so startling about a birthmark that looked somewhat like a snake?

"I say, Law, didn't the Incas worship snakes?"

I hadn't thought of that. "Yes, they did, but she's not an Inca."

"No, but superstitions die hard. If I had to guess, which I do, I would say that between our likeness and your little permanent bruise, she thinks we're a bit superhuman." He surveyed my clothes. "She must have a poor opinion of the gods' tastes in wardrobe."

"Superhuman or not, we need to get to Callao."

I asked her again about the boat, and she seemed only too glad to flee down the trail. We followed leisurely, still enjoying the shade and cool, tinkling water. The village was close by, and every man, woman, and child was awaiting us. They conducted us, almost as if we were superior beings, to the coast, and put us into their biggest boat, with four muscular men to row and work the sails.

Chester winked at me as we settled onto a pile of nets and the men rowed us out of the little harbor. "Charm, Law, charm."

"Hmph. It's *my* birthmark."

I rested my head on a rope coil and snuffed the salt and the fresh fish smell. The last scents of land reminded me of that fruity smell in the cabin of the enemy ship, and sent my brain spinning in a new web. How could a young, revengeful suitor have a prepared world-wide network of men either willing to do his bidding, or too frightened of him to not. Chester was right. Something much more sinister lay beneath these strange attacks.

"If only I had a corporal's squad," Chester said.

"What would you do with one?"

"I'd hunt that villain down and have a sea-trial, if he didn't die in the attack."

"Thankfully for me, it's our duty to find Garcia as fast as possible."

"Yes." He wrapped a cloth mat round his torso and stared up the coast. "If they've hurt her—" he spat into the ocean. "I won't wait for the corporal's squad."

Chapter 15

What with contrary winds, and coast-hugging, it took us nearly a week to arrive in Callao. We sailed between the island of San Lorenzo and the spit of land that protected Callao's harbor from the southern winds. The shore was low, with a yellowish grass, developing into a series of rolling hills, which rose in height until they melded with the soaring range of the Cordilleras. I congratulated myself for having bought some Peruvian geographies before our voyage.

"I say," said Chester, "there's our ship, *Miriam*."

Indeed, there she lay, surrounded by boats and taking on new stores. She looked homey, familiar, though slightly different because we were looking from the outside up, instead of the inverse.

"Lay us alongside, chaps," Chester said.

I translated the order, and we were soon bumping against the sturdy ship. We clambered up a rope ladder and stepped onto deck. Captain Mathers stood five feet away, directing the loading operation. He took one look at us and dropped his pipe.

"Is it ghosts?" he faltered.

Chester grinned. "Not a bit. We're quite flesh and blood, Captain, though a bit low in flesh, and with perhaps a few less pints of blood, than when you saw us last. Where is Señor Garcia?"

"By the way," I added, "may I borrow a few coins to pay these natives?"

The captain mechanically took some copper coins from his pocket and handed them to me. I paid the natives and dismissed them with hearty thanks. They had realized, by now, that we weren't gods, and gave us a hearty farewell yell as they pulled away.

"Come now," Chester continued, "you've no need to look at us like that, Captain. We're fully alive." He grasped Captain Mathers's hand and squeezed.

The old seaman started, looked at his hand, and shook his head like one leaving a daze.

"Aye, that's solid. Whew. Well, it's good to see you young'uns again. I thought for sure as ye'd been killed by those blackguards."

"Where is Señor Garcia?" I asked.

"The señor landed as soon as we anchored. I heard talk as he was traveling inland, though that's just sea-rumor. I believe as he took your chests with him, seeing as there was no one closer who had a claim to them."

"Inland?" I glanced at Chester. "That's rather sudden."

The captain removed his cap and raked his hair. "He seemed rather startled by that raid. Can't blame him myself."

"How is the señorita?" This from Chester.

"Oh, she's a plucky 'un. It's a shame her sister's so unlike her. She's been a bloomin' mess arter the attack, and we had to hoist her down in a sling. Oh, now I think of it, I've a letter for you."

He disappeared into his cabin, emerging a few moments later with an envelope in his hand.

"Some drunken marlinspike of a lubber stowed a bag of letters from England deep in the hold, and we only found it when unloading cargo." The characters on the envelope were as straight as rulers. My father's handwriting.

We shook hands again. "Thank you very much, Captain. We don't have any money now, but I'll make certain to repay you as soon as I can."

His leathery face gashed into a grin. "Forget the coppers, lad. It's an honor to help two fellows brave enough to board a ship on their lonesome."

I wish it *had* been bravery that prompted me.

Callao's streets were mostly narrow, with occasional piles of rotting garbage separating the wooden houses from the street-traffic. Sailors from half the world slouched alongside stolid-faced Quechua men, neither taking notice of the other. Both looked at us.

"We need new shirts, Chester."

"Aye, or better yet, just one, so we look less like the same man in two bodies."

We paused in a deserted alley to take bearings.

"Doesn't this entire situation strike you as rather strange, Chester?"

"Rather. Perhaps Garcia's afraid of meeting with this mystery villain. It would make sense, losing himself for a bit out in the wilds." He shook his head. "I've a feeling that our friends are in great danger."

"As are we, if we join them again."

Chester grasped my shoulder. "What would life be without danger?"

"Peaceful."

"Precisely. Let's join them as soon as possible."

I removed his hand. "How do you recommend that we do so? We have no money."

"Money isn't everything."

"No, but it purchases everything. We have no money, no means of transportation—"

"Our feet."

"—No *realistic* means of transportation, no knowledge of the country, and no idea of where we need to go."

Chester leaned against a convenient wall. "Very good, Professor. Now, let's forego the negatives for a bit. The positive fact is that we need to find Garcia and Company as soon as possible."

"And that will be after we get the necessary money."

Chester slapped his thigh. "Lawrence, can't you understand?"

I sighed. He looked the part of the noble knight readying himself to battle a host of dragons. I sometimes wonder if he considered me one of these dragons.

"Law, if we meet up with them, only to find that this other mysterious force got there first and sliced them up, or buried them in ant mounds, how will you feel?"

"Distinctly sorry that it happened to them. Distinctly regretful that we couldn't help. And distinctly thankful that we can finally be getting back to England."

He clenched his fist. "I will find them."

"Then of course, I'll be one step behind. But please, Chester, be rational. What means do we have of obtaining money?"

"The oft-quoted three. Beg, borrow, or steal." He resumed his leaning posture. "Stealing's obviously out of the question, and we don't know anyone to borrow from."

"And no Stoning will shame himself by begging." I looked at my tattered shirt. "No matter what we look like. You forgot to mention 'earn.' I know Spanish—assuredly someone needs an interpreter."

Chester pursed his lips. "Not a bad idea. Father would no doubt quote Socrates—something about virtue not being given by money, but money coming from virtue."

I felt the letter in my pocket. I had sent reports as regularly as possible. It was strange that he would write back.

We went to the main hotel, as the most likely place for Englishmen to resort. The room was pleasantly cool, sprinkled with tables, and occupied by a handful of ponderous gentlemen in day-dress, sporting thick cigars and repleted faces. The man behind the bar-counter seemed to be waiter, hotel clerk, and conversationalist tied together. He looked up as we approached.

"No tramps," he said in bad English. "Out."

I felt very self-conscious in my rags. "Please, sir, we're not tramps. We're gentlemen."

"Do I look like a fool?" His face darkened with anger. "Out, or I throw you out."

"Now look here—" Chester began.

"Softly does it," I interrupted. "Señor, we have come upon hard times and are in need of employment. I can interpret for any English gentleman who should require my services."

The man flexed his arms. "You want to be thrown out, pigs?"

Chester squared.

"No, Chester, they'll only put us in gaol. We'll try elsewhere."

Chester pushed past me and strode to the counter. "Look here, fellow, my name's Stoning, and no one calls a Stoning a 'pig.' I'll cut out of here if you want, but I'm not leaving without an apology."

Touring Englishmen often inspect foreign prisons as a sort of gauge of the national health. It looked that I would be allowed to continue the tradition, only in a very intimate manner.

To my surprise, the man behind the counter hadn't yelled for the authorities yet.

"You say 'Stoningk'?" he asked cautiously.

"Yes. You've a problem with the name?"

"Lawrence Stoningk?"

We both stared blankly.

"Er—no, I'm Chester."

The bar-man's face blossomed into a smile. "I did not expect to see you so soon! Have you gentlemen encountered a misfortune?"

I kept staring. "I beg your pardon?"

"I did not expect to see you so soon. You do know Señor Dedoras, do you not?"

"Er—yes."

"He left money with us, to give you if you ever came to us, but he said that this was unlikely, and that he expected to reclaim his money when he returned from the mountains."

"Oh." And men accused Garcia of being ruthless with money. The villains. "Well, here we are."

"And here you are." He unlocked a metal box beneath his counter and handed me a pile of coins.

The cold metal had the feel of power and security. In the past, I'd likened the idea of money to a man who has two volumes of an important work written, and is studying how he can fill more pages. I'd never been the man without ink or paper before.

"Don't you need to verify my identity in some way?" I asked.

The bar-man kept smiling. "The señor said that you were two brothers, twins, and now I see that so you are. I need no more."

After I recovered from Chester's exuberance, we made our way to the nearest shop and re-outfitted. Chester added pistols, a rifle, a sword, and the Eyesore's bloated first cousin. I bought a sword. Of course, we both re-wardrobed.

We stopped by the hotel once more, to hire two mules, and gained an unexpected piece of news.

"The señor," said our new friend, the bar-man, "he met with another señor. They seemed to know each other, and they are now traveling together."

"What was the other man like?" I asked.

"He digs in the mountains."

"A miner?"

"No, he digs to learn of the old people."

"Ah. An archeologist. Thank you."

Chapter 16

I tensed, every nerve straining to resemble sculpted marble. He sat motionless on my arm. *One. Two. Three.* I struck. A bead of dark red blood and half a wing stuck to my palm, the last remnants of the mosquito. I looked at the cloud of friends swarming to take his place and sighed.

Our guide grunted.

"What did he say?" Chester forced his hat down to his eyes and clapped a dozen of the pests between his hands.

I shrugged. "I don't speak Quechua."

The guide, a squat little fellow with his head stuck through a fringed poncho, pointed ahead. We were in a wide, meadowish place, which was covered with two-feet long yellow grass. We had been pushing our mules hard for three days and were well into the hills, though higher peaks rose ahead.

I squinted in the direction the guide was pointing. We were halfway up a hill, and over the rise I could barely see the next ridge. Over this ridge straggled two mules, the one in the rear carrying a slouching Indian.

"I say, I do hope it's them." Chester kicked his mule and trotted past me.

The guide clucked, and my mule instantly began an entirely new pace. The Quechua had become increasingly morose, and I think was quite happy to soon be rid of us. Perhaps it was our eerie likeness to each other—or Chester's nightly harmonica-playing.

At our increased pace we soon closed the distance between us and the riders. A long mule-train straddled the remains of the Inca road and wound up and over the next hill. The Indian on the last mule stared at us with blank eyes. I left our guide to socialize with him and followed Chester, who was prodding his contrary mule as fast as he could.

"Señor Chester! Señor Lawrence!"

I slouched in my saddle to see under Chester's hat and found Garcia riding toward us, his stubby face long with surprise. He reined his mule in front of us and gave each a hand.

"My dear friends, we thought that you were killed by the pirates, or had drowned in the storm!"

Chester shrugged. "Splendid to see you too, Señor. You didn't need to worry about us. I don't expect that I was born to be drowned."

"Hanging's more likely," I muttered.

"Señors!" Pacarina trotted down the line toward us, slapping her mule wildly. "You are alive!"

"Yes," I said, "no thanks to these cursed mosquitoes. Are they everywhere in Peru?"

She laughed. "No, Garcia says that they will not bother us much higher up." She looked at the bandage on my head. "What has happened to you both?"

"It's rather a long story," Chester said.

Garcia threw his right leg over his saddle and dismounted. "We will break now, and hear all. You!" He snapped his fingers at the closest Indian. "Tell your master to halt the caravan." He turned back to us. "You do not know how we have worried for you, my brave rescuers. My sister-in-law has not ceased to conjecture as to your fate."

Pacarina blushed. "Why shouldn't I? It is my right and duty, after all that you have done for me."

The sentimentality of the conversation was reaching an uncomfortable level, so I decided to put the stopper in the ink-bottle and calmly summarize our adventures. Between my summary and Chester's rather graphic interjections, we accomplished the retelling. I didn't mention my spitting and let Chester concentrate on his work with the sword-knife, so we were both satisfied.

It was very peaceful, sitting together in the tall grass on the gentle slope. But I still had unanswered questions.

"Now that we have spent a very self-centered half-hour, we have some questions for you, Señor."

His forehead wrinkled. "Is there something wrong?"

"I don't know yet. Would you mind explaining why you've taken this journey into the wilderness? It was my—our understanding that you were going to rent a villa in Lima or the surrounding area and settle for a time."

He steepled his fingers. "I planned to do so, but when we were attacked upon the sea—" he paused. "Whoever wishes to harm me has evidently followed us. I did not think it safe to remain in town, where he could easily find me, especially when you two brave young men were not here to protect us."

Chester coughed and cocked the Eyesore back a little.

Garcia continued. "When I was thinking of this danger, I met an old acquaintance, an archeologist, who I knew in my early days here in Peru. He was about to leave for the inland mountains to study ruins, so I said, why should we not also go?"

That sounded logical. I glanced up the long line of tail-flicking mules and their stolid Indian handlers. "I assume that this is the expedition?"

"It is. I will introduce you to the archeologist when we begin again."

"One moment, Señor." I glanced at Chester. "We have a few more questions."

"We do?" Chester scratched his chin. "Oh, right, we do." He cocked the Eyesore further and folded his arms. "With respect, Señor, there's more to this whole scenario than some unhappy suitor. Though, with respect to the señorita, I can understand why a rejected fellow would be unhappy."

I frowned. Those types of comments made England look much farther away.

"At any rate, I don't think that any rejected suitor is mad or rich enough to attempt your life, try his hand at capturing the senorita, and then follow us across the world with his own ship and men." Chester yanked a handful of grass and spread it on his trouser leg. "If this were one of old Aesop's fables, this would be about the point for the moral of the story, so I'll spell it clearly and simply. What's actually going on?"

I scrutinized their faces. Pacarina had joined Chester in the grass-yanking pursuit, and was apparently engrossed by the occupation. Garcia was sober.

"Señors, I have often thought the same as you." He looked at Chester, then at me. "At first, I thought it was the young gentleman who asked for my sister-in-law's hand, but the ship could not have been his. You are right. There must be more." He looked at Pacarina. "You are what this mysterious force wants. You alone know why."

Pacarina gazed at the hills below us. Her cheeks were flushed, but her chin was firm. I scratched the stubble on my own chin and waited. The circulation in my right leg slowed, and I had to uncross it and stick it straight out. Finally, her eyes focused on me.

"Long ago, these hills were Inca land." She slowly swept her right hand over the hills behind us. "All authority lay in the ruler, the Inca. They said he was divine. All gold belonged to him."

She looked toward the coast, a dim blue mist on the horizon. "The Spaniards came. They wanted gold. They got gold. But not all the gold."

She looked inland. "Much gold was hidden by the Inca, and his people swore terrible oaths to never reveal its hiding-place to the cruel Spanish. One by one, they died, by the sword, by the whip, and by age. One of the last to know was a woman, a daughter of the Inca. A conquistador took her to wife."

She held her right arm out, palm up, and traced the blue veins with her finger. "That woman's blood runs in my veins. Generation after generation, the secret was passed down, with the same oaths, to sons when there were sons, and daughters when there were not."

She stopped talking and looked at Chester. Garcia stared at her. My brain whirled. *Suitors, pirates, buried gold.* Chester spoke.

"So, Señorita, you're saying that there's a load of gold hidden somewhere in these mountains, and you know where?"

"That is what I am saying."

Chester whistled. "That's a stunner. Have you ever told anyone this before?"

"Never."

"Then how does this other fellow or fellows know about the secret?"

Pacarina shook her head. "I don't know."

Chapter 17

I took a few moments for reflection as our mules were brought back to us. The picture was exotic, but unwanted. I was traipsing into the mountains of Peru with a caravan of odoriferous mules and half-civilized Indians, bound by my duty to accompany Chester, who had bound himself to protect a pretty Spanish girl with a secret of blood and gold. And someone wanted that secret.

The breeze rustled the grass round my legs, and I drew my limbs closer, thinking of snakes. All I needed was to learn that Garcia was actually my long lost uncle to equal one of Chester's novels.

Garcia climbed into the saddle and waved for the mules to start.

My mule proved restive. By the time I had my feet firmly in the stirrups, Chester, Pacarina, and Garcia were far ahead. I straggled behind, content to be at peace with my own thoughts.

I was cresting the third hill when a man came riding back down the line toward me. His hat was wide-brimmed, but as he approached, I found that his cheeks were pinched and blotchy. He drew his beast across the path and tossed a half-eaten orange down the hillside.

"Señor Stoning!" He lifted his hat and bowed. "I trust you have not met any more robber coaches? Coach robbers, I mean."

I stared. "Sabas!"

He bowed again. "It is a pleasure to see you once more, Señor. Your name surprised me when Señor Dedoras said it. I was pained to think you dead. I am glad to see you again."

"The feeling is mutual, I'm certain."

As we rode together I thought of our last meeting. If he told Chester about my reaction—this could be very bad. My brother already thought I was a weakling. Now he would add coward to the list. Who would have thought that a momentary acquaintance in England would appear so inopportunely in Peru? I waved a dozen mosquitoes away from my nose. Along that train of thought, what *was* he doing here?

"How do you come to be with this expedition, Sabas?"

His cheeks rounded into a grin. "It is my expedition."

"Oh." So he was the archeologist. Life was complicating more every day.

We camped an hour before dark, the natives lighting fires, spitting meat, and pitching our tents. Terraces segmented the hill, forcing us to camp in three distinct parties. I sat on a rock and wrenched my boots from my tender feet. The pair I bought in Callao fit far better than the army pair, but my feet were still recovering from the desert journey. The smell of roasting fish and herbs filled the air and set my stomach grumbling.

An unfamiliar voice approached from the lower terrace, spewing a stream of angry Spanish and Latin. Chester appeared with sundry swords, knives, and firearms strapped to his body. I wished Garcia hadn't been so careful to preserve our baggage.

Chester's cheeks were scrunched as if he was in pain, and a fat friar with black robes and a few strands of scraggly gray hair criss-crossed round his tonsure was puffing at his heels.

"Law, I can't stand this fellow any longer. He's been jabbering at me for ten minutes as if I knew the language, and he smells like he's been rolling in a garlic garden."

Chester threw himself down next to me and folded his hands as if in prayer. "You must help me."

I grunted and rose to my stockinged feet.

"What can I do for you, Señor?" I asked in Spanish.

The priest glared at me. "I am Father Lorenzo. Have you been reading the Bible to Señorita Garnica?"

I blinked. "Er—yes, I have. Why?"

"How dare you!" His eyes bulged and his jowls quivered. I almost felt sorry for him, though. It must be torturous for a man with so little hair on the outside edges to have the pick of the crop shorn off in the center.

I offered him a convenient stone and resumed my own.

"It appears that you have a problem with my Bible-reading?"

He snorted like a bull who sees the matador coming. Had he been sitting, doubtless he would have jumped up. As he was already standing, he sat down instead.

"How dare you!" he repeated.

"It required very little daring, actually. The señorita had not read the Bible herself, and she was interested in the Word of God, so I read it to her."

Chester elbowed my lower right ribs. "What's the fellow want?"

"I think he wants us to be far away."

"You are English," Father Lorenzo said. I wouldn't go so far as to say that he spat the word, but it didn't roll off the tongue smoothly. "You are heretics. She is asking questions, doubting the authority of the Holy Father himself!" He crossed what little chest he had left above his stomach. "You are trying to corrupt a good Christian."

"Nothing is further from my thoughts, I assure you."

At the fire on the terrace below, Garcia, Atalya, Sabas, and Pacarina gathered to attack the roasted fish. Two Indians approached us with a steaming metal pan. The priest's nostrils twitched.

"Would you like to join us for a meal, Señor Lorenzo?" I asked.

He looked at us, then at the fish. His hands joined the twitching. "It is not proper to eat with heretics."

"Señor Garcia has not found it to be a problem."

One of the natives squatted in front of the priest with a fish at chin level.

He hesitated, then snatched the fish. "Then I will eat, but I am not done with you yet. The Holy Church is angry."

He addressed himself to the fish with zeal. I sniffed. Chester was right; he did smell like garlic.

Chapter 18

"Put away your weapons."

Chester grasped his pistol-butt.

"What did you say, Señor Sabas?"

"Put away your weapons."

The relatively open mountain terrain was quickly melding into a thick tangle of undergrowth, which ended in a wall of gloomy rainforest. Our mules plodded along the last remnants of the path. Sabas rode near the front, followed by Chester, myself, then Pacarina.

Sabas pointed at his men, who were strapping their muskets onto an empty mule, and then at the forest. "We are Mayamura territory entering. I have been here thrice, and am friendly with the tribe. They will not let me enter with weapons in hand. Do not worry. They will not attack."

Chester shook his head. "I'm sorry, Señor, but I'm here as a bodyguard, and fists aren't much good against guns or blow darts."

Sabas scowled. "I say, you may not go in armed. Do you want us all dead?"

I saw his point. "Come now, Chester, be sensible. With the premise laid out by Señor Sabas, you must recognize that in your current state you are practically a declaration of war."

Chester pursed his lips. "I thought *you* at least would be on my side. A gentleman never parts with his weapons."

"Perhaps so, but there are a large number of dead gentlemen. Señor, how long must we go without arms?"

"Only until we meet the Mayamura." Sabas smiled encouragingly. "Once we meet and an agreement arrange, we may do as we like."

Chester growled. We had been traveling for many days—I do not say how many—and in all that time I never once saw him without at least one pistol in his sash.

Pacarina prodded her mule between Chester and me. "I understand your sentiments, Señor Stoning, but a true gentleman does what is best for others. You can best do your job by hiding your weapons for a time."

Chester grunted and stuffed the offending pistol into his saddlebag.

Machetes were apparently considered necessaries, not weapons, as a group of our natives began chopping a path for us through the dense ground cover. Chester joined for a few minutes and came back flushed and panting.

"Why can't we use the path you used last time?" he asked Sabas.

"The path?" Sabas raised his eyebrows. "This is the jungle, Señor. The jungle lives. We cut, the jungle grows."

I stared into the trees until leaves, vines, and bark became an indistinguishable greenish mass. The thick trees reminded me of my solid desk at home, where I've passed so many pleasant hours. Its mahogany boards came from a forest just like this.

Whzz-thlop. An arrow shot over the choppers' heads and stuck quivering in a tree trunk. I threw myself flat on the mule, its coarse hair filling my mouth. Chester spun his mule in front of Pacarina's. Sabas chuckled.

"Do not fear, Señors. That is a welcome, else it would have struck one of you, not the tree."

A little native carrying a bow in his left hand stepped from behind a tree. He was no taller than four feet, with a broad slash of muted yellow paint across the bridge of his nose. One of our choppers approached him, and the two conversed in guttural tones. The language sounded like a drowning man's last cry, but the meeting must have gone well, because our arrow-shooting friend joined the choppers, apparently as guide.

"He will take us to his village." Sabas looked at the three of us in turn, his strangely dark eyes glittering. "Do as I say, and all will be well."

The village consisted of one to two dozen huts scattered haphazardly round a clearing in the thick jungle canopy. The huts were made of poles lashed together by vines and bits of rope and thatched with dead grass. A group of silent natives stood in the village entrance, but they stepped aside to let us enter, as it were, between their ranks. As soon as we passed each hut a string of men emerged from each low doorway, in their hands either bows or long, tube-like instruments, obviously the far-famed blow dart gun. The women followed their men clad in sack-like garments. Yellow bars or splashes of red paint decorated the faces of male and female. No one was smiling.

Sabas led, followed by Garcia and his wife. Father Lorenzo was off somewhere in the rear. I prodded my beast a bit closer to Chester's right flank. Pacarina edged towards his left. He looked at me, then nodded significantly to his saddlebag.

Sweat beads popped out on the backs of my hands. My sword was somewhere back in the baggage, but even if I got to it, I had no training. *How can Chester be so calm?*

A large hut, larger than all the others, stood at the farthest end of the clearing. Close by the door was a circle of blank-faced old women sitting cross-legged in front of large clay pots and spitting into them. As we approached, a native emerged from the hut's doorway and folded his arms. A curvy red line wound its way, snakelike, up each cheek. What seemed like yards of necklaces hung over his chest, full of teeth and bright stones.

Sabas dismounted before him, bowed, and motioned to one of his men, the same who had talked to the native in the jungle. He seemed to be the only man in the party who knew the language. He strung together a long sentence in the drowning-man dialect, but Snake Cheek remained expressionless. At last, he remarked something in a raspy voice, and the conversation continued.

Chester rested his hand on the saddlebag. The conversation became louder. I could have snapped a pen, I was so angry at myself for not bringing some books regarding linguistics. Presuming we stayed alive, this would have been the perfect chance to study a language.

Chester seized a momentary pause to speak. "I say, Sabas, what's the shirtless fellow chattering about?"

Sabas frowned. "He asks why we bring so many white faces."

"Hmph. Ask why he has so many brown faces."

"Be quiet."

The negotiations seemed to be concluding. The native raised his arm and pointed to his right, where twin mountain peaks rose high above the surrounding forest. Sabas bowed his head, and the deal seemed to be settled. At any rate, the silent natives broke into a clamoring throng of cheerful eyes and bright smiles.

Snake Cheek now greeted Sabas like a long-lost benefactor and sat us down, with some of the head men of the village, around the pots. One of the old women grabbed a stack of wooden bowls and started spooning a thick, purple substance into them from the pot. She looked strangely familiar.

"What is that?" Chester whispered.

"If it's what I've read about, they call it *masato*, or *manioc*."

"What's that?"

I shook my head at him. "You really should read, Chester. *Masato* is fermented cassava, which is a type of tuber."

Chester looked doubtfully at the bowl in his hand. "Is it safe?"

I looked at my own bowl. Little bits of green flecked the purple mush. "That depends on how you define 'safe.' The women of the tribe ferment it by chewing it up and spitting it back."

Chester was about to launch his bowl into the jungle, but I grabbed his arm. "It's our obligation as guests to drink it. You might as well shoot the chief as refuse it."

"I'd rather kiss a python." He rounded his shoulders, closed his eyes, and began draining his bowl.

I was sitting directly next to one of the pots. No one was watching. I lifted the bowl to my mouth, tilted it skyward, leaned right, and managed to drop the slime back into the pot.

Chester belched.

"Quite tasty, don't you think, Chester?"

He glared at me, then looked suspiciously at my bowl.

"It's horrible," he gasped.

I shrugged.

Shouts came from the jungle, and a line of natives filed into the village from the east. A thick-muscled man led them, with a head that rose probably a foot higher than the rest of his followers. He waved them away and joined our group, sitting between Snake Cheek and Sabas. He gave Snake Cheek a look which, in civilized society, would have been considered very unpleasant, and I believe it had the same meaning here, as the necklace-draped fellow scooted farther away.

Sabas turned to Garcia. "This is my friend, the chief."

Garcia raised his eyebrows. "I thought the other was the chief."

"Priest."

Two native girls collected our bowls and took them to the old women, who dipped them into the slime and handed them back.

"You may refuse second helping without offense," Sabas said.

Garcia smiled thankfully, and motioned the returning girls away.

"What did Sabas say?" Chester whispered as the girls approached us.

I contemplated. My mission was to keep Chester safe, not be his private interpreter. It wasn't my fault that he wouldn't take the trouble to learn Spanish. I skirted the question.

"We don't want to offend the natives. If they give you a bowl of the stuff, I would recommend drinking it."

One girl had red face paint, and one had yellow—the yellow one knelt before me and offered a bowl. I smiled, shook my head, and pointed to Chester. Then I resolutely turned my back and left him to the enjoyment of his drink.

Both girls reached Sabas at the same time, and both knelt before him. The chief smiled. Sabas paused a moment, then laughed and took both bowls—but he pinched the red girl's cheek. The priest frowned. I looked at Garcia, and he looked at me. Sabas seemed very familiar with these people. Any indiscretions on his part could seriously compromise our safety.

When the *masato*-drinking party finally ended, Sabas roused the caravan into motion and pushed off on a narrow path just wide enough for our mules to pass through, which led towards the mountains. This time, Sabas joined the end of the caravan, and I managed to position myself just behind him, hoping to learn the results of the palaver. After half a mile the mule in front of him, which had a heavy load, jammed between two trees, forcing us to halt.

Sabas jumped down to assist the natives, and I did the same.

"I beg pardon, Señor Sabas, but what arrangements did you make with that chief?"

He thrust his bowed back beneath the load of planks and resettled it on the mule's shoulders.

"The chief, he agreed to let me search for artifacts. But we must finish before the snake falls."

"Snake?" I eyed the long vines spilling across the path. "What snake?"

He smiled. "You will see."

Chapter 19

I said that there were two mountains, but the first was really only a hill. The second was indeed a mountain. We camped halfway up the hill, which was closer to the village, and summited it the next day around noon. Sabas immediately led us to a square stone building on the peak, measuring no more than five feet square, and still roofed by an enormous slab of stone.

A door opened in the south wall, but I had to maneuver round Chester's hat before I could see inside. There was nothing to see. The walls were firm, and the floor was smooth stone, perfectly clean.

Sabas pointed to the west wall. "There is the snake."

I gazed in surprise at a bright curvy line on the left wall that looked rather like a snake climbing or descending the wall. I glanced quickly to the right, and found a slit cut into the solid stone, almost like those used by medieval archers, except that it curved in and out to form the weird, twisted shadow.

"Splendid view," Chester remarked, looking out the slit.

"This is an ancient Inca sacred place." Sabas fished an orange out of one pocket and peeled it into another. "The natives do not worship the same religion, but they are superstitious. No foreigner is allowed in their lands when the ground touches the snake." He pointed at the shadow, or lack thereof, on the wall. It was a foot from the ground.

"I assume the position changes with the changing slant of the sun?" I asked.

"Yes."

"How long do you have to excavate, then?"

"Eighteen, perhaps twenty days."

Father Lorenzo puffed into our little group and crossed himself before the temple. "It is a shrine of paganism."

Chester nodded at me. I translated. He grunted. "He must be rather familiar with those."

The priest nodded at me, so I translated for him. He crossed himself again, glared at Chester, and puffed back down the hill. I didn't want him to be too offended, as I hoped to engage him in a badly needed intellectual discussion, but at least the air smelled better.

As we filed out of the shrine, or observatory, Pacarina touched my arm.

"Who decided to come to the ruins here?" she asked.

"Sabas, I believe. Why?"

She shook her head and said nothing, but her eyes looked puzzled. She knew something that the rest of us did not.

The natives began operations after lunch, Sabas carefully marking out areas to dig in, and Garcia accompanying. I left them to their own devices and arranged a comfortable bed in the grass with two saddles and an armful of blankets. I had finished Gibbon's *Decline and Fall*, as well as Stanhope's *History of the War of Succession in Spain*. There was so little left to read that I actually succumbed to Chester's offer of an American novel, *The Red Rover*. You can tell a man by what he reads.

I found myself picking absently at the grass and remembering making daisy chains once, when my mother was showing me off to some visiting friends. Funny things, daisy chains. One little white flower leading on to another. It reminded me of the chain of events developing before me—a simple reading of the Bible on *Miriam*, leading to Pacarina's questions, leading to my answers, leading to Father Lorenzo's fear that the girl was leaving the fold, leading to his constant lectures to her, leading to even more interaction between her and Chester, as she tried to keep away from the priest. This last most certainly did *not* lead back to England.

This line of reasoning, though sound according to the logic of geometric proofs, was giving me the chills. I rubbed my shoulders and rose.

"Chester, I'm going to walk around somewhat to warm myself."

"Warm yourself?" Chester stared at me. "You're cold?"

"Yes. I'll be back in a short while. I know you'll have no problem amusing the señorita until I return."

He laughed. "We were actually just talking about another shooting match."

Pacarina flashed a bright smile at me. "Yes, you must shoot again. I know that it was the swell that disturbed your aim on the *Miriam*." Her eyes sparkled. "I will make a wreath, and a prize. Tomorrow you two shall practice, and the next day we shall hold the match."

Her faith in me was touching. I was used to having to prove myself because I was doubted, not because I was believed.

"Very well," I said wearily. What was another shaming?

I longed for solitude, but there was none to be had among the busy natives on the summit and higher slopes of the mountain, so I descended the north slope and entered the jungle. I shivered in the cool shade. It felt wonderful to be the only human being in sight, the only human being in the jungle, for all that I could see. I walked carefully, watching the ground for snakes and ants. A few rogue mosquitoes buzzed around, but they could have been much more bothersome.

I pondered my situation. I was really a bodyguard's bodyguard, without training or any particular physical aptitude. Why was I here? Duty. Duty to bring back a fellow with arm-muscles larger than his brain, and a hat larger than my bedroll. Instead of scraping my shins on fallen trees, I could be sitting at a solid mahogany desk with a pen in my hand and a seven-thousand book library three rooms away.

A large tree blocked my path, so I stopped and leaned against the rough bark. It felt good to close my eyes. I must have been here for some time, until a sudden sound alerted my senses to a presence close by.

Something cracked among the trees to my right. I gripped my machete with cold hands. Pumas roamed these jungles.

Someone spoke. "I say, Señor Sabas, how much farther do we need to go? It's all very well for you to go ducking through a jungle, but I'm losing my breath."

It wasn't a puma. I opened my mouth to call to Chester, when Sabas spoke.

"Do you want gold?"

Something about his voice grated on me, and I slipped around the tree trunk, deciding to listen further before I revealed myself.

"Gold? I can't say that I would mind some. Why?"

"These mountains hide treasure. Inca treasure. The girl knows where."

There was silence. I couldn't see Chester through the thick foliage, but I expected a blow or a shot any moment. Instead, when he spoke, his voice was strangely quiet.

"How did you know that?"

Sabas chuckled. "I know many things. My job it is. You are English, you are not poor, but you are not rich. You like travel. With gold, you can go where you like, do what you like."

"That's so. What do you want from me?"

"We must get the secret from the girl. Garcia and your brother must die."

There was a long silence. I pressed my hot head against the bark, praying that they wouldn't come round the tree. At last, Chester spoke.

"You want me to kill my brother?"

Sabas emitted a dry, cracked laugh. "You are not, what they say, best friends, no?"

"No." Chester paused. "What if I don't agree?"

"You will."

Another pause. "What percentage do I get?"

"I give you one-sixth. I must pay my men, the expensive is expedition—I mean the expedition is expensive."

"Very well. Lawrence and I are supposed to practice shooting tomorrow. I'll take care of him."

My brain whirled.

Next thing I knew, something was pinching my right arm. I opened my eyes and smashed a penny-sized ant with my thumb. Trees towered above me, and four beetles were climbing up my shoe. I leaped to my feet. Had I been dreaming? I ran towards the spot where the voices had come from—no one was there, but a pile of orange-peels lay on an overgrown log. Orange-peels. A fruity, tangy smell. It all made sense. The smell on the man leaping out of Pacarina's window, the smell in the cabin of the pirate who attacked the *Miriam*—it was the same. Sabas was our mysterious pursuer.

I shook my head. It couldn't have been Chester that I heard. I glanced at the surrounding trees, and there, hanging from a thorn, was a piece of straw. The Eyesore had been here, and where Chester's hat was, there was the boy. My brother was going to kill me.

My stomach churned. *My brother is going to kill me!*

A monkey chattered at me from a tree branch. A bird squawked. The jungle was close, oppressive, alive. I fled toward the open.

Vines tripped me, bushes sprang into my path. My vision narrowed into one hazy tunnel. Could I be so afraid of death? Chester was right. I was a coward. My brain felt detached from my body. My ears heard my breath squeezing from my lungs in short rasps.

How could I protect myself from Chester? He could out-fence me with a butter knife. He could choke me with one hand. He could shoot my buttons off while I tried to load once. Shoot—of course—he would shoot me tomorrow, when we met, alone, for our practice match. I tripped over a root and rolled out of the wall of trees into open grass. The natives were still digging, and Sabas was with them.

I crept to my tent and dropped, exhausted, on my bedroll. This would be my last sunset—unless.

Chapter 20

I dreamed of burning trees. Light came to the outside world, but it couldn't penetrate my soul's darkness. My whole life for the past months had been centered on one duty—protect Chester, keep him safe, bring him back to England, and be free of my duty. I couldn't think clearly. I couldn't understand how a Stoning, even Chester, could murder an innocent man. But this was no rumor. I heard him say he would.

We shared a tent. Had he looked at me he must have seen that something was wrong, but he didn't look.

It was kill or be killed. If I killed him—I would have failed my duty—killed my brother. I would live under the shadow of his dead corpse. If he killed me—I would go to a better place, and the world would scarcely be the poorer. The only person I thought might depend on me was to be my murderer. And yet there was another. If I died, my knowledge died with me, and so died Pacarina and Garcia.

Chester loaded both braces of pistols and said he would follow in a moment. I entered the jungle, grasping the first pistol in my clammy right hand. My forehead was slick, and a great bead of sweat dripped into the corner of my mouth and stung my chapped lips. I turned toward camp and set my back against a tree. It was a fitting place to die, in the jungle half-gloom, as romantic as any of Chester's novels. And here Chester would die.

He rounded a tree ten feet distant and stopped. He held a pistol. Nothing blocked our line of sight.

"Quickly, Law, come here, I've something awfully important to tell you."

"You mean, to do to me." My voice was harsh, strained.

"What?" His eyes narrowed. "Lawrence, you look sick. What's wrong?"

"I am sick—sick at heart. I'm sorry this must happen, Chester. I wish it weren't so."

"Law, what are you babbling about?" He took a step closer.

"Goodbye, Chester. I'm sorry."

"Lawrence, stop sounding like a classical martyr and tell me what this is all about!"

I raised the pistol. His body jerked. "Law, what are you doing? You're pointing that at me! This is a shooting match, not a duel."

Frigid cold gripped me. I felt like Cain raising his club over Abel's head, but I knew I was right. It was my life or his. It was self-protection. I closed my eyes and squeezed the trigger.

Crack. The recoil slammed my elbow into the tree.

I tried to nerve my soul for the sickening sight and opened my eyes. There he stood, motionless, slack-jawed, his pistol half-raised. A chunk of his hat-brim was gone.

"Lawrence—Stoning," he gasped.

My eyes smarted and my stomach churned. "I missed."

He shuddered, his mouth snapped shut, and he raised his pistol.

That wicked barrel pointed at my heart. My dulling senses pulsed back to life and every tendon and sinew screamed to run away from Death.

No. I will not run. I dropped the pistol and locked my fingers together.

"Go on," I said. "Don't prolong the agony. Shoot and be done. I know it pleases you."

My temples throbbed like Indian drums, but I forced my eyes to stay open, to meet Death bravely. Perhaps I could prove, too late, that I wasn't a coward.

"Lawrence. You tried—to kill me."

Every fiber in my body tingled. "Shoot! Shoot! You've wanted to many times, I know. You despise me and all I love. You think I'm a coward, a weakling, half a man. You think I'm no good for anything but book-learning. So be it. Shoot! Shoot and be done!"

Tears dripped from my smarting eyes, but still he delayed. *Why will he not shoot?* Chills gripped my arms like tiny ice-spikes. "Yes, I see, of course, you enjoy this, you savor these last moments. I won't let you. I will make you shoot."

I grasped the second pistol. He stepped back, his eyes wide, his pistol still trained on my heaving chest.

"Traitor," I said. "Pacarina thinks you mean to protect her, and you will, until the dark moment when you tear away your mask and reveal your greed." I aimed as best I could with my trembling hand.

"Lawrence! You're mad! I'm not trying to kill you."

I sighted on his heart.

"Lawrence!" he cried.

"Lawrence!" It was another voice. A girl's voice.

I paused. "Pacarina?"

She bounded out of the trees and stood between us, her hands clasped on her heart. "Señor—Lawrence! What do you do? Will you murder your brother?"

"I do it for you, Pacarina. Move. He'll kill you for your gold."

Her brown eyes flashed and she whirled round to Chester. "What is this?" she demanded. "What is he speaking of?"

"Señorita, I'm totally confused, I was about to tell him—" he stopped abruptly. "Lawrence, were you in the jungle yesterday?"

I smiled bitterly. "Even a lowly scholar can stand behind a tree."

His eyes widened. "You heard Sabas and I talking!"

"I did. Pacarina, move, my aim is unsure even when my hand is steady, and I don't wish to kill you."

"Lawrence, I can explain." He threw the pistol to the jungle floor. "I had no idea what he was going to say, but when he revealed himself, I knew I must play along to figure out his game. I didn't agree to kill you, I only pretended to—I said I would take care of you, man. You thought I would kill you? My brother?"

"Why not?" I fought the urge to vomit and tried to steady the pistol-butt. "You don't understand me, you don't like me, you despise a brother who is not strong and fit and hearty like a true English gentleman."

His lips moved, but no sound came forth. "Well?"

"Lawrence, it's true that I haven't liked you, but to kill my brother—how could you think such a thing?"

His eyes were sincere. The pistol lay at his feet. Could it be? "You mean—you aren't going to kill me?"

"No! I was going to tell you what Sabas said, and ask you what we should do."

The pistol fell from my hand. "Then—I almost—" I looked at him, his green eyes wide and full of hurt and shock, and before him Pacarina, her hands still clasped, her beautiful hair spilling over her shoulders, and the picture swirled in my brain. I fell into blackness.

Chapter 21

Pain filled my stomach, and I tried to retch, but only brown phlegm came up. I lay back, exhausted, and felt a pillow beneath my damp hair.

"Drink." Someone held a cup to my lips. "It's quinine."

My throat was dry and hot, and I gulped the water greedily, vaguely knowing that it would come up again. It did. I lay back once more and felt clean, cold hands arranging my pillow.

"Pacarina?" I croaked.

"I'm here."

A wet cloth lay on my eyelids so that I couldn't see, but I felt her touch. It was strangely comforting, such as I had never felt before.

"That's right, old fellow, keep a strong heart." Chester's voice was low, almost embarrassed. "You've got malaria, old chap, but we're making you strong again."

The cloth lifted from my eyes for a moment, and Chester and Pacarina looked down on me with compassion, wonderfully different from my last memory of their eyes. A fresh cloth replaced the old one and cooled my burning forehead.

"Pacarina's a first-rate nurse, Law."

She laughed and smoothed my hair. "Me? You watch by him every night with a woman's care, if not a woman's touch."

Chester coughed. "Yes, well, he is my brother, after all."

I wracked my brain, trying to remember what had happened. The scene in the jungle came back only too clearly, and with it a strange, vague mixture of memories or dreams, of days of heat and cold, of burning pains in my stomach, and cooling cloths on my head.

"What—what has happened?"

Pacarina's cool hand touched my left arm. "I don't know that you are strong enough to hear."

"Nonsense, Law's a Stoning. If he's truly awake at last, then he's strong enough to hear." Chester grasped my other arm. "It's been a week since you decided to redecorate my hat. Thankfully, I never found time to teach you how to aim. Once you finally got the idea in your head that I actually wasn't trying to kill you, the malaria set in, and you were out. You may have something more than malaria, but we've been dosing you with quinine, and hopefully you'll now begin mending."

"But—Sabas. He thought you were going to kill me."

"So he did, which is why he wasn't surprised when we brought you into camp and said that an accident had occurred. You've been in our tent ever since, and Pacarina and I have taken turns watching."

"Where—where is Sabas?"

"That's a story for another day. Promise me that you'll get better, and I'll tell you tomorrow."

I didn't have much choice.

Chester removed his hand, and I heard him rise. "I'd best be out and about for a bit. You're in good hands." He coughed. "Do get better, Law."

He left, and Pacarina sat down beside me.

"You should know, he has watched over you like a mother, or a sister."

"Never had a sister," I croaked. "My mother left nursing to the servants."

"Your mother does not love you?"

I reflected. "I'm sure she loves me—or would, if she ever thought about it."

"I don't know your mother, but I do know your brother, and he has been by your side day and night."

Chester? My twin brother? After trying to shoot him?

She patted my arm. "Now rest, you've talked too much."

"Rest?" My body twitched, and I flung the rag from my eyes and struggled to sit up. "I can't rest with body and mind burning. Talk to me, I must think."

There were dark sacs under her eyes, but even so she looked fresh and cheerful. I waved her protests away and leaned my aching back against the tent pole.

"Tell me about your mother," I said.

She hesitated, but must have decided that it was best to humor me.

"My mother?" She smiled sadly. "She was the best mother a girl could have. She taught me to care for our home, even though we had servants. She taught me to love God, and to obey my father. She taught me how to be a good wife, by her teachings and her life."

"What of your sister?"

"Atalya?" She shrugged. "I love Atalya, but she is a silly girl. I don't know what Garcia saw in her, but I hope they are happy together."

It seemed a good opportunity to ask a question that had long bothered me. "Why was the secret passed to you, instead of your sister, Pacarina—I'm sorry, Señorita?"

"You may call me Pacarina."

I tried to shrug, but it turned to a shiver. I felt like someone was pouring ice water through my veins. "Very well, Pacarina. I suppose I should get used to it, if you're to be my sister."

She flushed. "What do you mean?"

I hadn't meant to say that. "Er, I mean, sister in Christ—oh, that's not so, er, I meant—"

"You think Chester loves me?"

I gulped. And I thought girls were diffident. "I do. Why else would he agree to cross the world to protect you, dragging me with him?" I pondered a moment. "I suppose I shouldn't say that. I came and gave him no choice."

She soaked the rag in a bowl of water, but I could see that her olive cheeks were bright.

"I don't think you know your brother well enough."

"I don't see any other reason for his actions."

"Have you never heard of knights?"

"Not ones with straw hats."

She laughed. "You have little experience with women, Señor—Lawrence, I shall call you—or you would not say such things. Now you must rest. You've spoken too much already."

It felt splendid, lying back down, with the cold rag on my eyes and another blanket over my shivering limbs.

I lifted the rag for one last peek. "Please, Pacarina, before you leave—why did the secret come to you?"

She hesitated a moment, and glanced through the tent flap. She looked back at me. "Atalya is a silly girl. Such a secret should not be entrusted to a silly girl."

No, I thought, when she was gone. *And it was not entrusted to a silly girl.*

Chapter 22

The disease turned that day. I slept restfully, and the next morning felt much better, though still weak and occasionally nauseous. I had much time for reflection that next day, and much to reflect upon. I thought of my relations with Chester over the previous months, indeed, the previous years, and for the first time I realized my own faults and inadequacies. Chester wasn't unintelligent—just as I wasn't cowardly—and now that I considered the matter, he had great strengths, and they matched my weaknesses. Why, working together, we could be so much greater than either—with my knowledge of science, mathematics, and so on, and Chester's physical abilities and unflagging spirit, we were a formidable pair.

I thought of how Pacarina treated Atalya. Atalya was worse than Chester, but Pacarina obviously loved her and gave her the respect an older sibling should receive. She rarely argued, but put up with Atalya's foolishness and insensibility. And she was a Catholic. Here I was, trying to teach her about true Christianity, and utterly wrecking my relationship with my own brother.

The realization of how I had mistreated Chester didn't help the sick feeling in my stomach, but I determined to act differently. Brotherly competition should contribute to the advancement of both, not the victory of one over the other. At that time, I didn't realize how important it would become that we could work together.

Garcia's head poked through the tent-flaps and interrupted my thoughts.

"And how are you feeling today, Señor Stoning?"

"Full recovery is in sight, thank you."

"I apologize for having not visited you earlier." He stepped over my legs and squatted on a camp stool. "My wife did not want me to come, because she feared that I would catch the fever."

"A just fear, no doubt."

He smiled. "She worries too much. You have heard of our situation?"

I shook my head.

The smile became a frown. "I fear I have made a great mistake by coming with Señor Sabas."

Ah. "So Chester told you of their conversation?"

He cocked his head a little. "What conversation?"

"Oh," I faltered, "they—they had a strange conversation, about archeology, or some such thing." So Chester hadn't told him. That was certainly strange.

"No, he did not mention that, but the archeologist has been in the village for half the week, bargaining with the priest for his daughter."

It was my turn to frown. What would an Indian girl have to do either with archeology or gold-seeking?

"His daughter?" I asked.

"Sabas wants her to wife." Garcia twirled a cigar between his first and second fingers. "I cannot help but feel, Señor, that his mind is in other places than the digging up of an ancient civilization."

I silently agreed.

"But I am sorry, Señor, that is not why I came. I came about my sister-in-law."

I raised an eyebrow. Surely he wasn't afraid that she'd catch the fever. "She has been very kind to me during my illness."

"Yes, very kind." He stuck the long cigar into his mouth, a humorous contrast to his stubby nose. "You are a gentleman, Señor Stoning?"

My stomach-muscles stiffened. "I am."

He held his right hand up. "Please, do not take offense, or misinterpret my words. You know that my sister-in-law is my ward, do you not?"

"I do."

He puffed a little fragrant cloud over my head. "I do not quite know how to say this, Señor. I do not know what your feelings towards the girl may be, but I must have you know that I am her guardian, and that you must come to me first."

I wracked my brain. What was he talking about? *No, it couldn't be. Could it?* "You mean to say, if I want to marry her?"

"Yes, yes, that is what I mean to say." He smiled encouragingly. "I do not say that I would be opposed, you understand, Señor, I but say that you must come to me first."

I laughed until my stomach threatened revolt.

"I wouldn't dream of doing anything else, Señor. I also wouldn't dream of doing that. I have largely accepted that she will be my sister, and I don't know a better young lady to fill that role."

His nose twitched. "Your sister?"

I nodded. "I think you're speaking to the wrong twin, Señor."

"Then you think your brother may be interested?"

"He's an impressionable young fellow. Not that that is necessarily wrong," I added hastily, thinking of my new resolves, "but he is used to romantic novels, where the hero and heroine must necessarily be betrothed, if not married, by the end of the story."

"I see." He continued puffing. "Then I must talk to him as well. It is a great responsibility, being responsible for a girl with such a secret."

"How do you think Sabas found out about it?"

He shook his head. "I do not know, but we must make sure that he cannot learn the secret."

"That's why Chester and I are here. If you will excuse me now, I think I'll take a short stroll. I'll need my strength soon, if we must leave in ten days."

Neither Chester or Pacarina were on hand to chide me, so I willed my flabby muscles into climbing the rise to the old Inca temple, or observatory, whichever it may have been. The sun hurt my tender skin, so that the shade inside was alluring. I stepped inside—and faced a little native with red facepaint and a slender blow gun.

My nerves jolted, but I knew that my weak arms weren't capable of fighting. I leaned against the wall and waited. He stared at me, then pointed at the shadow, or nonshadow, on the wall across from me. It was no more than six inches from the ground. The native stooped, touched the floor directly beneath it with his finger, put his lips to his blow gun, and then pointed at my throat. Music is not the only universal language.

This seemed to be the only message he wanted to communicate. He left me leaning on the wall and vanished down the hillside. Chester must have spotted him leaving, for he came up to investigate and vigorously chided me for venturing so far in my weakened state.

I told him about the man's gestures, then asked him why he hadn't told Garcia about Sabas.

"I don't know exactly, Law." He removed the Eyesore and twirled it round two of his fingers. His fingers stuck through a hole in the brim—a bullet hole. "I nearly told him when we brought you back to camp, but then Sabas left, and it wasn't as important. I suppose I'll tell him when Sabas returns, but I can't help feeling that something is wrong."

Eight days ago I would have told him that he wanted the glory of saving Pacarina to himself, but I kept my mouth closed.

He continued. "I'm awfully glad that you're up and about now, Law. That priest has been plaguing Pacarina and me all week."

"Why did he come?" I slid my back down the rough stones till I could rest my haunches on the floor.

Chester shrugged. "Some sort of penance, I believe. Garcia wanted a confessor along, and Father Garlic decided that the natives around here needed a good example of Catholicism."

He talked like the old Chester, but something was different. He kept licking his lips, and his words, though jolly, seemed somewhat forced.

"Is something wrong?" I asked.

He licked his lips. "Er—wrong? Oh, er—no. That is, er—maybe. Yes." He grabbed the loose ends of his sash and started tying them into tiny knots. "That letter from Father."

"Yes?"

"It was normal, right? Short, full of Socrates, talking about our educational experiment?"

"Yes. You saw it for yourself."

Yes. I—saw it for myself." He pulled something out of his sash and flung it next to me. It was a piece of paper.

"I'm rotten, Law. Rubbish through and through."

"What's this?" I picked the paper up and folded it on my knee. It looked like a letter with my father's handwriting.

"When I opened Father's letter I saw two pieces of paper. I wanted to read one first. So I just showed you the top piece. Then when I read the second one—well, I didn't want to give it to you."

I scanned the words.

> *My dear Lawrence,*
>
> *I write quickly, for the post leaves soon. I thought my first letter would suffice, but I have had new thoughts since writing, and thus enclose both. Since you both have left, I have strangely missed you. Yesterday I foolishly left a lighted cigar on the carpet, and a fire began. It destroyed my study, along with many of my papers, among which were most of the records I have so faithfully kept for yourself and Chester. I tried to behave as a philosopher, but it seemed almost as if you were gone, as if I only knew you through my notes. I hear James's horse at the door and must finish. I scarcely know what I write, for my brain spins strangely, but this I know; I was wrong to command you to follow Chester. You need do so no longer. I remove my command. Farewell.*
>
> *Adam Stoning*

I stared at Chester. "Our father wrote that?"

He nodded. "Can you forgive me?"

"But—I don't understand." I dropped the letter and pressed my thumbs to my aching temples. "It doesn't make sense. Why did you hide the letter? You didn't want me along, anyway."

"I didn't think I did, until I thought you might leave. I'm not sure how to say it, Law. I want adventure but—it seemed so strange to think of you not being along. You were the only familiar thing—I don't know. I'm sorry, Law."

"And then I tried to kill you."

He waved his hand quickly. "You had good reason, you thought, and let's let bygones be bygones. No harm done."

"Then this letter is bygone as well."

He smiled for the first time. "You forgive me? You're splendid, Law, thanks." He sobered. "I suppose you'll leave Peru as soon as you're looking less like a gingerbread man before baking?"

"I—I suppose I can leave." The realization finally filtered fully into my brain. I could hire some of the natives to take me back to Callao, and thence I could buy a passage to England. I could go back to my reading, and writing, and studying. I could leave—Chester, and Pacarina, and Garcia.

I looked up at him. "If I had read this on our way here, you're right, I would have left. But now—I can't, Chester. You need me. Or I need you. Or we need each other. I'm staying."

He grasped my hand and pulled me to my feet. No more words were needed.

The outside glare hurt my eyes after the dark room, and for a moment I stared blindly into the distance. Then my eyes focused. "Do you have your pistols, Chester?"

"Of course. Why?"

"Look."

Chapter 23

I pointed down the hillside. A crowd of armed natives was running toward our tents. Sabas had left five of his men with us, and these were pottering around among some ruins below us, the tents blocking the natives from their sight.

Chester slipped a pistol from his sash and drew his sword.

"Halloa!" he shouted. One of our men looked up, and I flung my arm at the approaching crowd. He ran to look between the tents, then yelled at his comrades.

"Run!" Chester bellowed.

The threat put power into my legs and I followed directly behind him, his scabbard slapping my shins every two steps. As I ran I tried to wrangle my pistol from its holster.

"No pistol," Chester gasped. "Don't want holes in the back of my head."

I saw his point and wrestled my sword out instead.

Garcia and his wife erupted from their tent, took one look at the rapidly closing natives, and raced toward us.

"What is happening?" Garcia shouted.

A low stone wall poked out of the grass some twenty yards behind the tents, and this is where we met. Chester jerked his hands at our natives and formed them into line behind this wall. All had picks or shovels, but their muskets were in the tents.

"No time for muskets," Chester said. "Where are Pacarina and the priest?"

Atalya whimpered. Garcia looked around wildly, his eyes bulging.

"He was to confess her at the stream."

Chester sucked a great draft of air into his lungs. "Are you strong enough to run, Law?"

I remembered that this was my first time out of bed for a week, but excitement left my legs tingling with nervous energy.

"Yes."

"Run to the stream—find them—hide them."

I hesitated a moment. My duty—then I remembered the letter. I didn't have to guard Chester anymore. Besides, my first duty was to protect women, and Pacarina was a woman.

I angled up and south so as to round the hill close to the ridge—hopefully the enemy would be too occupied to see me. My big toes scraped raw against the insides of my boots and a sharp running pain started somewhere below my right ribs. The stream was on the opposite side of the hill, really only a small brook that flowed down from a spring.

I finally came within sight of the running water. The priest sat on a rock, talking and gesturing violently at Pacarina. The girl stood before him, her head bowed, but also somewhat defiant. I scanned the slope. No trees, no cover. We must make for the jungle.

"Quick," I gasped, "the natives are attacking our camp, we must hide."

The priest struggled to his feet and nearly fell into the stream. Pacarina's head shot up, and she looked at me with wide eyes.

"Why are they attacking?"

"I didn't ask."

The priest fell to his knees and raised his hands heavenward. "Hail Mary, full of grace, the Lord is with thee—"

I yanked him to his feet. "Mary was human—if you want help, pray to God Almighty as I've already done and follow me."

He let Mary be and trotted behind us at a surprising rate. I kept glancing over my left shoulder, fearing to see a painted face rise out of the grass. Just as we reached the cover of the trees something did move in the grass, but we were out of sight in a moment. There had been no shots from Chester's party.

We dashed through the jungle, tripping over vines and dodging trees. "Here." I pushed the priest into a patch of four-foot leafy stalks. "Smaller numbers hide easier. Crawl to the middle and don't make a sound."

He clung to my arm, lips quivering and eyes bulging. "B-but there are snakes, and ants, and other unholy vermin!"

"If you prefer blow darts then run along back to camp."

I shook the priest off, grabbed the girl's arm, and led her farther through the jungle, twenty yards or so, to a similar patch of cover. "In here." We crawled through the stalks, trying to crush as few as possible, and stopped when we could no longer see the brown tree trunks outside.

We lay side by side, regaining breath in quick heaves. Pacarina turned her head to me, her eyes wide, but her chin firm.

"Do you think we can escape the natives in their own jungle?"

"I don't know." Something tickled my leg but I forced myself to remain calm. My fingers closed round a hard-shelled beetle on my calf, as thick as an apple-rind. I tossed it the way we had come.

Pacarina covered my forehead with her palm. "You are sick. You should still be in bed."

"Don't worry about me, worry about Chester."

She nodded. At least, her eyes nodded, for it's hard to nod one's head when it is cheek down on the jungle floor.

"Your brother is in great danger."

"And so is your sister." We whispered, and I felt sure that we could not be heard outside the stalks. My mind was surprisingly clear. "Now that I think of it, you barely interact with your sister. But you said that sibling relationships are important."

"You can trust your brother."

I paused. "Well, yes, I think I can. But can't you trust your sister?"

She was silent.

"Is that why the secret came to you, and not your elder sister?"

She was still silent. The crawling sensation returned, and I removed another beetle. The ants were probably nearby. Leaves rustled in the distance, and a faint murmur came from the priest's direction.

"That fellow better not give us away." We waited. Nothing. Looking into the girl's calm eyes, I could only thank God that she was the one with the priest, and not Atalya. "By the way, the priest looked unhappy when I came upon you two. What was the problem?"

Her eyelashes drooped. "He wanted me to confess."

"Confess what?"

"My sins."

"What sins?"

"Any I had committed."

There was nothing surprising about that. He was a priest, and that's what Catholics did. And Pacarina was Catholic.

"Did you?" I asked. "No."

I wrinkled my forehead. "I thought you believed in the confessional."

She smiled a weak, half-smile. "Didn't you read from the Bible itself, the verse, 'there is one God, and one mediator between God and men, the man Christ Jesus'?"

"Are you turning Protestant, Pacarina?"

"I don't know."

Here was a heavy stack of papers for mental sorting. Something snapped nearby, and I touched my lips with a finger. I felt her body tense, and we waited. Nothing happened. *Strange,* I thought, as my muscles slowly relaxed, *that she should be changing her mind because of what I read. Perhaps there was a reason that I came on this wild journey. Perhaps*—I felt someone's eyes looking at me from above. The stalks separated. I rolled to my back, and there stood three natives, blowguns pointed at our necks.

Chapter 24

They wrapped tough vines round our wrists and pushed us into the open. The little native whom I had found in the Inca ruin led the way, and his two friends brought up the rear, their blowguns jabbing our backs at whim. Pacarina and I walked side by side, with the trembling priest behind. I hoped his bulk might protect Pacarina from rearward darts.

The wind was at our backs, and our leader sniffed suspiciously at us. I nearly smiled. Though it was a colorful name, Chester didn't call the priest Father Garlic without cause.

They led us back to camp. The tents still stood, and a crowd of natives surged round our cooking fires. There were no bodies near the wall. I strained my neck to look over their heads. There was Chester! He stood next to the Dedorases and Sabas's men.

Our leader moved aside and helped push us to the center of the crowd. Chester stood there, erect, arms akimbo.

"Why didn't you hide?" he asked.

"We did. The little fellow who was in the Inca ruin must have followed me."

He nodded. "They're looking for Sabas."

"I thought he was at the village."

"He was."

I recognized the chief and Snake Cheek in the angry crowd circling us. The Indian priest was hopping mad, literally. Sabas had taken his interpreter with him, but the Mayamuras somehow had him as a prisoner. Snake Cheek barked at the fellow, and he translated the question to me.

"Where is the Sallow Man?"

"I don't know."

Snake Cheek glowered at me.

"You must know," he said through the interpreter. "He would fly to friends."

"I didn't know he was flying from anything."

The chief stepped forward.

"He has stolen our priest's daughter. He wanted her to be his woman."

I shrugged. "I know nothing of the priest's daughter, or where the Sallow Man, as you call him, now is."

Snake Cheek grunted at the chief, and the combination of his words, which sounded like a dying man's gurgle, and his finger, which he slid suggestively across his neck, made my Adam's apple bob.

The chief squinted at us. I tensed my muscles—if I was to die, I would at least make Chester proud. We locked eyes.

"Pacarina dies dearly," he muttered.

The chief raised his hand. Twenty-five bows and blowguns panted for our blood.

Chester's hands clenched. *Oh, for a plan.* Then I had a happy thought.

"Are the Mayamura liars?" I asked.

The chief bent his ear to the interpreter.

"What say you?" he replied.

"You promised us safety until the snake fell."

He frowned. "My priest promised you that."

"He promised for your people. Will you not stand by your word?"

He scratched his painted cheek. "The Sallow Man has stolen my priest's daughter without our agreement. Had he waited, he could have had her."

"Is the Mayamura word to be trusted?"

Snake Cheek exploded into a stream of words, but the chief glared him into silence.

"Your lives are mine. I say you—" a shout from the jungle interrupted him. Looking between the tents, I saw a native running toward us. He bowed before the chief and poured out his story in short, violent sentences.

In a moment the natives were waving their weapons and shouting. The paint lines rippled over their contorted features like bright snakes. Snake Cheek threw his arms up and danced like a drunken Chinese sailor I saw when I first visited Liverpool. The chief turned to me.

"We have found the Sallow Man and his men. They wait for us with the long sticks that shoot fire. I stand by our word—you may live until the snake falls. The Sallow Man may also live until then, but we will not let him leave. When it falls we will kill him. I have spoken."

They trotted away.

Chester plucked his hat from his head, bit the brim, and spit out a mouthful of straw. "I don't know what you said, Law, but you're a brick, and no mistake."

With the danger gone my muscles turned to jelly and my legs trembled.

"He is still not well," Pacarina said quickly. They lowered me gently to a sitting position.

Garcia sat beside me. His hand trembled as he selected a cigar from his case.

"I am very sorry, Señors Stoning, that I brought you here. I should not have trusted this man, Sabas."

"I think Chester has something to tell you that will make you even sorrier."

He swiveled his head toward Chester.

"What is that?"

I nodded at Chester.

Chester shrugged. "I think I know who our mysterious follower is."

Garcia looked up eagerly. "Who?"

"Sabas." He told the story of Sabas's words, and our near-duel.

Garcia leaned forward, his cigar still unlighted. "Then he knows of the secret? And he has brought us to the vicinity of the treasure?" He sprang to his feet and faced Pacarina. "Sister-in-law, if he escapes the natives he will come for us. We must find the treasure quickly and leave this cursed land at once!"

Pacarina stepped back. "I have sworn, Garcia, I cannot reveal the secret."

Garcia scanned the jungle as if he expected to see Sabas marching out at any moment. "You have sworn, girl, but you are only flesh and blood, and if that villain returns, may he not use means which you cannot resist?"

She drew herself tall. "I have the blood of the Incas. I can stand."

Garcia shook his head. "It would mean death for all the rest of us as well. Is there not some way to free yourself of this oath? If he tried the torture and was successful, you would be perjured." He snapped his fingers. "Could not the Father absolve you?"

Her cheeks reddened. "No."

The priest pushed himself forward. "But I could, child, it is my authority as a priest of the Holy Church."

"He can," Garcia pressed, "and would that not be better than risking violating your oath, and letting such a villain gain such a treasure?"

"I made my oath before God. A man cannot absolve such an oath."

Garcia stared at her blankly. "But he is a priest!"

She covered her face with her hands. "What of the Bible? Where does it give him that authority?"

"What's all this jabbering about, Law?" Chester demanded.

Garcia stared at Chester and me. "Have you perverted her religion?" he said in English.

"Perverted her religion?" Chester raised his right hand. "Absolutely not, I plead innocent, please see the Professor for my defense."

Garcia looked down at me.

"I read her the Bible. If that's a crime for your religion, then I recommend reevaluating your religion, not blaming us."

For several minutes, no one spoke. Finally Garcia sighed. "Then we must wait."

Chapter 25

Chester and I took turns that night, watching, but no further threats appeared. I slept until noon the next day, and even then was only wakened by the screeching harmonica somewhere outside.

I think Chester was trying to wake me, because I had hardly poked my head out of the tent when he was on me, thrusting me back in, and shutting the flaps behind us.

"You'll never guess what Garcia's been saying to me, Law." He tossed his hat at the tent pole and flung himself onto a pile of cushions.

I took a stool. "Then I won't try to guess. Where is he?"

"Hmm? Oh, he's out in the jungle with the priest, but he's a splendid chap. He seems to have forgiven us already for reading the Bible to Pacarina. He's not a fiery-blooded papist—more of a traditionalist, you might say."

"I conjectured that long ago. You say he's not angry with us?"

"Angry?" Chester thrust his hand through his hair and grinned sheepishly. "Not quite. He practically just offered me Pacarina."

"Excuse me?"

"Bracing, isn't it?" He whisked a knife from his boot top and scraped at the mud on his heels. "He called me in, said some nice things about the two of us, and then started talking a load of rot about guardians, and wards, and legal jargon."

"Ah. I think I know exactly what you mean."

"Yes, well, at any rate, I told him to hit the bull's-eye, and he certainly did. He said that if I wanted to marry Pacarina, I had to go through him, but he wouldn't be opposed, because he liked me, and he would feel a load safer if the girl had a natural protector."

I rested my chin on my thumbs. "He made the same essential speech to me yesterday, though at the time, the danger wasn't as great."

"Oh." Chester looked a bit crestfallen. "Well, I suppose he likes both of us." His face twitched. "I suppose you—turned her down?"

"Indeed. I congratulate you, Chester, she's a splendid girl, and now that she's coming to our faith, the last barrier is removed."

"Eh? What's that?" He stared at me.

"She's a great girl. Lively, but self-governed. She's no Kate, though you could probably play Petruchio if it were required."

He stopped scraping. "First off, Law, since when do you reference Shakespeare, and what *are* you talking about?"

Chester is not an actor. He couldn't be faking the amazement on his face. "You *are* going to marry her, aren't you, Chester?"

"Marry her? Me?"

"Yes, marry her, are you a parrot?"

He shook his head slowly. "No, I'm not going to marry her. I like her a great deal, certainly, but not in that way."

I tried to grasp this.

"You mean to say, that all this time we've been trailing along, you haven't loved her?"

"Not a bit. At least, not in a romantic way. I like her greatly, perhaps you could even say love, as a sister, but that's all. Whatever gave you the thought?"

I pulled the stool from under me and bumped the floor. "It seemed—natural.

It just seemed—well then why were you so insistent on coming with them?"

He leaned close. "Because she needed protection. Haven't you ever heard of *noblesse oblige*? Chivalry?"

"Well of course, but I thought knights always married the damsels they saved."

"Haven't you ever read about the Knights of the Round Table?"

"Just a discourse upon the likelihood of their existence."

He folded his arms. "You're hopeless, Law. Look, knights rescued damsels because they needed help. They couldn't have married them all, even if they'd wanted to. It's a gentleman's duty to protect, and a Christian's, what's more. Now, what about Shakespeare? I would have expected some Socrates from you, perhaps 'call no man unhappy until he is married,' or something like."

"I'm not a philosopher, Chester. I do enjoy certain of Shakespeare's plays, though."

He grinned. "Then that makes two things in common. We've both turned down the same girl, and we both like old Bill the poet."

Chester likes Shakespeare?

"'To be, or not to be?'" I said.

"'Friends, Romans, countrymen.'"

"'All's well that ends well.'"

"Let's hope this whole dilemma does end well." He paused and stared at me. "It's hard to put into words," he said slowly, "but it's nice working *with* you, not against you." For a moment, he looked at me seriously, his forehead wrinkling. Then the corner of his mouth twitched. "You're not a bad brother."

In a moment we were grinning at each other. "You're pretty good yourself, Chester."

We said little more. He produced his harmonica from his sash, and I pulled out pen and paper.

About an hour or so later we were interrupted by a muffled crack. It was far away, but I instantly knew that that grating ring could only come from a pistol.

Chester froze with the harmonica to his lips. There was another shot.

He dived through the tent flaps and I followed a scabbard-length behind.

Our five natives stood motionless on the hill, staring at the jungle. Atalya dashed from her tent with splaying hair and a pocket-mirror in her hand.

"What has happened? Where is my husband?" She dropped the mirror and wrung her hands.

Pacarina slipped out of her own tent. "He was walking with Priest Lorenzo, Señors. They left some time ago."

Why would they walk in the jungle? It certainly wasn't pleasant walking, save the path that Sabas's natives had been keeping clear for our return journey. The priest hated the jungle, and I didn't think Garcia was much fonder.

Chester cocked a pistol. "Wait."

We stood silently, even Atalya, for six minutes, watching, waiting. Nothing. Then a sound—was it cracking stalks, ripping vines? Something moved in the edge of the trees.

Garcia burst into the open and raced toward us. He was carrying a pistol. Chester and I sprinted to his side.

"Stop—him!" he gasped.

"Who?" I squinted at the jungle. Chester leveled his pistol. Nothing moved.

"There's no one there," I said at last.

Garcia was shivering. Something terrible had happened under those gloomy treetops.

We walked him to Pacarina and his wife, one of us on each side. Pacarina fetched a flask of wine and poured three or four glugs down his throat.

"We are in—great danger." He ripped the collar off his neck. "The priest—he tried to kill me."

Chester took the flask and gave him another drink. "Please, Señor, talk in English so that I can understand you."

He nodded, and removed the flask from his lips. "The priest asked me to walk with him. I walked, though I was surprised that he should want to. We were on the path." He shuddered. "He asked if I knew the secret of the gold, and when I said I didn't, he pulled a knife from beneath his robe and ran toward me."

My head felt like a desk-full of papers caught in a winter gale. "Why?"

"He must have been in league with that cursed archeologist."

Chester raised his hand. "Please, let me understand this fully. Our fat garlic-gulping friar tried to knife you in the jungle, and then chased you all the way back?"

"No. I shot him when he attacked me."

"Then why were you running?"

"Someone *else* attacked me."

The gale in my head was definitely a Nor'easter.

"A native?" I asked.

"He fired a pistol, it could not have been a native."

"Sabas?"

"No. I would have recognized Sabas, and besides he is surrounded by the savages."

Chester scratched his head. "But there aren't any other options."

Garcia swiveled his head, as if afraid of being heard, and lowered his voice to a near-whisper.

"I fear there is someone else. Someone greater than Sabas. Think, Sabas is not rich, how could he have his own ship? But it must have been he who attacked us on the ocean. I fear there is someone else."

I rubbed my chin. "Then you think there's a mastermind behind him?"

He shuddered. "I do not know, but whoever attacked me hides there in the jungle."

Chapter 26

Garcia went into his tent to calm down. Chester lugged a stool onto the hillside overlooking the tents and took guard with his rifle over his knees. I settled down in our tent, slipped off my boots, and started writing my will. I didn't feel dramatic, or particularly emotional. It was simply logical, facing the danger of death, to settle my earthly affairs. I bequeathed most of my possessions to Chester, but this was really just a gesture. If I died, Chester was unlikely to survive me.

I toured my room in my mind, writing down each book as I saw it on the shelves. History, science, theology, mathematics—if Chester were to survive me, I hoped that he would appreciate their worth. A shout from Chester yanked me back to Peru.

I leaped for the door, but my feet felt wrong. Of course, I was still in my stockings. I groped for my boots and thrust my feet in, first left, then right. My right heel stuck slantwise, so I let it be and wobbled out of the tent. A haze of smoke clung to the north mountain-slope. Chester ran down the hill toward me, his rifle slung over his back.

"Blankets!"

I wobbled back inside and grabbed a load of blankets. There was no time to play with my boots. I slammed my heel down—my stocking ripped at the heel, but my foot flattened into the proper shape. Blood was pumping to my heart.

The fire was several hundred yards from camp, and by the time we reached it, Chester was puffing. We each grasped a blanket and attacked the burning grass. Garcia soon joined, followed by the five natives. The fire-encompassed area was not large, but it was growing quickly.

I turned my face from the fire, but the heat scorched my neck and arms. The tough wool blankets scratched my hands as I beat down at the flames. The air smelled like a concentration of the cheapest cigars imaginable.

We formed a ring, first containing, then narrowing. The charred ground smoked under my feet as we advanced, but if we didn't kill the fire at its heart the wind might toss sparks past the circle we had beaten out and into the dry grass beyond.

At last, the fire was conquered, leaving a black bald patch of smoking earth and stubble.

"This was no accident," Chester said, panting.

I wiped my forehead, transferring a thick streak of soot to my blackened sleeve. A thought came to mind, and I whirled round to look at the distant tents. "Chester, we've left Pacarina unprotected."

He was doubled over, spitting black phlegm. "Run back and see to them. I'll be along in a moment, I—I need to make certain the fire's dead."

I ran back to camp, Garcia following. No one was in sight. Pacarina's tent was empty. I poked my head into Garcia's tent. His wife was on her knees before a crucifix.

"Where is your sister?" I asked in Spanish.

She jumped. "I—I don't know."

I ran to my tent. She wasn't there.

"Could she have gone to the stream for water?" Garcia's face was red from the fire-heat, but I think it would have been white otherwise.

I shook my head. "No. She's intelligent, she knows that one bucket of water wouldn't have helped."

"Sabas's tents?"

The second grouping of tents was twenty yards away, where Sabas's natives ate and slept.

"We'll search."

We entered the sleeping-tents first, but there was nothing save the natives' blankets, clothing, and food. Only the two supply tents remained. I darted into one—it was stocked with all manner of equipment, tools, weapons, crates, barrels, but no Pacarina. Garcia's eyes were wide.

I walked to the last tent and slowly pulled the flap back. A pile of planks lay on the ground, with two thick coils of rope beside them. Otherwise, the room was bare. No Pacarina.

I clasped my wrist. Garcia cracked his knuckles. Chester came puffing up to us, his sash untied and draped over his shoulder, and the front of the Eyesore's brim scorched.

"Where is she?"

I lifted my shoulders.

He punched his left palm. "The fire was a ruse, man-set. We're going to find her."

"I will come," Garcia said.

"I'm sorry, Señor, but you're not fit enough."

He stared at Chester.

"It will be no pleasure-trot, you can be certain of that. Lawrence, grab your sword."

Garcia stepped in front of me, blocking my path. "Señor Chester, your brother is hardly more fit than myself. He has been sick, he is recovering. I will go in his place."

Chester shook his head decidedly. "My brother will have time to be sick later. If you see us again, we'll have saved her. If you don't, well—how do you say it? *Bon jour.*"

That was that. We armed, then trotted the jungle-path to the village. A troop of monkeys followed us overhead, their brown bodies flitting through the green foliage, and their strange hiccuping cry, as if the whole group had persistent indigestion, filling the air. Chester, running at my side, was emitting noises not so very dissimilar.

"Are you all right, Chester?"

He swallowed. "Yes, quite. The smoke—it's made my lungs scratchy."

We leaped a log. "What if the natives took her?" I asked.

"Then we get her back."

We leaped another log. "What if someone else did, but the natives stop us to ask questions?"

"We keep going. We don't speak the language."

"I suppose we could try sign language."

He clenched his fist. "That's the only sign language they'll get out of me."

But when we ran out of the jungle into the village, the first man I saw was Sabas's interpreter. He stood, arms akimbo, by the *masato* pots while the chief harangued his followers, who were gathered in a dense body at the center of the clearing. The chief stopped and glowered at us.

"You talk," Chester said.

I skipped preliminary compliments and got to my point as quickly as Chester might.

"Have you seen the Spanish girl?" I asked through the interpreter.

"Why do you come here?" the chief countered. Every man was holding his weapons.

I bit back my fear. "We look for the Spanish girl. Did she pass?"

The chief paused, his beady eyes staring into mine. He said something to the interpreter.

The man spoke rapidly. "He doesn't want to tell you, but I will. She ran through not long ago with a man, they thought he was one of Señor Sabas's men, but he was not. They went the path we came."

"God bless you."

The chief looked suspicious.

"We go," I said, pointing toward the path.

He nodded and turned back to his men.

"Are you safe?" I whispered to the interpreter.

"Yes. I am half Mayamura, they will not harm me, but I must obey. Sabas has sent messenger, they think he means to fight. We go to meet him."

Chester tugged my arm. "Well?"

"He saw Pacarina and a man heading for the outside."

Chester trotted away without a word. The jungle soon blocked the village from sight, boxing us into the narrow, twisty lane that Sabas's men had kept clear. We ran silently, stopping frequently for breath.

Even these breaks weren't enough. Chester was soon bent almost double, waddling like a duck, the air hissing from his lungs.

"Which side is the pain?" I asked.

"Left."

I felt new excitement. Could I actually use my knowledge of anatomical processes to help Chester in the physical realm?

"Inhale only when you put your right foot down. Exhale the same way."

At first, he slowed until he was nearly walking, then it began to work, and his pace gradually increased. It nearly always works. Breathe when the foot opposite to the running pain hits the ground, and the pain should gradually die away. His breath was still short, but he stopped bending.

After half an hour we stopped and Chester pulled a slice of bread from his pocket. He broke it in two, and we munched together.

"Do you think they're making for civilization?" I asked.

He shrugged. "Don't know. She's plucky, but she won't run her fastest if she's been kidnapped. They'll have to stop the night in the jungle, and if we keep on with short breaks, we'll catch them."

"What then?"

He touched his sword-hilt.

Chapter 27

Little is worse than a night in the jungle. Perhaps some Englishmen tolerate such nights. Perhaps some don't notice them. Perhaps some even enjoy them. None of the three apply to me. At times, as we blundered along the path, I thought that the creeping creatures beneath my feet were the worst, and the occasional sting or bite would make me certain.

Attempting to remove my mind from these physical discomforts, I would stare at the dark forms around, the trees, and stalks, and vines, and they would change to horrid beasts, dragons, and hobgoblins, as in the stories my nurse told long ago. I believe these are the worst fears—when you know that there's nothing really there, but you're afraid anyway.

For once, my fear didn't try to stop me from going forward. The path we'd come was just as dark.

Chester was quiet, but he seemed not to notice the dark.

In the early morning light, when the sun and the trees fought for the conquest of the dark jungle floor, we heard footsteps. They were irregular, probably tired like ours, and moving away. Chester's eyes were just visible in the gloom. They were bright.

I pushed my aching legs harder. The footsteps quickened—we had been heard.

Chester pulled his pistol.

The sunlight conquered the shadows and our path took more shape. The hobgoblins fled. Our quarry was close enough that I heard quick breaths, and the footsteps were louder. One more bend.

Click. Chester cocked his pistol.

"Don't shoot too soon," I gasped.

We rounded the bend. Ten feet away stood Pacarina, and beside her a man, his dirty clothing in shreds, stubble covering his chin and cheeks, and a strange light in his eyes. Chester stopped and leveled his pistol. The man opened his mouth. Pacarina screamed. *Crack.*

When I opened my eyes, they were both on the ground.

"You've shot her!"

Chester shoved his pistol into his sash. "She fainted."

He gently lifted her off the man's body, and I knelt to examine him. The bullet hit slightly above the nose, causing instant death. I swallowed against the rising vomit and forced myself to check his pockets. They were empty, save for a few coins and a crumpled piece of paper. I unfolded this and smoothed the creases between my palms. Crude triangles and circles dotted the paper, and in the top center was a square. It must be a rough sketch of our camp, with the Inca ruin above.

"Recognize him?" Chester asked.

"There's not much to recognize, after your bullet, but he doesn't seem familiar. I hope he wasn't a friend."

He looked at me. "No friend would be stealing her."

I shook my head. "I'm beginning to think that any true friend would want to steal her out of this place." Chester loosened the stiff collar round Pacarina's neck, and her breathing came more regularly.

He chewed his thumb-knuckle. "Should we carry her?"

My knees twitched at the thought. Yes, she was slim, but my legs, still recovering from my illness, were over-tasked just to carry my own weight.

"What would the knights do?" I asked.

"They always had horses."

"Then I think we should wait."

I took his place by her side, so that he could drag the man's body into the jungle. Her wrist-pulse strengthened. Red tinges spread over her white cheeks. Her head twitched.

"Pacarina? Pacarina, can you hear me?"

Her eyelids fluttered, then opened, and she looked up at me with dim, uncertain eyes. "Father?" They cleared further. "Juan?"

"Try Lawrence."

Her eyes sharpened, and she struggled to sit up. "What—what happened? Why are you holding me?"

She had a point there. I propped her against a tree trunk and let go.

"You've had a trying experience, Pacarina, but you're safe now."

"Chester?"

"Present." His shadow bled over my shoulder and covered her face. "I'm awfully sorry for the whole thing. Couldn't be helped. It's done now. He won't bother you anymore."

"Juan?" She searched the path with her eyes.

"Who is Juan?" I asked gently.

"My father's servant—he was just here."

My knees gave way and I crumbled into a sitting Turk's position. My mouth went dry. I think Chester's knees gave way also, for he was suddenly kneeling at my side.

"Who?" he asked hoarsely.

"An old man was with me." She started. "The shot—did you—is he—"

Chester nodded. "Who was he?"

Her head dropped onto her bosom. "Juan. He was my father's servant. I thought he died with my father and mother." She looked into the distance.

I took her hand. "Why was he here?"

"He said to rescue me." Her dark eyes darted to meet mine. "Lawrence, he said that it was no accident that killed them. Someone was on the hill, someone started those rocks—" she covered her face.

I looked at Chester. His face was white, almost green.

"I killed him. I thought he was an enemy. I didn't ask. I killed him." It was his turn to stare into the distance.

The realization crept into my mind. We had just killed a friend who was trying to protect Pacarina. What secrets did he know? What knowledge did he possess that we didn't?

I wasn't sure which of them needed consoling more, so I picked Pacarina.

"Did he say who was on the hill? Who pushed the rocks?"

She shook her head. "He couldn't see." She took a deep breath and uncovered her eyes. "Señors, I don't know what is happening, but I am very afraid."

Chester groaned. "I can't believe I killed him." He sat on his haunches and thrust his head between his knees.

Pacarina sobbed, and crawled to his side. "Señor—Chester, it was not your fault, you could not have known."

He shook his head fiercely. "I should have waited, asked. It's all my cursed hastiness. Lawrence wouldn't have done it."

I licked my dry lips. "Lawrence couldn't have hit him even if he *were* bad," I said.

She touched his shoulder. "Please, don't."

He looked at her, and a tear was in his eye. I'd never seen that. "You can't forgive me, and I can't blame you."

For a long moment she said nothing. I almost thought she agreed with him. Then she tried to smile through her tears. "You did it for me, how could I not forgive you? Come, I will show you that I do. I will call you Brother."

He raised his head. "Brother?"

"Brother."

He grasped her hand and sobbed. "Lawrence." I stretched my legs and managed to kneel beside them. "Lawrence—Brother—we have a sister."

I took her other hand. My nerves were overwrought. I wanted to blubber like a little boy, but I knew I must be a man. *Oh, what would a knight say?* Then I knew. I didn't have to be a knight. If she wanted me to be a brother, then I must simply be me.

"Welcome, Sister. Our future is uncertain, but for as long as it lasts, our lives are yours."

She smiled a little wider. "Thank-you—Brother. You sound like a knight. Like Don Quixote."

Chester took a deep breath and rose to his feet. "Then let's find him some windmills. Come, I've done enough harm for a week. We have a long journey back, and strength needed when we arrive."

Chapter 28

My shins were tight, and my feet felt wet from blisters or blood. Little streams of sweat tickled my ribs. The sun's rays battled with the treetops, but few penetrated the leafy shield-wall to reach us down below, and these seemed weary from long warfare. The humid air had no battles to fight, so my chest was heavy from breathing thick oxygen.

Noises filled the jungle around us, but they were no longer the nameless fears of night. Trees were trees, and vines were vines. My waist was raw from my sword-belt chafing it all night. I wondered if the knives in Chester's boots bothered him. He was plodding at our lead with a mule's tenacity. Pacarina followed him, her chin high, her voice cheerful, circumstances considered, but when she looked back at me there were dark circles beneath her eyes. It had been a long night for us all.

Chester spoke. "I say, Pacarina, did you ever read Shakespeare?"

"A little. Why?"

"Just curious. Law once compared you to Kate, the shrew."

"Lawrence?"

"Hold now, that's not true," I countered.

Chester grunted. "I heard you with my own ears."

Pacarina smiled back at me and lifted those thin eyelashes.

I frowned. "Don't believe him. I said that you were *not* Kate, and the context—" I paused. "Actually, the context isn't important, but I was speaking in your defense. You're much closer to Bianca."

She mock-curtseyed. "A lovesick goose with more suitors than wits? Thank you, Brother."

I feel quite capable at battling wits with men, but girls are another matter. I ducked a low-hanging vine. "Chester, I leave flattery to you from now on, along with your pistols and knives. I scarce know which is more dangerous, either to the deliverer or recipient."

"The pistol is much more dangerous to you, if you're the deliverer. Let's pause a moment."

We paused for many moments all that day. I kept a careful eye to our rear, but no natives appeared. They must be watching Sabas. The interpreter seemed to be a decent fellow. I wondered what his role was in the scheme.

Twilight was nearly changed to night-darkness when we stepped out from the trees and finally saw our campfires beckoning on the hill. Too many fires. I used my fingers to count the number of people there should be—five of the archeologist's men, plus Garcia and his wife. Seven. I counted eight fires. Why would they light more fires than there were people to use them?

The closeness of rest gave us a last burst of strength. It wasn't that my legs stopped feeling like thin curved bones tied to my ankles with wire, but that the wire was holding more tightly. The brave girl took a few more steps at our faster pace, then her knees buckled and she would have collapsed had we not caught her. I slipped my hand round her waist from the left, and Chester supported her right, so that we half-helped, half-carried her into camp.

"Pacarina! Señors Stoning!"

I could only see his silhouette against the main cooking-fire, but I would recognize that stub-nose in Africa or the Antarctic. Another man stood next to Garcia, and he also seemed familiar. His back was hunched, and his profile was angular. *Sabas?*

"Good evening, Señors Stoning." Sabas bowed.

Chester almost dropped Pacarina. "You—I thought—didn't the natives have you holed up?"

Sabas smiled, and his dark eyes searched the girl's face. "They did, but I am friends old with the chief, we soon agreed. We are friends once more."

"But what about the priest's daughter?" I asked.

He shrugged. "The chief does not like the priest. What cares he for his daughter? Priest is unhappy, no matter. I returned the girl, all is well."

I looked at Garcia sharply. He bit his lip, half-nodded at the archeologist, and lifted his shoulders helplessly.

"The señorita needs to go to bed immediately," I said abruptly.

We gave her to her sister and sought our own beds. All was dark in the tent, but I quickly found the pole with my head and knocked myself woozy. At the same time my scabbard managed to angle between my legs, and I tripped into a pile of scratchy wool blankets. I had no desire to get up. The blankets smelled of smoke, and my right thumb poked a hole in the charred wool.

"Should we take turns watching?" Chester asked, his voice muffled.

I tensed my neck muscles and managed to lift my head a few inches. "I can't stay awake much longer, Chester."

He snored.

I sighed and let my head fall. Tomorrow's problems were just that—tomorrow's.

Chapter 29

Tomorrow became today. I woke with a confused impression that someone had been watching me during the night. Some sharp, thin, ghoulish face.

I breathed deeply. The smoke scent was still there. "Chester?"

No answer.

I raised my head and looked at his side of the tent. The blankets were mounded, and his harmonica sat on top. His sword and pistols were gone.

My feet felt pinched, and I realized that I had never removed my boots. Efficient, yes, but not particularly comfortable.

My head felt dense. I wondered if that was the feeling drunks experienced after a wet night. I never drink myself, so I wouldn't know, but if there is any parallel between the feelings, then that is just one more good reason not to drink.

All of Sabas's men were back and were scattered over the hillside with shovels and picks. It looked like Sabas was actually an archeologist, as well as a treasure-seeker. The two professions merged admirably. I didn't see Sabas himself, but Garcia and his wife were arguing by the smoldering fire. They stopped when I approached.

"I am glad to see you walking, Señor Stoning," Garcia said.

Atalya's cheeks were an angry red, but she smoothed her dress and motioned me to a seat.

"You—you risked much yesterday, Señor Stoning."

I shrugged. "Only a gentleman's duty, Señora. May I ask where the others of our party are?"

Garcia coughed. "Señor Sabas is doing something in his supply tents, I believe. Your brother escorted my wife's sister to the stream."

"I see." I glanced round. No one was within earshot. I leaned closer. "Señor, what has happened? Why is Sabas here again?"

He also looked round nervously, and hunched closer to me. "As he told the story, he is an old friend of the chief's, and once the chief was past his first burst of anger, Sabas negotiated through messengers. The archeologist agreed to return the girl and resume his regular negotiations for her, and the chief promised him free passage until the snake falls."

"And the priest?"

Garcia shook his head. "He is furious, I think."

"Quite understandable. What are you going to do now?"

He chewed his cigar. "We are in his power. We cannot leave without his knowing. But if we stay after the snake falls—" he shook his head. "Could your brother not have been mistaken? Perhaps it was a joke, a misunderstanding?"

I frowned. "Then who attacked us aboard ship?"

Garcia sighed. "You are right, all points to him. And the friar said that they were working together."

The friar. "Yes, Lorenzo." I pondered a moment. "You said that the priest tried to kill you with a knife, and you shot him—and then the other man shot at you?"

"Yes." Garcia shifted to the edge of his camp-chair. "Who was this man? Your brother said very little this morning."

"Yes, he's taken to brevity for variety, but I'll explain that later. Do you know why this man attacked you?"

He raised his hands. "I know no more than you. As I told you, he fired, a close shot, and I ran."

"Very interesting."

The more I thought of the whole scenario, the less logic there seemed to be. Why did this old servant track us all the way to Peru and try to kill Garcia? What's more, who tried to kill *him*, and did kill Pacarina's parents, in Spain? Why? I had more questions running through my head than are on the final exam at Eton.

They were soon to be answered.

We spent a quiet, watchful day. Sabas stayed busy on the hillside. I read the Psalms to Pacarina.

Dark clouds gathered in the sky at the end of the day, a brisk breeze started, and the whole feeling of the air changed. A storm was coming.

Chester and I went to bed early. He took first watch, and I nestled into my blankets.

I scarce knew that I was asleep when a slap on my shoulder wakened me. I stared up groggily into the darkness.

"Mmugh. My watch already?"

"Wake up, Law, we have a visitor." Chester's voice was low and tense.

I scrambled to my knees and groped for my boots, but my hand closed on a cold pistol-butt instead.

"Only shoot if I'm behind you," he whispered.

I swallowed.

The canvas walls snapped in the gusts of wind. Rain dribbled. Lightning flashed, followed almost immediately by a thunderclap. The momentary light left a long thin shadow on the tent-flaps. Someone was nearby.

"Qui va la?"

The light was gone, and all was black.

"What's with the French?" I whispered.

"Sentries say that in the books."

"This isn't a book." I cleared my throat loudly. "Who goes there?"

"I am my friend." The voice was loud to be heard over the rain. *What manner of answer is that?* "I mean, I am your friend." *Sabas.*

"What do you want?"

"Come with me."

Chester snorted. "Why should we do that?"

"You must."

"Why?"

"Because the camp is full of my men. If you come not, they will bring you."

That was sound logic.

Chester grunted. "Very well, but if you try any tricks I'll redecorate your forehead."

I crammed my feet into my boots and slipped a poncho over my shoulders. Sabas waited for us outside, his face hidden in shadow, his back hunched more than ever. The rain was coming down hard, and soon had little rivulets running down my back. Silently he turned and led up the hill. We passed the last tent without sign of pausing.

"We're going to the Inca ruin," I whispered.

Chester nodded.

Lightning flashed again as we neared the top, showing a glimpse of the squat temple. Blankets were tied somehow over the door and snakish window. I remembered my sword, hanging on our tent-pole, and wished I had brought it along. The pistol in my hand did not bolster my confidence.

Sabas pulled the blanket away from the door and pointed inside. Chester didn't hesitate, but entered boldly. I swallowed my heart and followed.

"Umph." Never stop suddenly in a dark room when an unsuspecting brother is following. My nose lost a one-sided battle with the back of Chester's skull and water clouded my squinting eyes.

"Hello?" Chester said. "Anybody home?"

The blanket swished back into place behind me.

"Welcome," said a man's voice. "I apologize for this inconvenience."

I pointed my pistol in the direction of the voice and accidentally speared Chester in the back. He winced.

"What's all this about, whoever you are?" Chester demanded.

"I need your help." Something rustled in the far-right corner, and I thought I could see a dark shape outlined against the wall.

"What kind of help?"

"Would you like gold?"

"You didn't drag us here just to offer us gold."

The man in the corner chuckled. "Not entirely, you are right. However, you will gain gold if you help me."

I licked my lips. "Are you after this Inca treasure?"

"I am."

Chester grunted. "So you're the fellow that has been causing us so much trouble. You're the archeologist's boss, aren't you? Come now, be a man and show us your face. Or are you a coward?"

For a moment, the man was silent. "Ah," he said slowly, "but you have seen my face." A bright beam of light lit the room from a dark-lantern in the corner. Two legs stood over the lantern. And above those legs, a body. And above that body, a head.

"Good evening, Señors Stoning." *Garcia!*

My lower jaw dropped. "You!" I gasped.

He smiled, but it was no longer a cheerful merchant's grin. "A pleasant surprise, I hope, Señors?"

"What—but you—but they were after you!"

Two chairs were between us and him, facing him. He chuckled and pointed at them. "Please, sit."

Chester, who hadn't said a word since the revelation, sat down mechanically, and I followed his example.

"A cigar, Señors? No? Then I will have one if you do not mind." He placed the end of his cigar into the lantern, then stuck it between his lips and puffed peacefully.

"You say, Señors, that 'they' were after me, but it was actually I who was after myself." He crossed his right leg over his left knee. "You see, Señors, the world does not look kindly upon men who force their sisters-in-law to give away long-hid secrets. They think much of men who chase kidnappers into wilderness places."

Chester spoke. "Then you arranged for her to be kidnapped?"

"Yes. All was pleasantly arranged between myself and Sabas, until you so opportunely saved my life."

"From Sabas?"

He frowned. "No. I had not planned for that. It was the same man who ran away with the girl two days ago, I believe. It must have been one of her father's servants. Perhaps her parents' driver did not die when they did, as he was supposed to."

I gasped. "*You* killed her parents?"

"Not personally. Señors Stoning, you must understand that you walked into a very carefully thought plan. Mine is not the half-calculated scheme of a desperate man. I have waited and watched, and now the game is almost through."

"Why? Is money worth so much to you?"

He frowned. "Who cares for money, but for what money buys! Money will buy Don Carlos his kingdom, and I will be his most powerful adviser." He stopped abruptly.

"But they said you were against Don Carlos."

"That is what I intended the world to think."

"But, you turned in some of his adherents."

"Ah, so you heard? Yes, I did. Suspicion was rising, I had to prove myself. The men were poor spies, mere liabilities."

The whirling in my brain had slowed a bit, and I was rapidly picking up the pieces of my shattered thought-patterns. So many questions, and strange looks, and oddities, and holes, now made sense. But why us? Where did we come into this dastardly scheme?

"Then what are we here for?"

Garcia puffed at his cigar. "A good merchant always has many available options. When you saved my life, you offered me another option. Several options, in fact. First, by making much of the attack on my life, I had an excuse to come to Peru. Taking you with me gave more—what is the English word—*credence*, to my actions. Who could blame me if the girl was abducted upon the ocean? Had I not brought two bodyguards?"

"That was the only reason?"

"No. I also brought you because you are English. That is why you are here tonight."

Chester fidgeted with his pistol. "How does our being members of the greatest nation on earth affect your scheme, Garcia?"

He smiled. "You English are such patriots. You know of the girl's oath. She cannot tell the secret to Spaniards. But you are English."

Chester bristled. "So you want us to trick her into telling us?"

"No, she is more intelligent than that. I had hoped that she would love one of you, and so be willing to tell all, but you did not advantage yourselves of opportunities."

"Leave talk of love out of this treacherous mess. If you don't want us to trick her, how are we of any use to you?"

Garcia knocked his cigar-end against the lantern and let a heap of ashes drift to the stone floor. "I brought the silly priest to absolve her of her oath, but your cursed talk of religion spoiled that plan." He glowered at us. "You saved her from Sabas on the ocean, and you saved her from the priest. It is only fitting that now, in the end, you should be the means of getting the secret from her."

"How?" I asked.

"I am not a bloody man. I do not like violence. I want peace, and money buys peace." He looked at us narrowly. "Tomorrow, Sabas will at last be happy. The secret will be wrenched from her. He will begin it, but you will finish it, and it will not need to be so long or so painful, because by telling you she will not break her oath."

Thunder cracked outside.

"But then you want us to tell you."

"When the pain comes, she will be glad enough that she does not break her oath in letter as well as spirit."

Chester rose. "You're a cold-blooded monster."

"I? A monster?" He jumped to his feet and dashed his cigar to the floor. "You young fool! I have plotted and schemed to make this an unnecessary step. The priest, you—do you think I want her to be tortured? She is still my wife's sister."

"Yes," I said. "She is. Is that how you found out about her secret? Your wife?"

Garcia shook himself, muttering as he picked up the cigar. "The silly woman has wide ears. Her parents were right not to give her the secret—but she overheard bits of it anyway. She was in the next room when they swore Pacarina to secrecy."

"And then she told you when you married her." Chester sneered. "A touching display of conjugal trust, I must say."

"Chester, sit down." My overloaded nerves were stretched tight, like the limbs of the men offered as sacrifices here in the olden days. "Garcia, you don't deserve this gold."

"But I do!" He exploded. "Years of toil, years of planning. Is that nothing? Only a girl's foolish obstinacy is between me and my treasure, and no one has better right to it than me. The Incas are dead. Why should I not take it? It is mine, by justice."

"Then we will help you to that end."

Chester choked. "What, Law?"

"Be quiet. Garcia, we will help see that justice is carried out. Tomorrow, we will be ready."

Garcia squinted at me. "You speak the truth?"

"Gentlemen don't lie."

He winced. "Then you make me happy. I did not want to kill you. Sleep well. Tomorrow you will be rich."

Garcia covered the lantern, and Chester and I slipped out of the darkness of the ruin into the storm. Sabas stood next to the entrance, impervious to the wet, his teeth gleaming and his long fingers twining about each other like a den of baby snakes.

"Tomorrow you see the work of Sabas," he hissed.

I prayed that Chester wouldn't strike or behead him. He didn't. In fact, Chester didn't breathe a word until we were back in the privacy of our tent. Then, he turned on me with glaring eyes and clenched teeth.

"What are you doing?" he asked, barely restraining his voice to a vehement whisper. "You just promised us to help a pair of filthy villains torture a pure, innocent, beautiful, trusting—"

"Stow the adjectives, I know what Pacarina's like just as well as you."

"Then tell me what you're thinking! Do you have no honor?"

"Chester—" I forced the air from my lungs. "Chester, listen. I thought you trusted me more. What did I promise to do?"

"To help the fiends." He spat and glared at me.

"To help them do what?"

"I'm not here to play word games with you, Lawrence Stoning."

"But I'm playing them all the same." I grasped his shoulders. He shook me off. I grabbed him again. "Listen, Brother. I promised Garcia that justice would be carried out. Do you consider the torture of an innocent girl to be justice?"

He stared at me. "N-no," he said slowly.

"Then we don't have to help in it. In fact, justice requires that we hinder it."

He locked eyes with me and stared until the water sprang to my eyes from holding my eyelids open too long.

Finally, he sighed. "I'm sorry, Law. I should have trusted you. You're right, as usual." He patted my arms and took my hands from his shoulders. "You're worth your weight in gold, Law."

"An apt metaphor."

He shook his head. "Tomorrow will be red, not golden."

"What's your plan?"

He sat down on his blankets and took one of his pistols from his sash. Lovingly, he wiped an oily rag over the barrel. "Kill and be killed, I suppose."

I sat down on my own blankets. "That's your entire plan?"

He stopped rubbing and looked at me across the tent. "Do you have a better one?"

I thought for a moment. "Perhaps. It may have the same end, but—perhaps. Listen."

Chapter 30

The storm was over the next morning, but the grass was beaten down, showing the strength of the rain. Everyone gathered round the fire for breakfast and was quiet and solemn, except for Pacarina, who chatted cheerfully as normal.

"Have you found the artifacts you have been so earnestly searching for, Señor Sabas?" she asked.

The archeologist bit a hunk of bread and wrenched off a piece. "Not yet. I will today."

"Oh? You've found the place you have been looking for?"

"Yes. Very pretty place."

He stopped chewing and looked at her hungrily. Her cheeks reddened and she edged away from him.

"Now, Garcia," he growled. "We've waited too long already. We have little time left before the snake falls."

She looked at Garcia. He sighed and dusted crumbs from his hands. She looked at Chester and me, and fear was in her eyes. That was when I realized how hard our part would be to play.

"My dear sister-in-law," Garcia began, "I hope you will be willing to oblige me, after all of the troubles I have taken on your behalf?"

Her neck muscles bulged slightly as she swallowed hard. "What do you mean?"

"Treasure is meant for human hands, not the centipedes of the mountains. Do you understand my meaning?"

"No."

Garcia sighed. "How do we get to the Inca treasure?"

Her cheeks went white. "Chester—Lawrence!" she gasped.

I looked at Chester. Chester looked at the fire. "You'd best tell, Pacarina."

She gasped again, and looked at us with true horror in her beautiful brown eyes. Then, the look changed. Slowly, she rose to her feet. I'm not a sentimentalist, but I freely confess that the thought of her standing there still chills me. Her brown hair flowed over her neck and back, her cheeks were white, her lips parted slightly, her breath quick. She looked like an olive-skinned version of a fairy queen from one of Chester's books.

"You know my oath."

"That oath began centuries ago. Forget it."

She looked at her sister, and Atalya cowered under her piercing eyes. "You told him, didn't you?"

"Father and Mother wouldn't trust me," Atalya whined.

Pacarina laughed bitterly. "Why do you think they didn't trust you? So that's why we came here, to these mountains. Very well." She raised her chin and looked down on Garcia. "If this traitoress heard the secret, why do you need it from me?"

Garcia smiled through his teeth. "She only heard a little. It's somewhere in these mountains, but we don't know where. You do. Tell us."

"Or?"

Sabas grinned, pieces of bread clinging to his teeth. "Don't talk now, Sweet. I am here for that."

He barked at his natives, and two of them grabbed Pacarina's arms. I grasped Chester's arm, squeezed with all my strength, and pulled him to his feet. I seemed to hear a faint thumping—I think it was his heart.

I forced myself to speak levelly. "We'll bring our cloaks, if you don't mind," I said. "Rather chilly."

I picked up my cloak, a long, dark affair stretching from my shoulders to my ankles. Chester tied his sash on the outside of his cloak and put on his hat.

Garcia and Sabas led the way up to the Inca ruin. Atalya remained seated, rocking back and forth and weeping into her hands. We followed the natives and Pacarina. Blankets still covered the door and window, but lanterns lit the interior. A large contraption filled the middle of the room, as tall as a man, and built of wood and rope.

"What is that?" Chester burst out.

Sabas capered about the cramped room, fondling the thing like a child. "I do not care for priests, but they are not stupid," he crooned. "Yes, darling, not stupid. Have you never heard of the rack?"

Chester gasped. My windpipe closed for a moment, and I staggered against the wall. Pacarina turned her head and looked at us wildly, her hair now disordered, and her white cheeks blotched by fiery red.

"Cursed traitors." She spat at my feet. "You are no brothers of mine."

I couldn't meet her eyes.

The rack was built of planks, with a wooden roller near the top of the frame, and another at the foot. Ropes stretched between them. The natives lifted Pacarina onto it, and Sabas himself bound her ankles to two ropes stretched round the bottom roller.

"Where did this come from?" I asked. My voice sounded hoarse, strangely distant.

Sabas chuckled. "I always bring my daughter with me. Do you not recognize her? You helped me tend to her on the path from the village."

The strange load of wood and rope. The piles in the second supply tent. If our plan fails. . . .

Sabas tied her wrists to the top roller. Her eyes were dilated, terrified, staring straight ahead—straight at me.

"Shall we try fire too?" Sabas grinned and picked up one of the lanterns.

Garcia grabbed it from him. His hand was shaking. "Don't you think the rack's enough, demon?"

"Now am I a demon?" Sabas kept grinning that horrible, evil grin, beneath unsmiling, hungry eyes. "You paid me for this."

Garcia pushed him aside and stepped next to the rack, by Pacarina's head. "This need not be, girl—tell me where the gold is, tell me how to get there, and all will be well."

She turned her head toward him. "I am defenseless. Betrayed. I cannot break my oath. Do your worst."

Sabas pushed past Garcia and grabbed a handle at the top of the rack. "Gladly, Sweet, gladly." He slowly pulled the handle toward us, half-inch by half-inch. The rollers creaked. The ropes tightened. Pacarina closed her eyes. Her ankles tightened.

"Enough."

Sabas paused. We all looked at Chester.

"Enough." He knocked Sabas's hand from the handle, though he didn't loosen the tension. "It's obvious no one can stand this fiendish tool. She'll talk in a minute, and it will be sooner if it's just we English to hear."

Garcia nodded and wiped his forehead with an already sweaty handkerchief. "You are right, that is why we brought you. Come, Sabas."

Sabas glared at him. "What do you mean? I wait for this for a long time. You tried your plans; they failed. This is my time!"

"My plans have not failed. This is my plan, and she'll talk before her bones break. Come. We are leaving. Now."

Sabas folded his arms. "No. I do not trust them."

"Who cares?" the merchant snapped. "They can't go anywhere."

I cleared my throat. "We gave you our word."

"There, you see?" Garcia waved his hand in the other's face. "They are not fools to court Death, and marry her too. You work for me, and I tell you to come with me, now!"

Sabas spat and stormed out. Garcia slipped after him, and we were alone with the girl.

"Well, false brothers," she said bitterly, looking at me. "Pull away."

Chapter 31

Chester eased the lever backwards, releasing the tension, and letting the girl's ankles fall limp. "I'm awfully sorry it had to happen this way."

"Why should you be? I am sure you will be well paid."

"Eh?" Chester dropped the handle as if it had burnt him.

I jumped to her left side. "Pacarina, you don't think we're actually against you, do you?"

Her eyes were red, but brave and disdainful. "The rack isn't enough? You must torture me with words as well?"

Chester groaned. "Pacarina, this is all a plan to save you!"

"Assuredly. As was the plan to come here, to Peru."

I thought I had run my plan through every possible grid. Yes, there were many areas where it could fail, but I never thought that Pacarina herself might disbelieve us.

Chester slammed his fist against the wooden frame. "Law, we need to work quickly or they'll be impatient."

I tried to stay calm. "Pacarina, we need you to scream."

She laughed, or sobbed, I'm not sure which. "I'm sure I'll scream loud enough when the wheels begin turning."

I grabbed her hand. "Pacarina, don't you understand! We haven't betrayed you. We're saving you. We're your brothers, Sister!"

She shook her head. "You betray me, you let them tie me to this—" she shuddered. "Then you ask me to believe you again?"

"Lawrence," Chester hissed, "she needs to scream."

I raked my long fingernails through my hair. "Pacarina, listen. You must scream, or they'll be back in to see what we're doing." I heard a voice close by outside.

Tears coursed down her cheeks. She shook her head.

"Lawrence!" Chester cried.

I swiveled toward him. Something blurred the air and struck me just below my left collar bone. Pain wrenched the breath from my lungs and I staggered backwards, bashing my shoulder-blades against the stone wall. Pacarina screamed.

I gasped for breath and looked with blurred eyes at Chester, who stood on the other side of the rack, nursing his right hand.

"Law, do you have rocks under your skin?"

"What happened?" I gasped.

"Sorry, we needed her to scream."

I pulled myself up and gingerly flexed my left arm. "Was that the only way?"

"Seemed good at the time."

Pacarina looked from one to the other of us with wide eyes. "Are you—are you saying the truth?"

"Absolutely, Pacarina." Carefully, I took her hand, still tied to the horrible rack. "Won't you believe us?" I smiled encouragingly. "I just sacrificed a quarter of my body for you."

"Not to mention my knuckles," Chester added.

Her lips trembled—I prepared for a scream. She searched my face with those earnest brown eyes, and I stared straight back, knowing that this moment meant life or death for the three of us. Then, she sobbed.

"Forgive me."

A leaden ball melted away from my chest.

"You believe?"

She nodded, the tears still flowing, but now from whatever odd source makes girls cry when they're half-happy, half-something else. "Yes." She tried to smile through the falling salt water.

Chester grunted. "I say, we should probably take her down."

We rapidly untied the ropes around her wrists and ankles and lifted her down.

"Take my cloak." I handed the garment to her. "I'm sorry, but you'll have to be Chester for a time."

She stared at me. "What do you mean?"

I plucked the Eyesore off Chester's head and gave it to her. "I don't envy you. You're going to walk outside with Chester, and you're going to have your hair bunched under that hat—it could hide a lion's mane, probably—and you'll have the cloak over you, up to your face, and you'll be him, and he'll be me. Thank God that we're twins."

"Hold," Chester said. "You'll be you. I'm staying."

"You're most certainly not. I'm the oldest, it's my place."

He choked. "You? The oldest? Is your brain cooked? I'm obviously the oldest."

I grabbed his shoulders. "Chester, you're taking Pacarina out of here, and I'm staying. Do you know why?"

"Because you want to be a hero."

"I don't feel a bit like being a hero. I'd much rather be inking a pen nib at my desk in England. I'm staying because I came along to protect you—"

"Father released you." He quietly removed his cloak. "You don't have to guard me anymore."

"I know I don't. But I'm going to. Because you're my brother. No, don't speak—" I lifted my hand, "—there's another reason. You can fight, and I can't, and she needs a fighter if she's going to survive."

He opened his mouth, but nothing came out. There was nothing to say. I draped the cloak back round his shoulders and turned. "Goodbye, Sister."

She grabbed my hands, her eyes wide and wet. "Lawrence, you can't stay! They'll kill you!"

I forced a smile. "Only two entered, only two can leave. You'll have plenty of danger yourself. Follow Chester implicitly, and try to keep him in character. I do wish I could see him playing me."

"That's the rough." Chester's voice was choked. "I don't know Spanish. What do I do?"

"We already went over this." I helped Pacarina into the cloak, tied the strings around her neck, and pushed the hat lower over her eyes. "I often use English. Your voice is the same as mine. Just try to speak intelligently, and you'll be fine."

He grunted. "You've—you've a nice opinion of yourself." His voice was thick.

"And don't grunt. I never grunt like you. If they ask you which way east is, it's toward the village. Geometry is shapes—algebra is letters and numbers. Feather pens are less convenient than the new nibbed pens."

"All right, all right, it's just Garcia and Sabas, not an Eton headmaster."

I stepped back and surveyed the girl. With the Eyesore, sash, pistols, and cloak, she looked convincing enough for a summary inspection.

"You now look remarkably like Chester, Sister, more's the pity. Our time is up. Go."

Chester pulled a knife from his boot and slashed the ropes on the rack. "They won't use that on you," he muttered. "I wish I were staying."

"I know you do, and I know you would, but she's your responsibility now. Go." I pushed back the blankets that hung over the doorway. Chester squeezed my arm.

Pacarina lifted her hat brim and looked me in the eyes. "Goodbye, Brother."

The blankets swished, and they were gone.

Chapter 32

I stared disconsolately at the rack. It's much easier being brave when there is someone to watch. Standing alone is the real test of bravery. Standing alone in a lantern-lit, centuries-old ruin next to a slashed rack with a camp-full of enemies on the other side of a blanket takes a great deal of bravery.

Or does it? I knew I was not brave. I knew the sharp stab of fear. If what I was doing was really brave, then it was only accomplished through God's help.

Voices spoke outside, but the thick blankets and thicker walls muffled the words. My plan was laughably simple. I feel that if I were writing this as a novel, instead of a history, any self-respecting reader would promptly ridicule it. The plan was simply that Chester and Lawrence would walk out, say that they had gotten the secret, that Pacarina was still inside, and that they needed to draw a map immediately in their tent. Of course, Chester would actually be Pacarina. Hopefully, Garcia and Sabas would come to check on Pacarina, and the others could somehow escape to the jungle in the short minutes available.

It sounds desperate. We were.

Chester thought we should make a last stand with swords and pistols in the doorway, like Horatius guarding his bridge. My main problem with that idea was that Horatius's opponents didn't have firearms—ours did.

I waited for a shout of discovery, but there was none. Might they make it? I opened the slide on each lantern and blew out the flame. Only the barest bit of light managed to sneak past the blankets, and for all practical purposes, the room was black. I wiped my sweating forehead and leaned back. With a start, I realized that I was leaning on the rack, and quickly shifted to the far wall.

Light streamed through the doorway. For a moment, a woman's figure was outlined against the sky, then the blanket fell back, and all was dark.

Atalya—it could only be she—sniffled.

"I didn't know—I was angry that Father and Mother didn't trust me—I didn't know he would kill them—I am so sorry, Sister." Sobs punctuated her broken lamentations.

Her fingernails scratched against the rack. "Pacarina? Pacarina! Where are you?"

I sprang forward and reached into the inky darkness. My hands brushed a pair of ears, so I grabbed lower, found her mouth, and clamped my right hand over her upper lip and chin.

"Say nothing."

She went absolutely limp, her full weight leaning against me, and her feet twitched. I presume that she believed in ghosts.

"Where are Chester and Pacarina?"

She didn't move.

I tightened my grasp. "Where are they?"

She gurgled something.

Oh. I should probably move my hand. I gave her an inch of breathing space and repeated the question.

"Pacarina—here," she gasped, her breath hot and clammy against my palm.

I had forgotten. "Where are the Señors Stoning?"

"Tent."

I closed my hand back over her mouth and considered. If they were in our tent, then the first step had been successful. Now, they needed an opportunity to slip away. There was very little time. *Of course.*

I removed my hand once more. "Scream."

Nothing.

"Scream, woman, or aren't you afraid of ghosts?"

She didn't just scream—she caterwauled. I squinted to ease the pressure in my eardrums and dragged her backwards, wondering when she would run out of air. *That should bring the whole camp, and a decent percentage of Peru as well.*

It definitely brought Garcia and Sabas. They plunged through the doorway, tearing the blanket to the ground, and blinked into the darkness.

"Pacarina!" Garcia shouted.

"I have your wife, Garcia, and I have a pistol."

I pointed the pistol at her head. Something looked wrong. *Right.* I cocked the hammer with my left hand.

Garcia gasped. "Where is she?" He stared stupidly at the rack.

"My rack!" Sabas howled. "You have cut my rack! English dog, you die!" He drew a knife from his belt, but Garcia jumped between us and grabbed his arm.

"Stop! He has my wife."

Sabas foamed, white specks spouting from his mouth. "You fool! You said you trusted them, you said they would not lie—where is she? Where is my gold?"

Garcia turned on me. "How can you be here? You just went to your tent."

"It's called a dual personality. Twins often suffer from it."

"The girl!" Sabas cursed. "She is out there. I kill you!"

Again he raised the knife. Atalya screamed. Garcia grabbed his arm and threw him back against the wall. "Do you want to kill my wife, fool?"

"You and your wife." Sabas glared at him, his knife still poised. "What have you done? Do we have the gold?" He spat at Garcia's feet. "You let the cursed girl go. I would have broken her. I would know where the gold is now."

I could only see the back of Garcia's head, but I could imagine the look in his eyes.

"You dare to insult me! You are a fool, jabbering at me while the girl escapes."

Sabas slashed the blanket over the window and yelled out to his men. Canvas ripped outside, and a yell came back.

"The tent is empty." Sabas cursed again. "I follow now, but I will kill you English dog." He gnashed his teeth, then darted away with his stooped, trot-like run.

"Hold." Garcia turned back to me. "Do not hurt my wife." His eyes were wide, pleading. "Please, let her go."

"So that you can shoot me dead the moment she's behind you?"

He bit his lip. "You called me a monster because I would hurt her sister. You say you will hurt her. We are the same, are we not?"

I hadn't thought of it in that way. I thought of Chester. He would scorn to hide behind a woman. Atalya trembled in my grasp, and Garcia brightened. He must have realized my weakness.

"What makes you good, and me evil, eh?"

I tried to justify myself. Self-preservation, preventing him from doing murder, protecting Chester and Pacarina. No. I couldn't justify it.

I sighed. "This." I let her go, and she dived, sobbing, into Garcia's arms. "You're right. Christians and gentlemen don't hide behind women. Take your wife, and I'll take the consequences." I folded my arms.

He pointed a pistol at my head, his fingers quivering round the trigger. "Should I kill you?"

Atalya wailed.

"I'd rather you didn't," I said.

"Are you a liability, or an asset?"

"Was the priest a liability?"

"Yes. I no longer needed him, so I disposed of him." He lowered the pistol. "But you are not. Yet. I brought you for yet another reason." He grabbed my right sleeve and tore the worn fabric apart. "There." He jabbed his finger into my arm, just before the elbow-crook. He was touching my birthmark.

"My birthmark?"

"You are a twin with a snake on your arm. The natives will think you divine, if we have problems with them."

Sabas's men bound my hands tightly behind my back with thin cord. They were about to drag me outside when one of them grunted, and pointed at the wall. We all turned. The sun was shining through the window and filtered through the open spaces in the rack. There, on the opposite wall, was the twisted, snakish light. It touched the ground. Garcia grasped his throat.

"It has fallen," he gasped.

"And with it your hopes of any gold." I might have pitied him, but for the cords creasing my flesh.

His stubby nose wiggled, the nostrils flaring wide. "I have lied and killed for that gold, and it will be mine." He smashed his fist against the rack. "I will hunt them down."

"Then be prepared for the hunters to become the hunted."

Chapter 33

My hair clung to my sweaty, oily forehead. The cords cut most of the circulation from my hands. I couldn't see them, because they were tied behind my back, but I imagined the strips of dark red flesh that must border the cord-grooves. The indignity was even worse than the pain. These godless villains didn't deserve the shelter of a sewage-filled London alley, but here they were my masters. I was a freak show, valued only because of the strange mark on my skin.

I stood in the path to the village while Sabas and his men hacked in the jungle to my right, searching for signs of Chester and Pacarina. Two tall men and the interpreter guarded me. The two listened eagerly to the squelching blows of the machetes slicing through waterlogged plants, hardly looking at the interpreter and me, though I knew that if I tried to run they would be upon me in a moment.

The interpreter looked sorry for me. He gently prodded me until I was turned to face my guards, then he slipped behind me. For a moment, my hopes soared. Was he going to cut me free? Water trickled over my burning wrists. He slipped back into my periphery and stuck the stopper back into the neck of his water-flask.

"The cords will stretch a little," he said in Spanish. "It will ease the pain."

"Thank you."

He looked fearfully at the guards, but they paid him no attention. "I am sorry that this has happened. I—I am not a bad man."

"Then why are you here?"

"I—I worked for Sabas, before I married. I did wrong things, of which I am ashamed." He looked sideways again at the guards, but they were still watching the search. "I am now a fisherman on the coast. One day Sabas came in a ship, and told me that if I did not come with him, he would report me to the authorities. I would die, and my wife would be a widow."

I stared at him. Hadn't I heard pieces of this story before?

"My old mother was Mayamura, though she left the tribe. She taught me their language."

His old mother. I remembered the old woman in the hut on the coast, squatting and staring at me. That's what the Mayamura crones had reminded me of—his mother.

"Please, believe me, I do not want to be here."

"I believe you. I've seen your wife and mother."

His jaw dropped. "When?"

The searchers burst out of the jungle. "Nothing," Sabas growled. "Try the other side. You," he pointed to the interpreter, "in and search."

In a few minutes someone howled. My guards pushed me into the jungle until we found the others clustered on a trail of slashed vines and undergrowth that started about thirty-five feet from the path and led north. Chester and Pacarina must have pushed through the jungle, until they were far out of sight of the path and then started chopping.

"Why are they heading north?" Garcia asked Sabas. "The coast is west."

"How should I know?" Sabas snapped. "Ask the English dog you keep alive."

Garcia looked at me. "Well?"

I smiled dryly. "Perhaps they're making a side-trip to El Dorado."

He cuffed my right ear. It smarted as if an enormous bee had sunk his stingers into the earlobe, but I couldn't touch it because of my bound hands.

"Do not provoke me," Garcia said.

We plunged along the trail, the natives ahead widening it with their machetes. Each man had a bundle strapped to his back with tools, torches, ammunition, and food. Once the Mayamuras found that the snake had fallen, we wouldn't have access to our camp. Sabas, Garcia, Atalya, myself, and my two guards formed a close group.

The mosquitoes quickly realized that I couldn't guard my face and attacked, their wings tickling my skin, their horrible buzzing bodies climbing up my nostrils and ear canals. I started to grind my canine teeth, but two flew into my open mouth.

We had a great advantage. Chester had to make his path through the jungle, but we could use the same path and travel far faster. If they were to escape, we either had to lose the path or delay for some reason. *I must be that reason.*

I flipped through my mental notebook, trying to find bits and pieces of historical adventures, travel books, and Chester's ramblings. *How to delay?* I remembered something about stooping to tie one's shoes, but that didn't seem to fit the occasion. Anyway, my hands were behind my back.

I could throw myself on someone, but that would hardly stop them for a minute, and I would probably get a bullet or a knife blade in me for my trouble. Sabas's keen eyes, when I could see them, were alive with anger, as if he could see Chester on his rack in his mind. The cheerful, kind, friendly merchant whom I had known, or thought I had known, was turned into a glowering man with twitching fingers and a burnt-out cigar stub between his lips.

What if I could turn these two against each other? They're already on bad terms. A few well-placed words might do it. Greed and treachery—fear, greed, and treachery.

This called for versatile thinking.

I stepped a little faster, until I was walking only two feet behind them. I tried to clasp my wrist, but couldn't.

"So, Garcia, was Sabas supposed to kidnap Pacarina that night in your villa?"

Garcia eyed me. "Yes."

"Then why didn't he?"

Sabas glared at me. "You stopped me, dog."

"Actually, that was Chester, but I don't blame you for mistaking him for me." Sabas glared. *Careful, Lawrence, don't get too witty.* "But of course, you must have expected us to stop you, since Garcia told us to be there."

The archeologist turned on the merchant. "You told them to be there?"

"Of course." Garcia smirked. "It became part of my plan. I thought I could be sure of the servant, once they saw in what danger I was."

The servant? Oh, of course. I was a servant.

Sabas spat at a tree trunk. "You never told me." He wrenched an orange out of his waistcoat as if it had no right to be there and bit into it without peeling the skin.

Garcia smiled. "As long as you both were punctual, you didn't need to know."

This was the opening I needed to exploit. "So Sabas really did think he was kidnapping her?"

I could see that Garcia was suspicious of my inquiries, but it was struggling with the pride of a master-conspirator. Pride won.

"He was to kidnap her, and I was to follow as a good guardian should." He flung the cigar stub into the trees. "I would not find her until after the gold was found, though."

One of the natives picked something off the ground and showed it to Sabas. He thrust it into my face.

"What is that?"

It was a blackened rectangle of straw. "It's from the Eyesore—er, my brother's hat."

Sabas threw it away. "His skin will look like that when he is done with me." He barked at the natives and we moved even faster.

"So, what else have you not told Sabas?" I asked, regulating my voice so that it would sound nonchalant.

Garcia half-turned. "What do you mean?" he asked sharply.

I shrugged. "Oh, I just assumed that a master-planner such as yourself would have even deeper plans. After all, someone must be blamed for this escapade, and it can't be you if you want to return to society, gold or no gold."

"Be quiet." Garcia struck me again, this time choosing the left ear. I thought that the pains on both sides might balance each other, but they didn't.

Sabas spat a glob of orange-rind into a swarm of mosquitoes. "What does he mean by that?" he demanded of Garcia.

"He is trying to make me angry."

"I will kill him." Sabas drew his knife. One of my native guards chuckled.

"No." Garcia waved him back. "I tell you, he is an asset—the snake."

I nodded. "Assets must be protected. It's only when their worth is used up and they become liabilities that they should be disposed of. Like the priest. Now Chester. Soon, Pacarina. After her?"

Sabas was visibly shaken. "The dog is right."

"Stop jabbering, both of you." Garcia flailed his arms at the swarming mosquitoes. "Cursed pests! I paid you to help me find the treasure, not talk."

Sabas stopped in the middle of the path and turned, squaring his hunched body in front of Garcia. His natives stopped as well. Garcia swiveled back and forth between Sabas with the men in front, and me and my two guards behind. Atalya gasped.

"What are you doing, fool?" Garcia said. "You're wasting time."

Sabas glared at him. "You have not paid me for anything. I *am* a fool. I help you do everything, and then you say it is all your plan, and that I am a paid fool. You said that I will be paid from the gold. How do I know that you do not lie? Why you not betray me?"

Garcia's face turned livid. "You call me a liar and a traitor to my face?"

I coughed. "You did betray your wife's sister," I reminded gently. "Along with a bit of lying."

Garcia pulled a pistol from his waistcoat. "Do you mean treachery?" he shouted.

Sabas laughed. "You would not dare to shoot me. My men would roast you alive and pluck your skin like a roasting feather's chickens."

I twisted my head slightly. My guards were staring at the two leaders, their breath coming in irregular draws. Their arm-muscles bulged. They looked ready to spring on Garcia if Sabas gave the word. I edged backwards. Sabas and Garcia stared at each other. I was now slightly behind my guards. The tension was nearly palpable.

Tendons bulged on my guards' bare legs. Another inch. I aimed just below the back of the larger man's knee, right where the tendons bulged, and kicked with all my force. He crumpled. I plunged into the left guard with my shoulder. He fell into a pile of vines.

"Get him!" Sabas screamed.

No one was behind me. I raced back along the path, the whole crew of miscreants in furious pursuit. Something tugged at my foot and nearly tripped me. My balance was distorted because of my bound hands.

"Don't kill him!" Garcia shouted. "He has the snake! A pocket of gold to the man who captures him."

I regained my balance and pressed forward, churning the ground with my feet and dashing through thick clouds of mosquitoes. Sweat soaked my forehead and trickled into my eyes. The soggy air caught in my throat and seemed to coat my lungs in layers of wet. Running pains burned beneath the ribs on my right side.

I sucked the air in, trying to regulate my breathing with my steps to ease the pain. Footsteps crunched behind me, and I ran faster, forgetting all thought of breathing. The footsteps mingled with sharp hissing exhales. I glanced over my left shoulder—only two natives were in sight, but they were gaining.

What if they kill me in the heat of chase? Garcia isn't here to stop them. Should I have let them catch me sooner?

Arms grasped my waist and I fell. My hands were bound and useless, the ground rushing up at me—I flung my head up to protect my eyes and nose and slammed my chest and chin into the ground. Splinters of pain coursed through my skull. My eyes swirled in black haze.

Bony fingers tore at my arms, pulling me to my wobbly legs. Trees, vines, all spun around and rocked like the *Miriam*. My stomach churned and rose toward my throat. I vomited.

My two captors clenched my elbows and dragged me back. Vines grabbed at my knees and toes. The rest of the pursuit party quickly sighted us and closed, their cheeks puffing and sagging with each breath and exhale.

Garcia struck me with the back of his hand and his wedding ring tore a strip of flesh from my right cheek. The mosquitoes must have cheered.

He poked his blotchy face into mine, nose to nose. "If you did not have the snake, I would watch Sabas kill you for five hours." He spat into my eye.

Chester probably would have had a snappy reply. I kept my mouth shut and silently thanked God for the strange birthmark.

Sabas was strangely wary. "You die soon, dog." Then he looked at Garcia. "They gained much time. We will talk later. Follow."

Chapter 34

At first I thought my ears were ringing. A strange noise like a scream sounded vaguely in my throbbing eardrums. Then I looked at the rest of the party, and they too were standing still, heads strained in the direction of our camp. The sound came again, this time louder.

Sabas cursed. "They have seen the fallen snake. The Mayamuras are on our trail." He turned savagely to Garcia. "You waited too long. Our blood is on your head."

The merchant trembled. "W-we have guns. Can't we fight?"

Sabas sneered. "Guns are no good in thick jungle. Only in the clearings. They will shoot us down with poison darts and arrows."

"C-can't we escape?"

"We are in the middle of their country."

Sabas's men crowded round, their faces contorted with fear. Angry Mayamuras evidently had a reputation. One of the fellows said something to Sabas in their native language. The villain nodded.

"We have one chance."

Garcia gulped. "What is that?"

"You have led long enough. I lead now. You ask, no listen. Listen, no ask I mean."

He waved his arm and his men broke into a run, dragging me along. I thought I was spent. I couldn't stop my knees and ankle-joints from wobbling. My two new guards paused a moment to hoist me into the air, one grabbing my legs, the other locking his elbow round my neck and supporting my chest with his shoulders.

I gurgled a complaint, but he just tightened the headlock.

The path kept curving to the left, so we must be approaching the second mountain. Indeed, the trees began to be fewer and thinner-trunked, and light shone through ahead. It was then that I finally realized where Chester and Pacarina were going.

The hiding-place of the gold. She knows where it's hidden, and they must be able to hide there too. But we're following.

We ran out of the trees into thick grass. Someone called softly, and a man's head rose from the grass. Sabas ran to meet him. They talked rapidly, pointing to the mountain ahead.

Garcia wrung his fingers. He was no longer the master-schemer. He was a trembling, frightened merchant in a land full of enemies. "Who is he?" he finally blurted.

Sabas scowled. "I sent him on when we turned back to chase the dog. He knows which way they head."

My lungs sagged. *All of this, and we bring them to the very treasure at last?*

The native said something. "They go high," Sabas translated. "Follow."

Without warning my carriers dropped me and I slammed into the grass-covered ground. The one who had been holding my head kicked my side. I struggled to my knees, then my feet, and looked up. Terrace after terrace cut the mountain side and rose into the clouds, each terrace covered by luscious, fresh-smelling grass. Wispy clouds hid the peak.

"I can't climb with my hands tied," I said.

Garcia sliced the ropes. "Try to run and you die."

There were no paths at this low level, but the climbing wasn't hard. The terraces were about a yard high, sometimes treacherous because of the loose stones. Twice they crumbled and dropped me on the level below, tearing my trousers and lacerating my shins. The terraced sections were wide, but they grew steeper higher up. It was every man for himself. Sabas was soon far ahead, his hunch accentuated as he twisted and crawled to each new level.

The grass smelled fresh. How could the world look so clean and good while villains scrambled toward their evil objective?

My guards scarcely looked at me, and I realized that I could easily slip away. But where was I to go? Yes, we were hunters, but we were also hunted. Probable death ahead was better than certain death behind. I wondered what kind of poison the Mayamuras used. Would it swell my throat and seal my windpipe? Would it disintegrate my stomach lining? Would it swell my brain? The latter would be fitting, as Chester used to say that I had a swelled brain. I kept climbing.

Garcia and Atalya looked terrible, their faces splotched and their sides heaving. I offered the woman my hand. She shrank back as if I were a snake and clung to Garcia. He pushed her away. The silk handkerchief in his hand was dark with sweat.

"I will help you, Señora," I said.

Her eyes darted, wholly unlike Pacarina's steady brown orbs. "Y-you want to hurt me."

"Your husband, perhaps, but not you, Señora. I'm a Christian gentleman. We don't make war on women." I extended my hand again.

She looked pleadingly at Garcia.

He glared back. "If the fool wants to burden himself, let him."

Slowly, hesitatingly, she gave me her hand. It trembled. For the first time I realized how really young she was—she could scarcely be twenty-two. Pacarina was my age, eighteen, so a three- or four-year difference was quite likely. I supported her elbow and pushed her up onto the next terrace, following myself. I wondered what made her marry Garcia. A strength of character which she lacked, perhaps? I had neither breath nor time to ask now.

An hour passed. Our group was scattered over the mountain-side, the weakest and slowest at the bottom, the fastest, or those most driven by hate, like Sabas, at the lead. Garcia, Atalya, and I were among the last. Though not one of the fastest, I could have made a better pace but for the woman. I would like to say that Garcia stayed to help his wife, but he was only with us because he was so slow himself. Web-weaving exercises the brain, but it does little for the calves.

A chorus of yells sounded far below. I looked down. Little brown specks were running across the grassy plain between the jungle-edge and the mountain-base. I might soon be able to answer my questions about Mayamura poison.

Sabas came bounding down the mountain-side and grabbed me by the arm.

"You and your snake stay with me."

I'd had enough. He could kill me if he wanted, but I would submit to no more indignities. I shook his arm off. "It's not a snake. It's an overgrowth of blood vessels beneath my skin, and I'm not going with you."

"Looks like snake." He grabbed me again and pulled me away from Atalya.

I yanked back. "Stop, you blackguard, I'm helping the woman."

"She has husband for that."

Garcia gulped the thin air like wine. "You—will—not—leave—me. I brought him." He weakly grabbed my other hand. Atalya collapsed against a terrace-wall and sobbed.

"What good are you?" Sabas asked Garcia.

"I had the plan. I brought us here."

"Yes. Here." Sabas pointed at the brown dots, now climbing the bottom terraces. He stamped his foot. "Follow, but keep up."

Atalya moaned.

"Leave the woman."

I looked at Garcia, expecting an explosion. He said nothing.

"You can't leave your wife!" I burst out.

The merchant just wiped his forehead.

"Have you no humanity, man? Are you a man? Is the gold that can make you a nice wealthy little trader more valuable than your wife?"

Garcia crumpled his handkerchief convulsively. "It is not just for myself. This is all not just for myself. It is for Don Carlos. With that money, he can win the war."

"So a brutal little Spanish pretender means more to you than your wife?"

His face turned red. Sabas hissed with impatience.

"My wife goes with us," Garcia said at last.

Sabas yelled at one of his men to help her, and we continued the climb.

The slope lessened. Looking up, I realized that we were entering a rift, or valley. Walls rose on either side, and our pursuers were no longer visible. What was better, they couldn't see us.

"Did Pacarina come this way?" Garcia asked.

Sabas pointed up. A man stood near the top of the valley. *Chester?* I squinted. *No, couldn't be. Chester doesn't slouch.* We scrambled closer and I recognized him to be one of Sabas's men. The archeologist must have sent more than one man ahead when I did my delaying trick.

The native said nothing, but pointed even higher, and led us forward. The nature of the ground brought our group closer, and we were now climbing in a spacey body. A massive chunk of rock thirty feet thick and ranging from five to twelve feet high nearly blocked the valley. Only a small passage remained on each side. It didn't look like a regular outcropping. It was more like a rock dropped by a child into mud to hear the squelch.

Behind this rock was a cliff, or steep slope. Fissures scarred the cliff-side like spider-legs, while a giant splotch of less weather-beaten rock formed the body. It was clear that at some time probably in the last fifty years an earthquake had split this ground and torn off the mass of rock behind us. Soil had eroded down the cliff-side, so that grasses grew over the rock, like setae, the little hairs on spider-legs.

The man pointed to one of these clumps of grass.

"They went in there," he said in Spanish.

"In where?" Sabas demanded.

"Cave."

He ran up the steep slope and groped at the grass. It lifted like a mat, revealing a small dark hole in the mountainside. Recently-severed tendrils of grass dangled from the bottom of the mat.

So we had reached the treasure. A secret cave in a little-known mountain far away from main Inca land.

Sabas pushed forward, still holding my arm, and crawled into the hole. A cool wind kissed my sweaty forehead.

"It is dark," Sabas said.

"Caves generally are."

I couldn't tell how large the cave was, but I had to keep edging forward as more sweating bodies pushed me from behind.

"Light torches," Sabas commanded. His voice echoed, but I couldn't determine whether we were in a small room or a cavern.

Flint and steel scraped. I braced. If Chester was in here, then as soon as those torches lit, there would be a shot. Blood once soaked these lands for the sake of treasure. More blood would flow. One by one the torches caught and flashed their light, but there was no shot. It was a small room. The walls were solid rock covered here and there by lichens.

Three holes gaped in the far wall.

Sabas looked at me. "Which one?"

I shrugged. "Just because I'm English doesn't mean I know all things."

"Which would your brother take?"

"Whichever Pacarina said was the right one."

Sabas swore.

One of his men pointed at the middle hole. Sabas held his torch close. A section of lichens had been torn off recently. Something was carved into the stone, not new, but ancient. Probably Inca.

"It is an animal carving," Sabas muttered. "Looks like alpaca."

I rubbed my hands over the hole on the right and found another bare spot. "Try here."

Torchlight showed a carved snake.

"There's a bird over here," Garcia said, standing by the third hole.

I rubbed my chin. "That's actually quite brilliant of the Incas. They evidently left code-like carvings to direct others in the future. The secret of the codes must have been passed down along with the cave's location."

"And Pacarina knows it."

"Yes, well, she has a right to. We don't."

Sabas balled his hands in the lichens and tore off a great swath. "We will!"

The last man pulled the tangle of grass back into place behind us.

Sabas released my arm. He twined his fingers and popped his knuckle-joints. His eyes twitched. Finally, he spoke. "We take the right." He pointed ten of his men to guard the entrance, should the natives have seen us enter.

I cleared my throat. "What if the Incas set traps? Pits, and the like?"

Sabas said nothing, but sent five of his men ahead. I ducked into the hole. I knew that these next few minutes would determine my future life. Or the lack thereof.

Chapter 35

Water-drops trickled down the walls and shimmered in the torchlight. Sabas crawled directly ahead of me and I was followed by Garcia, then his wife, then the rest of the men in single file. Grunting and panting echoed from the five men in the vanguard. I clung as close as possible to Sabas's shirt tails, willing to bear the stench of oranges, tobacco, and sweat, because he held a torch. All this talk of snakes made me very wary of resting my hand in dark wall-niches.

The men called back from ahead. We crawled even more cautiously, extending our hands so as to touch the rock on both sides of the tunnel. Sabas breathed sharply. My hands slipped off the rock and groped empty air.

The torchlight showed rock for a few feet, then nothingness. There was no bottom to the chasm in the range of our torchlight. A rope bridge stretched into the darkness.

Can the ropes still be safe?

We stood. Two massive grass rope-ends anchored our end of the bridge round two stone pillars. Each rope was no less than a foot in diameter. I touched one—it was dry, crinkly. Material like this could last only a few years at most in the elements. Here in the cool, protected dark, it obviously lasted much longer, but could it still be trusted? Many of the strands were snapped or frayed. Could the rope-heart still hold true?

Two of the natives with us on the ledge had rope-coils slung over their shoulders.

Sabas pointed to the closest man. "You, cross. You will take both ropes, we will hold the ends here, and you will tie them there. We will cross on new rope."

The man faltered. "Is—is it safe, Señor?"

"Of course not, fool, that is why you take new ropes over."

He gulped.

"Couldn't we try one of the other passages?" I suggested.

Sabas struck me across the face with the back of his hand. "I say we come this way, we come." He looked at the native. "Go!"

I fingered my tingling cheek. *What drives Sabas? Hate? Greed? Fear?* Fear was definitely what drove his men.

The bridge sagged dreadfully, so that it appeared to lead, not across, but down into a bottomless pit of night. The walking-surface consisted of mat rolls tied to the main ropes by individual strands, thus creating a prickly network of cords.

The native took a deep breath and gingerly put his foot on the first roll. It crunched.

"Faster!" Sabas shouted.

He stepped again. His foot broke through the mat in its center and dangled below. He pulled himself up by his arms and stepped to the third roll. This held.

Step after step he advanced. A torch was strapped to his back, but he couldn't carry one because he needed both hands to grab the main ropes. I stroked the huge rope-ends. They were tighter than before, and more strands had snapped. The native's form grew dimmer as he reached the edge of our torchlight, then he disappeared altogether. A distant crunch marked each rotten mat he encountered.

"Where are you?" Sabas shouted.

"Here," came the faint reply.

We waited in tense silence. Minutes passed. The new ropes kept rubbing on the rock, moving out a few inches at a time, so we knew that the man was still advancing. Then they stopped. A dot of light flared in the distance.

"I am here!" the man shouted.

Sabas wound the ends of rope round the pillar and knotted them together.

"Cross," he said to the other four natives.

One by one they stepped out onto the bridge, their hands grasping the new ropes. These could not be held taut, as that would leave them many feet above the disintegrating bridge-deck. Mats crunched and crumbled as each advanced. The fourth had to haul himself by his arms over many gaps. Sabas pushed me forward and followed close on my heels.

I clenched the new ropes and prayed God for safety. Heights frighten me, even safe heights. These were not safe. The fourth mat broke under my weight and I dangled, my armpits gripping the ropes.

"Keep going," Sabas growled.

It wasn't the last time. Six broken mats later I reached the other side and clung trembling to the solid stone ledge. Yes, the air was cool, but my shirt was soggy with sweat. Finally our party was over save for those tasked to wait by the entrance. The crossing had used up much time, so the Mayamuras would be close to the little valley.

We faced a solid rock wall broken only by a small tunnel-mouth which yawned at us. We entered, keeping the same order as before.

We crawled, but I think there were occasional open spaces above my head. The air was thick with the resinous odor of the torches. Voices mumbled ahead.

Sabas stopped without warning and my head rammed his back. He yelped and dropped his torch. There was a horrible scream and a bright flash of orange light—Sabas's torch had set fire to the closest man's shirt, and two of his companions were wrestling with him, trying to stifle the flames. Atalya screamed.

Something crashed far away from where we had come. Two more followed in quick succession.

"Shots! The Mayamuras have tracked us!" Sabas pushed frantically through the struggling natives and disappeared around a corner. I crawled to the still-burning torch and held it over my head. The path forked ahead, no doubt why the men stopped. Sabas had just crawled down the right fork.

Now is my chance! I flung my torch at the struggling natives, and they shrank back against the walls.

Garcia grasped my ankle. I kicked and he let go with a scream of pain. It took but a moment to rush through the confused natives, reclaim the torch, and squeeze into the left fork. Garcia bellowed, and the natives sprang after me. The roof rose high, so I ran holding the torch over my head, afraid to smash my head on low-hanging rock, but also afraid that I would trip or fall into a pit. My boots click-clacked on the stone floor, but only a padding and a panting warned of my pursuers.

Three men are behind me, but five went ahead. What if—something clattered ahead, and it wasn't an echo. *I must put out the torch!* Drops of water glistened in a small niche in the right wall. They were too few to extinguish the flame, but they gave me an idea. I dropped the torch, slipped out of my waistcoat, flung it over the flame, and ground it with my boot until the fire was smothered. We were in total darkness.

I slipped into the niche and clung to the walls. The cold wet rock chilled my burning cheeks. The padding feet came closer. Someone hissed, and bodies thudded. The silence cracked with shouts, grunts, and screams, the sound of mortal combat. My pursuers had met the other two who had gone in advance, and in the dark could not recognize them. Souls were about to leave earth.

Moving by ear, I tiptoed from my niche, skipping to avoid the flying limbs and knives that scraped the rock. As soon as I was a safe distance from the fight I ran, feeling the wall on my right with both hands. I changed direction every time the rock disappeared under my fingertips. The path kept turning, and me with it. The screams grew farther away until they finally ceased altogether.

I paused for breath. I had no light, no weapons, no waistcoat, and no idea where I was or where I wanted to be. Sweat soaked my clothing, but I shivered in the cold air. Shapes loomed in the dark. Something slithered behind me. I swallowed my heart and clung to the wall. I had once said that little is worse than night in the jungle. I now found the 'little.'

What would Chester do? I ran possible scenarios through my brain. I could shout, but with twenty or thirty of Sabas's men and an angry native tribe roaming around, it didn't seem to be the best plan. I prayed instead.

Lord, help me find Chester and Pacarina, and help us survive. Give me strength.

I expanded my lungs and sucked in a deep breath. My back was to a wall, but there seemed to be a great open space all around, and a faint trickling sound far away in the right corner. A distant waterfall, perhaps?

It was a different world down here. Centuries ago these tunnels were lit by torches as Inca priests and Inca slaves buried part of that empire's vast wealth. If the tales of the conquistadors were true, the gold under this mountain could enrich a nation.

What happened to those who knew the hiding-place? Such a secret could only hope to be kept by a few, but many men must have carried the treasure. Did their skeletons lie in these dark passages? I shifted a little closer to the wall.

That sound came again from the corner. What if it were flowing water? I licked my lips at the thought. They were dry, and my breath was hot.

Gathering my nerves, I stepped away from the wall and toward the sound. I edged cautiously, testing the ground ahead with one foot while leaving the other firmly planted. We had already seen one chasm—might not there be more?

The sound grew louder, but it wasn't continuous. It kept stopping, then starting, then stopping. Waterfalls don't do that. I cupped my right ear. *Breathing?* Something clicked. It sounded like a pistol-hammer.

"Stop!" I shouted. "I'm a friend—er, maybe—depending on who you are."

"Lawrence?"

"Pacarina!" I leaped into the darkness, tripped over a boot which could only be Chester's, and found my arm around Pacarina's shoulder.

Relief flooded my soul. "You have no idea how splendid it is to see you two." I stared into the darkness. "Well, feel you, at any rate."

That strange sound started again, this time right below my ear.

"Chester?" I gasped. "What's wrong?"

Pacarina gripped my shoulder convulsively. Fear clenched my innards. Was Chester injured? He was lying flat. His stomach heaved with each breath and the air hissed from his mouth.

"What's wrong, Chester? Are you hurt?"

His fingers clenched my right hand with a drowning man's strength.

"No," he gasped. "No—breath."

No breath? Chester was the physical one, the hearty one, the horse-riding fence-vaulting hero. Out of breath? I gripped Pacarina's shoulders and gently pushed her away until I saw the whites of her eyes.

"What's wrong, girl?" I whispered.

She kept her voice firm, but her body quivered. "I don't know, Lawrence. We ran, and ran, and ran, and his face grew red, and his chest heaved, but he wouldn't stop. I pretended to faint once, to make him rest, but he only picked me up and kept walking."

Chester grunted weakly.

"We kept going, and going, and going, and at last we reached the cave, and I guided us on the right paths. Then he collapsed." She shuddered. "I thought you were Sabas. I was going to shoot you."

I stooped and put my ear to his mouth. A short blast of hot air brushed my cheek. "What's wrong, old fellow?"

"I'm—sorry," he gasped. "Never—told—you. Asthma."

Chapter 36

Chester's fingers were cold. My brain slowly comprehended. "Asthma. I see. Right. Stay calm." My nerves tingled. *How can he have asthma? He's always been so active.* Then I remembered him panting that night in San Sebastian, and his savage reply when I joked about it. And those constant rests in the jungle. Other memories flooded my brain. Now it made sense. *Control yourself, Lawrence. This is a time for action.*

"We need to clear your air passages." I sat down and propped his shoulders against me. This would help the air flow. His shoulders slouched, and his arms dangled.

"I need water," I said.

Pacarina tore the hem from her skirt and rubbed it along the rough floor, soaking up moisture that had gathered in the cracks and fissures. She handed the wet rag to me.

"Bottoms up," I whispered.

Chester tilted his head back and I squeezed a dribble of water into his mouth. He swallowed. I think the wheezing lessened slightly.

"Good, Chester, now regulate your breathing. In, and out, that's right. Think about something steady."

Pacarina was at my side wiping the dank hair from his forehead. "Think of

Lawrence," she whispered. "There's nothing steadier."

I nearly laughed. Me, steady? My nerves were twittering.

Slowly, very slowly, the heaving lessened.

"That's right, you're doing splendidly, Chester." I sat back on my haunches and wiped my forehead.

Pacarina handed me another wet strip and I gratefully sucked it. The water was gritty but heavenly.

"You have had some?" I asked.

Pacarina laughed. "No. My dress isn't so long that I can keep shredding it."

I chuckled and handed her the rag. My throat felt odd. It seemed ages since I had laughed.

"How did you get over the rope bridge?" I asked.

"Rope bridge? There was no rope bridge. You must have taken a different passage. We followed the sign of the condor. I know some of the basic signs, but I don't know where all of these other passages lead. Yours must have connected with ours at some point."

"Where are we?" I asked.

"Not far from the entrance."

A pinpoint of light pricked the gloom. We froze. More pinpoints joined the first and came steadily closer from the direction I had come.

"Sabas," I hissed. "Quick, farther in."

We grabbed Chester's arms and slid him away from the light, deeper into the gloomy nothingness. I thrust my left hand forward, prepared to meet any obstruction, and it was good I did so, for without warning my fingers jammed into solid rock. I didn't realize we were so close to the wall.

"Look for a hiding place."

We propped Chester against the wall and crawled in opposite directions. The lights were coming closer, and the darkness was beginning to lighten.

"Here," Pacarina whispered. She had found a pile of rubble. By lying on this with our faces to the wall we might blend with the shadows.

Pacarina stiffened. She pointed to the ground we had just vacated. A dark object lay on the rock. It was the torch they had used. If Sabas saw it he would certainly investigate, and then we would be spotted. The pinpoints had grown to flickering balls.

I slithered toward the stick of wood. *Lord, please don't let them see me.* Three more inches. My fingers touched the end and I clenched it in my fist. Voices hissed near at hand. I pushed back on my elbows, lifting my boots so that they wouldn't scrape.

"The Mayamuras are following." It was Sabas talking.

I reached the base of the rubble and hugged a lump of stone to my chest, my face pointing to the wall. I closed my eyes, as if that would stop them from seeing me.

"We must find a good place to defend." Sabas's voice was very, very near.

Even with my eyes shut I could sense the torch-glow. The resinous odor was powerful. If I should sneeze—I held my breath to keep down the urge.

"This place is too big to defend. Check weapons."

Ramrods scraped, steel clattered on steel, and men muttered in Spanish and Quechua. The sounds slowly quieted, fading into the dull swish of tightening leather and shuffling feet.

"All ready? Good. You, go ahead, then I, take second passage."

Three pairs of shoes clicked, followed by an indistinct patter of bare feet. The light dimmed. At last, the voices faded away and all was pit-black.

"How are you?" I whispered to Pacarina.

"Well."

"Brave girl."

Chester spoke. "I say, shouldn't we be moving on?"

His wheezing had nearly stopped.

I patted his shoulder. "It's good to hear you talking regularly, not like an asthmatic old—man. I mean—I didn't mean to say that."

"You meant an asthmatic young man." His teeth showed white in the darkness. "Are you ready to escape?"

I grinned back. "That's my brother."

Using my shoulder as a crutch, he cautiously rose. We had to get out of that huge room before the Mayamuras arrived. We followed the path Sabas had taken into a tunnel about a head taller than Chester and me. Though Chester sounded stronger, his legs were weak, and he leaned heavily on us. The first passage gaped in the left wall.

"Sabas is taking the second passage," I whispered, "so it's safe for us to take the first."

The walls were still wet, but the floor was mostly dry. The passage was too wide to touch both walls, so we kept to the middle. Then disaster struck.

An arm crooked round my neck and dragged me to the left. I tried to strike out but strong hands pinioned my arms. Metal scraped and torches flared.

"It is them!" someone yelled in triumph.

I blinked in the glare. Sabas, Garcia, Atalya, and a group of natives clustered together, staring at the three of us.

"But you were taking the second passage!" Chester blurted.

Sabas's lip curled up over his spotted teeth. "So, you listened, dog? Bad things happen to English who eavesdrop. You see, you misheard me."

"But you said the second passage," Chester insisted.

"I said I would go second in the passage."

I frowned. Chester was right, Sabas *had* said the second passage. *Wait. Of course.* Sabas constantly misplaced his words. He had said that he would take the second passage, but he had meant that he would go second in the passage. *The first passage.*

I wanted to throttle him. All this work, and now we were back in his hands. But it would be worst for Pacarina.

Sabas shoved me against the wall and grabbed the girl's arm. "Where is the gold?" He whisked a knife against her throat.

Chester's eyes flamed. His hand slipped to his sash, where his pistol must be hidden.

Pacarina was pale, but calm. "The Indians will be here soon, and then we will all be dead. Why would I break my oath to lengthen my life a few moments? Cut."

"Not without confession," Atalya said, sobbing. "Let her say her *Ave Marias*."

"Mary won't help me, Sister." Pacarina smiled. "My soul is in God's hands, and His alone."

Sabas cursed. "Gold is god. Where is the gold?"

She said nothing. The knife quivered.

"Mayamuras!" a man called from down the passage.

A musket crashed, followed by screams. Sabas flung Pacarina away and rushed at the head of his men into the passage. I caught Pacarina and held her close. She clung to me, her head pressed into my shoulder.

Garcia covered the three of us with his pistol. It looked like our fates depended on the contest in the passage, and judging by the yells of the combatants, the Mayamuras were winning.

"Is there another way out?" I asked Garcia.

"Not for you." His face was yellow with fear. I think he was sick at heart at the failure of his plans and wanted to bring us to the grave with him, but he knew that if he fired his pistol the remaining man would attack.

Talk was useless. Neither my wits nor Chester's muscles could get around that pistol. *What's that?* Something moved in the shadows. A pair of eyes gleamed. Could we possibly have a friend here in the bowels of the earth? Garcia suddenly pitched forward and the pistol clattered on the floor. I scooped it up and clubbed it against Garcia's head.

The interpreter stood before us, his face-muscles twitching spasmodically. He bounded to me.

"You said you saw my wife, my mother? Were they well? Were they safe?"

"Yes, they were well."

He smiled. "If you live, tell them I died happy. I hope they believe it." He slipped into the passage and was gone.

Atalya looked at us. Her face was weary—simply weary. I think the stresses and emotions had drained her until she had nothing left to lose. She handed me a torch.

Pacarina took one long look. "Goodbye, Sister."

We entered a tunnel on the far end. Distance muffled the war-cries. Pacarina sobbed.

Chapter 37

Now that we had a torch, Pacarina could see the symbols above each passage.

"Is there another way out?" I asked.

"If there is, the secret was not passed down."

"So we have two parties of enemies to get through before we can get out." I sighed. "It's a chain of predators. It's like a lion hunting a dog who is hunting a mouse. We're the mouse."

"I'll handle the squeaking." Chester talked little to save his breath, but his humor hadn't faded.

A fresh burst of shouts sounded close at hand.

"Where are they coming from?" I asked Pacarina.

She put her hand to her head. "I don't know, I only know the signs for one path. I don't know how the rest mingle."

We stopped in a long, wide room. Two tunnels entered it from the right and there was one more straight ahead in addition to the way we'd just come.

Chester held up his hand. "We can't just keep wandering. We need a plan. What do you think, Law?"

"If we knew the full plan of these caves, we might be able to outflank the enemy and get back to the entrance. As it is, we're trapped." I gnawed my thumb-knuckle. "If we go deeper into the cave, perhaps we can hide until someone wins the battle and leaves."

A rock bounded out of one of the two passages on the right and slammed into the wall.

"Lights out," Chester whispered.

I had already sacrificed my waistcoat. I wasn't about to become shirtless. I reached for Chester's sash, but he knocked my hand away and handed his waistcoat instead. Another second and the room was totally dark.

His pistol clicked.

My eyes had grown accustomed to the light, so that now I couldn't see anything, but someone was definitely coming through that passage. Several someones.

They were gurgling to each other—Mayamuras. My hands grasped the torch handle so hard that the rough grain dug into my palms. Chester touched me and guided my hand until the flammable torch head was directly beneath the pistol barrel. The voices came closer.

A man-sized blotch loomed out of the darkness. Chester sucked a breath of air. The pistol blasted and the flames shooting out of the barrel lit my torch. Sharp echoes melded with human screams and the orange flame showed a painted native crumpled on the ground and two more frozen beside him.

"Fight!" Chester shouted.

I charged them brandishing the torch before me. They jumped apart. If I attacked either I must leave an exposed flank. They raised their bows.

"Duck!" Chester cried.

I dropped on my palms and knees. Air brushed my hair and two arrows splintered against the far wall. *Do they soak their arrowheads in poison?*

"Now!" Chester called.

I swung the torch at the closest fellow's ankles. He leaped, screamed, and hobbled back into the passage. I rolled to my back and looked up. The second native stood over me with a club in the air, strange shadows dancing in his eye sockets. I clenched my jaw. This was death.

But the blow didn't fall. The man fell instead, clutching at his back. A knife-hilt stuck between his shoulder-blades.

I lay stunned, my nerves quivering. Pacarina bounded to my side.

"Are you hurt?"

"No. Just—shaken."

"Can I have my knife?" Chester asked.

Gritting my teeth, I wrenched the knife out of the native's back. A bright stream of blood followed. Chester didn't smile when I returned the knife, but stared up at the ceiling with tight lips. His breathing was still irregular.

"I can't do it." He shook his head. "I'm too weak."

I retrieved the torch and lighted his pale face. "What are you saying, Chester?"

"I'm too weak to fight. Too weak to run." He looked me in the eyes. "I've never wanted to admit weakness before, Law, but pride won't do any good now. If I try to fight or run, my windpipe will close, and I'll be another dead Englishman."

Pacarina wiped his forehead with one of the rags. "Then we will stay with you, Brother."

"Not a bit." He kept looking into my eyes. "Take her, Law. The natives must have heard the shot. They'll be here in a few minutes. You've had your chance at being a hero, now it's my turn. Go."

"No, Chester, we can stay together, we can help you on."

"It's no use. I'd only be the death of you. I thought I'd be older when the time came, but I'm ready to look Death in the eye. I go to a better place." He sat down.

Tears clouded my eyes. "Chester—my noble, fearless brother."

"Noble, I hope. Not fearless. Remember this, Law, every man's afraid. Being afraid doesn't make a man a coward. Running from the fear makes the coward."

What could I say? When we were in the Inca ruin, Chester was the most able to protect Pacarina, so it was his duty to go. Now the page had turned. He was disabled, and it was my duty to go.

"Chester—Brother—I love you."

"I love you, Lawrence."

"I won't leave you, Chester." Pacarina fought back her tears, bravely trying to keep a cheerful face. "I never thought I would see Lawrence again. Now God has brought us back together, and I can't bear to lose you. You're all I have in the world."

I realized that she really was alone. I had parents, and familiar surroundings to return to. She had nothing.

Angry voices echoed in the distance.

"Pacarina, we must leave him. Of course you don't want to, but it's my duty to make you. I have to protect you."

"Why?" She turned on me. Her voice cracked. "Why? What am I to you? A Spanish girl who has only brought you trouble. You came to save your brother, not me."

The voices were approaching. I grabbed her arm. "You're a girl, that's why."

Her lips trembled. "We must do something!"

I met her pleading eyes, feeling utterly helpless. "Can you run like the wind?"

She nodded eagerly.

"Good, because we'll need to go even faster." I pulled her toward the far passage but stopped just outside. The gurgling voices changed from a trickle to a roar, and the first passage discharged a torrent of Mayamuras.

"Looking for someone?" I called.

They yelled and raced toward us. We squeezed into the passage and scurried like rabbits, bent almost double in the low-roofed tunnel. Lord willing, the Mayamuras would be so intent on us that they wouldn't see Chester, but would be after us as fast as their feet could pound. My own poor feet had that uncomfortable wet feeling again, as of a dozen blisters having popped and sprayed water into my socks.

Chapter 38

Pacarina and I crouched together against the cold stone. We had shaken the natives off our trail, at least for the time being. The torch was burning low. I held it carefully balanced so that the flame would not eat away at any particular side, and would thus burn more slowly. We had been threading the tunnels for half an hour.

We rested at the end of a passage and drank from the dripping walls. Pacarina's face was haggard. This must be very different from her quiet life in Spain. I had always thought of girls as they were in Chester's novels—giggly, flighty little things that were pretty to look at but good for very little else. Of course, the authors would never say that of them, but that's how they were painted. The words 'sensible girl' seemed oxymoronic.

Then there was Pacarina. She was all that I could want in a sister. What possessed Chester to not want to marry her? Life is a continual round of opposites. I spend months trying to prevent them from loving each other, and now wish they did. It did seem hard, though, knowing that some unknown man would enter her life in the future and take her full love and devotion.

"Is there something wrong with my face?"

I started. "Eh?"

"You've been staring at me for some time."

"Oh. Yes, well, you don't look very good, Pacarina."

"That's not a nice thing to say to ladies."

"Oh, I mean, you're pretty, and all that, I just meant that you look tired."

"Yes, you're not supposed to say that to ladies."

"I'm sorry, Pacarina. I never know the right things to say to ladies."

She sighed. "Can't you shorten my name?"

I blinked. "Pardon me?"

She looked a little wistful. "Chester calls you 'Law.' Can't you call me something special?"

Special? Girls are the most unpredictable creatures. "I always thought of nicknames as being disrespectful."

She shook her head seriously. "No, not at all. My father called me his '*pequeño rayo*,' his little ray of light. A special name—unless of course it is an insult—means that you care for the person. A special name is a special link."

I scratched my chin. "That appears to be sound logic."

She smiled. "But don't you agree? What will you call me?"

I sighed. "Perhaps 'Goose,' for instigating this world-encompassing goose-chase. Or I could follow native naming patterns and name you for a physical feature—'Brown Eyes,' for instance."

"But I could call you the same."

"Never mind. What about 'Sister'?"

"A good name, but shared by many."

"I don't know, Pacarina. I do know that we're running out of light."

"What about 'Dear'?"

I cocked an eyebrow. "Deer? As in, the family *Cervidae*? That is, as in stags and does?"

She laughed at me. "No, you silly boy, as in 'my dear sister.'"

"Oh." I coughed. "Well, I suppose it wouldn't be problematic. Er—Dear."

The torch hissed out. We were in complete darkness.

"Now where?" I asked.

"To Chester." She grabbed my arm and pulled me out of the tunnel. "We have circled back around. I pray that the natives are lost in this maze."

All was silent.

"Chester?" she whispered.

No answer.

"Chester!" I called, louder.

Silence.

"This can't be the right place," I said.

"It is. I saw the carving, that's why I waited for the torch to die. I know my way out from here."

"But Chester doesn't."

We groped to the far wall and felt along the rough stone. I stepped on something hard, like a stick. It was the arrow the native had shot at me. Two more steps, and Pacarina gasped. She handed me a piece of wet cloth. It was one of the strips she had torn from her skirt hem.

"Where is he?" Her voice quavered.

Someone gurgled.

I turned. "Chester?"

Sparks leapt out of the darkness and spots of light shot at my eyes. I jumped back, blocking the light with my hands. Something sharp pricked my right side.

"Law!" Pacarina clung to me and the hazy objects surrounding us shot into focus. Red- and yellow-streaked faces glowered beneath spitting torches. Snake Cheek stood two feet from me, grimacing and holding the short spear that was trying to ventilate my shirt.

"Oh." I smiled weakly. "H-how do you do? Have you seen my brother?"

They stepped closer.

Chapter 39

Terraced valleys covered the mountain for thousands of feet below. Our procession wound snake-like up the mountainside, the Mayamuras chanting a ceaseless ditty that would have made one of Chester's noble American savages stop cold in the middle of his death-chant. This would be no common jungle execution. To the mountains we had fled, and from the mountains our souls would fly.

Snake Cheek had ordered my boots torn off, but that caused me no great anguish. I was surprised to see all ten toes still firmly attached. The grass was tough at times, and the rocks tougher, but at least my feet could breathe. Our captors let Pacarina keep her shoes.

Snake Cheek and twenty-one more Mayamuras guarded us, prodding with their spears and patting their bows when we missed our footing. Many of the spear tips were splashed red. *Chester's blood?*

On we climbed, up, up, jagged stones tearing my trousers and scratching my legs, spear-points prodding, the air thin and unsatisfying, thirst, blisters, the panting girl just behind me—that horrid chanting. I stopped looking up or down. All that mattered was the rock in front of me, the tuft of grass that would ease my foot-pain, the sharp thorns that would not.

I don't know how long it took. It was nightmarish, a green Dante's *Inferno*. All I know is that at some point I tried to step to the next tuft of grass, and there was a pair of legs already there. I stumbled into the man ahead. He pushed me. I fell, rolled, the ground below me disappeared, a mist was engulfing me—a hand grasped my right and held me dangling in the air.

"Climb, old man, climb!"

Chester? I looked up dully into his face.

His teeth were clenched. "Climb, Law!"

The blood pumped through my extended arm and my head cleared. That mist below was clouds, through which I was about to fall. Climb, indeed. I grasped a handful of grass on the cliff edge, but the dirt gave way and dropped into the clouds. I reached again, and this time I grasped a solid rock. The jagged edge sliced into my palm, but I couldn't let go. Chester pulled on my right arm, and inch by inch I moved higher, the pain increasing in my palm, until my upper ribs stretched over the edge. One last pull, and I lay panting on the top of the mountain.

"Rather a long way down."

I turned on my back and looked up at Chester. The tattered remnants of the Eyesore covered his head, and his face was weary, but his eyes still had a suggestion of that old mischievous sparkle.

"Thanks," I said.

"Not a bit." The sparkle faded. "I didn't want to die alone."

We were almost to the mountain peak, on a side-shoulder which surpassed the surrounding shoulders and was flat enough to hold the entire group. More natives came up the path, and in their midst trudged Garcia, his wife, Sabas, and a handful of his men. The rest of the men were missing, but many of the grinning Mayamuras had muskets over their shoulders. There were certainly skeletons in that cave now.

The actual mountain peak was close by, protruding like a tumor from the flat shoulder. It was no more than fifty feet high, and looked climbable. As best as I could see from my back, the ground at the top leveled, but it could only hold a few people.

Chester pulled me to my feet. "Where there's life, there's hope," he whispered. "Stay by me."

As the new prisoners joined us the horrid chant ceased and silence ruled. The Mayamuras jostled us toward the far edge.

When Sabas saw us, he howled and tried to wrench free from the men holding his arms. Spots of saliva and Spanish curses spattered from between his lips. His pupils were dilated, his cheeks sunken, his hair splayed. I thought of a picture I once saw of a hollow-mouthed African snake sticking its head out of a box and hissing at its captors. I edged a little closer to Chester.

Garcia stood watching him with folded arms. "Fool."

Sabas wrenched his head around and spat at him. "You! It is all your fault! I die because you are a pig greedy!"

Garcia unfolded his arms. "I did not want it for myself, I wanted it for my king." He glared at the archeologist.

Sabas gurgled. "And you would be rich, advise him, he would be your puppet."

Garcia flushed crimson and raised his right arm. Two Mayamuras grabbed him and dragged him towards a flat boulder on the cliff edge. Others grabbed Chester, and me, and Pacarina. They forced our knees into the earth beside the boulder so that our chins rested on the sun-warmed stone.

The chief and Snake Cheek stood before us. Snake Cheek drew a stone knife from his girdle. The sun beat down from above.

I was first in the line. The priest grabbed my hair and forced my chin down. With loud, screaming tones he shouted to the heavens, the knife-shadow undulating on the rock face. A strange whizzing noise sounded nearby, and a condor glided close to the mountain edge. They feed on carrion. At least my body wouldn't be wasted.

Snake Cheek stopped. I closed my eyes. I didn't need the interpreter to tell me the import of his words.

Forgive me of my sins, O God.

I felt detached. What would the knife feel like? Would death come quickly? Would it hurt? My cut hand throbbed faintly.

"Take the priest." Chester's breath tickled my ear. "I'll take Pacarina and the interpreter. To the peak."

Blood coursed through my veins. How could we survive? What if I failed?

What if I didn't knock him down?

Chester's elbow punched my ribs. I tensed every tendon, ligament, and nerve in my legs and exploded upwards. My hand caught the descending arm and shook the knife loose. The priest was totally unprepared. Another wrench and I had his arms clamped behind his back.

Mayamuras shouted and every man leveled his bow, or blow gun, or spear. Chester burst through them, the interpreter draped over his back and Pacarina running by his side. I followed, spinning the priest round and round so that any shot would likely hit him. The natives fell back in awe and we scrambled up the peak, slipping, sliding, scraping, on the steep rock. There was barely enough space at the top for all of us to stand.

Chester dumped the interpreter. "Tell them that if they shoot or attack, their little priestly friend is going to go condor-hunting." He pushed the trembling Snake Cheek to the edge.

The interpreter cowered. I repeated the command in Spanish. He crawled to the edge and looked down on the natives, his hands held in front of his face as if to guard him from arrows. He gurgled to the men below. The chief strode out of the group and looked angrily up.

"He says that you have mistreated the Snake Priest," said the interpreter. "You will surely die."

"Tell him I'd mistreat a regiment of Snake Priests," Chester said. I translated.

The answer was more satisfactory. "The chief asks what you want."

"Tell him what the Americans told us. 'Life, liberty, and the pursuit of happiness.'" Chester tightened his hold on the wriggling priest. "At the moment the pursuit of happiness sounds awfully like fox-chasing on the fields at home."

The answer came. "The chief says not to harm the priest."

"Tell him that we want to go free."

"He says that you did not abide by his terms. You stayed after the snake fell."

Snake Cheek gurgled something.

"The priest says that he would rather die than let us live."

Chester grunted. "Very nice of him. Tell him to keep his mouth shut. Better yet—" he wrapped his arm round the priest's neck. The gurgles stopped abruptly. "Much better."

The Mayamuras had closed around their other prisoners.

"The chief says that they will kill our friends," the interpreter said.

Chester snorted. "It's a long trip to England, and that's where the only friends we have are. Wish we were there too."

I wholeheartedly agreed. "Tell them that they're no friends of—wait, what about Garcia's wife?"

The native cocked his head. "Señor?"

"Hmm? Oh, never mind, don't say anything." I turned anxiously to Chester. "What about Atalya?"

"What about her?"

"She's a woman. We can't simply condemn her to die. The men are responsible for themselves, but it's our duty to save a woman."

Chester sighed. "I'm afraid you're right. Well, you have the brains, what do you propose?"

We negotiated. It was eerie, standing at the top of the world, looking down on a group of angry brown splotches on the green grass, with clouds circling lazily below us, and birds flying at foot-level. Glimpses of green jungle-canopy peeked through momentary clefts in the cloud cover.

The chief offered Atalya in exchange for Snake Cheek. I declined, knowing that I would resemble a pin-cushion two minutes after the proposed exchange took place. The chief realized that he had a valuable prisoner, and he was intent to make the most of her. What was worse, he didn't seem particularly concerned that Chester was holding Snake Cheek by the scruff of the neck over the mountain-edge like a boy dangling a kitten over a pond.

Then Atalya realized that we were bargaining for her. A sensible woman would have kept quiet and let the negotiations continue, but Atalya was *not* a sensible woman. The moment she realized that we proposed to save her and leave Garcia to his own devices, she screamed and clung to the villain. She wouldn't go without him.

Chester looked at me over his shoulder and shook his head.

"It's hard to believe she's Pacarina's sister."

I looked at Pacarina. She was sitting by the edge, her knees drawn up to support her chin.

"Do you want your sister saved?" I asked.

"Of course. I still love her."

"Right." I scratched my head. *How do I talk us out of this?*

Chester shifted his legs. "Can you challenge them to single combat?"

I stared at him. "Are you joking?"

"Not a bit. Haven't you ever read history? I hear that some of our chaps have brought single combats back a bit in Siberia, too."

"This is Peru." I tried to coalesce my scattered brain cells into a concentrated thought. What could we give them? Snake Cheek. But once they had him, they could shoot us at their leisure. Gold?

"Dear, is there really gold in that cave?"

Chester started. "Dear?"

"Quiet."

Pacarina nodded.

"Do you know where?"

She nodded again.

The interpreter tugged on my sleeve. "The chief, he is not patient.

"Ask him if he wants gold," I said.

The interpreter's eyes widened. "Gold?"

"Yes, *oro*, gold."

I watched the chief as the message was delivered. We were too high to clearly see his face, but he didn't appear to be impressed.

"He says he needs no gold, that only greedy fools like my master and Señor

Dedoras need gold. He says that you have angered his gods, and that you must die." The interpreter gulped. "We must all die."

God works in mysterious ways. Sabas must have understood bits of the native language, for when the chief made this speech, he utterly lost his head. With a scream, he sent the nearest two natives sprawling and turned on Garcia.

"You! You have ruined all, my life, my gold, it is gone, you are stupid, you are fool!"

The ceremonial stone knife lay near his foot. He stooped, grasped it, and plunged toward Garcia. Atalya screamed. The next moment her body sprawled on the altar, blood pouring from a gaping chest-wound. I don't know if she purposely jumped in front of Garcia, or if it was an accident, but there she lay, and above her stood Sabas, the blood-dripping knife in hand and foam dribbling down his chin.

Garcia roared. Sabas struck with the knife, but Garcia grasped his hand and they locked in a deathly embrace. They spun round and round, grunting, squeezing, jabbing, biting.

A bow twanged. *Thomp.* Sabas fell over the dead woman's body, an arrow sticking out of his neck. Another moment and the natives fell on the helpless prisoners.

My stomach churned, and I turned my face. The screams soon ended, then the groans. Something crashed down the mountain-side, and I looked back. Pooled blood covered the altar, but the bodies were gone. The clouds had received them. Condors screamed below.

Pacarina sobbed. I knelt beside her, dizzy with horror and the fearsome heights we stood upon.

"Oh, Lawrence!" She buried her face in my shoulder. "My sister!"

"I'm sorry, Dear. I tried."

Chester spoke, and his voice was tense. "Come here, Law."

I squeezed Pacarina's hand and rose. The natives were clustered round the foot of the pinnacle, brandishing their weapons and screaming at us. They had tasted blood.

"You like history, Law. Ever read about Horatius and his bridge?"

"Of course."

He pushed Snake Cheek down so that his head was hanging over the edge. "The audience is demanding an encore." He pulled a knife from his left boot and handed it to me. "Too bad there aren't any historians around to write about us."

The handle was warm from touching his flesh, and it felt ridiculously small compared to the native spears. The entire tribe clustered round the bottom. Priest or no priest, they were coming up.

Chester planted his foot on Snake Cheek's back and looked at Pacarina. "Goodbye, Sister. I'm glad to have known you."

She rose, like they say princesses do, and wiped the tears from her eyes. "Goodbye, Brother. Thank you."

He turned to me. "I've been rotten to you most of your life, Law."

I extended my hand. "It's been mutual."

He grasped it. "I'm proud to be your brother."

"I'm proud to be yours."

We turned and faced the enemy side by side. Nine were already climbing the hill, and as fast as each man's legs left room, another joined the line.

Chester sighed. "Some loose stones would be splendid. One dropped now would take out half a dozen of the beggars."

Something flickered in my peripheral vision. Chester's feet flung up and he thudded on the grass, his head hanging over the edge and the Eyesore fluttering down into space. By reflex my arms shot out and I grasped for Snake Cheek. Someone screamed—the interpreter had been crouching on the ledge nearest the attacking natives, but he was there no longer. Shouts rose from below and I glimpsed a crumpled brown body smashing against the hillside and sweeping off the climbing Mayamuras like ants from a stick.

The priest was struggling with me, struggling to throw me off just as he had pushed the poor interpreter, struggling to free himself from my encircling arms. My chin rammed into a hard ball of bone on the back of his neck, and he shot forward. For a moment I thought we would slip off the mountain together, but he managed to twist his momentum sideways and we fell at the edge, myself on top.

I sensed Chester prancing beside us. "Come, Law, let me at the rascal."

I couldn't let go. His elbows jabbed my ribs like alternating pistons, and he tried to bite my right arm. I could withstand blunt rib-jabs, but the idea of his filthy teeth sucking my blood twisted my brain, and I shot my arm back out of his reach. Thankfully, he only had shirt, not skin, in his teeth, and the fabric ripped from mid-muscle to forearm.

I tried to reach round his neck and throttle him, but he dropped his chin into the dirt and my arm struck his nose, mucus wetting my bared flesh.

Without warning, his tensed muscles relaxed, and he lay limp on the mountain edge. I tensed, fearing a trick, but he was as motionless as a dead fish.

"Did you knife him?" I asked Chester.

"How could I when you've got yourself draped over him like a kite on a kitten."

Snake Cheek gurgled. I tightened my grasp, but still he made no movement. A head popped over the peak's edge, the face streaked with dull yellow stripes. Snake Cheek howled. The attacker stopped motionless and stared at me with dilated eyes. I stared back, with as much wonder, if not as much width, in my own eyes.

Hot breath blew my back neck-hairs, and I felt Chester kneeling behind me. "Either this is a mountain of sudden sunstroke or something very odd is happening."

Another head popped up beside the first, but a word from the priest froze it.

"Law, they're looking at your arm."

My arm? I looked. There, with the sleeve torn off and the sunlight shining full upon it, was my birthmark. The bulging veins beneath the skin ran below the snakish swirl, the whole effect standing out darkly against my white skin.

Of course. That was why Garcia had kept me alive. Chester's strong arm couldn't save us, but my weak arm might. A plan formed.

I freed my left arm from under the priest's body and rose. "Drop your knife, Chester. We bluff."

The knife fell. Snake Cheek slowly rose, his eyes still focused on my birthmark.

I raised my chin. "Let us go down," I said in English, trying to sound majestic. Of course, they couldn't understand my words, but they could understand my gestures, and they might notice that my language was different from the Spanish they were accustomed to hearing.

I repeated the command and waved him back. For a long moment he stared at me, awe and hate struggling in his eyes. Then he ordered the natives down.

"What if they knife us in the back?" Chester asked.

"It's very similar to being knifed in the front. Help Pacarina and be quiet. This is my job."

A string of natives clung to the peak from top to bottom, but they somehow squeezed themselves into nooks and crannies so that we could pass down. Snake Cheek preceded us, swaying like a drunken sailor.

"What's it all about?" Chester demanded.

I looked back up at him. "I recommend circumspect behavior, Chester. They think we're gods."

Chapter 40

My ears were hot, and I knew without looking that they bloomed bright-red.

"This is rather awkward," Chester said.

I nodded. We stood in the center of the native village trembling with exhaustion but unable to show it. The entire village was spread out before us, face-down, except for Snake Cheek, who was on his knees gurgling some sort of oration at us.

Pacarina's mouth was tight and her eyes were wide. The horror of the mountain was fresh upon us all.

I touched Chester's arm. "Can you try to cheer her?"

He shook his head. "She's a right to be downcast, Law. She just watched her sister die. She's a good girl, give her time, and she'll be herself again."

Snake Cheek rose from his knees. The whole village rose at this signal, and one by one they began forming snaky lines across the open ground.

Chester snorted. "I say, it looks like a country dance."

It was, Mayamura style. The natives began by shuffling their feet and locking arms, winding like snakes round the clearing. Then here and there a young fellow would break from the line and execute a wild pirouette. Chanting began, low and fierce at first, but growing louder and fiercer.

Chester laughed. "If you have an unbiased perspective, this scenario is rather amusing."

He grinned at me. His chest was moving well, free of asthma for the time, and what with his smile, and his tired but commanding face, he looked handsome. I felt proud to be a twin.

"What's amusing, Chester?"

"Two tattered English boys and a pretty Spanish girl standing in front of a hundred chanting natives who are inventing entirely new dance moves in the middle of a jungle."

Things didn't look very amusing to me. I decided that my perspective must be biased.

Snake Cheek sidled next to me and pointed at the dancers, then at us.

"What's he saying, Law?"

"I think he wants us to dance."

"Oh." Chester scratched his chin. "Tell him I'll consider it if he brings some suitable partners."

The priest pointed more insistently, and I could sense him becoming annoyed beneath the mask of deference. Between our twinhood and my birthmark, the rest of the natives seemed to have firmly accepted us as gods, but I felt that the priest didn't appreciate competition. Even if he did believe in his religion, he couldn't be blamed for being surprised that two gods would tamely follow a crooked Spanish trader and then let him chase them around a miserable cave.

"I think we need to dance, Chester."

"Oh, very well. As Hamlet once said, we must suffer the blow darts and arrows of outrageous fortune." He swung his arms windmill fashion and puffed his chest. "I've wanted to practice the highland fling for some time now. I say, Pacarina, can you dance?"

She blinked at him. "I know a few Spanish dances."

"Splendid. Well, here goes." He pointed his toes, squared his left arm on his hip, and began prancing up and down.

I shook my head. *Dance? Me? I can't dance.* Snake Cheek looked at me. Well, perhaps I could try a hornpipe. I put my hands on my hips like a sailor I once saw in Liverpool and tried to dance. My feet instantly doubled in size, and the ground began jumping up and down at me in the most peculiar fashion.

The natives shouted with glee and redoubled their efforts. I thought I had already sweated away all my internal moisture, but I found that I was wrong.

In the rare moments I snatched to look at the other two, I saw that Pacarina was doing something graceful with her feet, and Chester looked splendid, his head flung back in excitement.

Somehow my right foot hit the ground much before it was supposed to, and my liver executed some painful gymnastics.

"What are you doing?" Chester asked.

"It's—a—hornpipe," I gasped between steps. "But—don't—you think—this is—rather—blasphemous?"

"Dancing?"

"I mean—aren't we—worshiping?"

His head wagged back and forth, and I think he was shaking it, but it might have been part of the dance. "I'm not worshiping anything. Besides, I would hardly call a Spanish dance, a highland fling, and a poorly executed hornpipe 'blasphemous.'"

My foot size tripled.

Just when I thought that my joints would disintegrate, Chester pulled his harmonica from his pocket and started playing. Mayamuras have no appreciation of music. They screamed with delight and danced harder.

Twenty minutes passed, and I expected every moment to find myself sitting on the ground with missing knee-bones. Thankfully, the natives were also human, and they finally tired of the game. The dance stopped abruptly, and five old men crawled toward us.

I grasped Chester's shoulder. "Do you think gods are allowed to sit down?"

"Yes." We collapsed, and Pacarina sat down beside us. That girl is wonderful. Her cheeks were red and her breathing was hard, but she looked fresher than when she started.

The old men indicated the priest's hut and led us to it. We evidently had the freedom of the village, at least for the present time.

I was about to wave the fellows off and collapse into whatever bed or pile of leaves the hut held, but Chester stopped me.

"They're not finished."

I forced myself to look up, and there was Snake Cheek and the chief advancing, each leading a girl by the hand. One of the girls had red face-paint, and the other, yellow. They were the same girls who served us that first day at the village.

All four bowed before us.

"These fellows do enough bowing and scraping for Frenchmen," Chester muttered.

Snake Cheek pointed at the red girl, touched his chest, touched the girl's head, and patted the girl's hand. The chief did the same to the yellow girl.

"I believe they're both father and daughter," I said.

The priest then pointed to me, and patted his daughter's head. The chief did the same, but pointed at Chester instead of me.

Chester frowned. "Are they saying they're our daughters now?"

Pacarina smiled. "Silly boys. They are giving you wives."

I collapsed against the doorpost. I feared heart-failure. I couldn't stand any more.

"You don't say." Chester folded his arms and looked at the girls. "Never been in this situation before."

I gasped. "Chester, you can't think of marrying a pagan!"

"I can't?" His eyebrows twitched. "Why not?"

"Chester!"

For a moment his face remained serious, then, like water seeping through a dyke, a smile seeped out of the left corner of his mouth and spread across his face. "Don't worry, Law, I'd never make you have a sister-in-law with cosmetics like that." He nodded at the face-paint.

Snake Cheek pushed his daughter at me and gurgled.

"What do I do, Chester?"

"Can't say. Never been proposed to before. First-time experience."

Pacarina touched my arm. "May I help?"

I nodded gratefully.

She stepped between the little pagan and me and shook her head at Snake Cheek. His eyes opened wide as half-sovereigns. She pointed at herself, then at Chester and me.

The chief nodded vaguely and turned his daughter around. Snake Cheek had to follow. I staggered inside.

"I say, what do you think *they'll* think?" Chester said.

My fumbling hands found a pile of grass, and I threw myself face-down upon it.

"I don't care," I mumbled. "I've thought enough for a year. Good night."

I slept.

Chapter 41

Strange dreams twirled and twisted in my brain, strange now that I think of them, but perfectly reasonable at the time. Someone kept talking, shouting, muttering, a constant chorus, like monotonous strings on a classical piece.

"You awake?"

Chester's voice wrenched me from dream-land. I realized how shot my nerves were when my first instinct was to jump up and grasp my sword. I lay in shadow, but sunlight pierced through the doorway and illuminated the hut's center. Long blades of grass clung to my hair and clothes. Outside, there were rows of bobbing heads attached to thin bodies sitting in the dirt facing the hut. Snake Cheek was prancing and gurgling in front of them.

"He'd make quite a professor," Chester said dryly.

"What's going on?"

"He's giving a little lecture. It's either an architectural lesson or a theological discussion, since he keeps pointing at our hut."

"Where's Pacarina?"

"I'm here." She leaned out of the shadows in the back. "What do we do now?"

I combed my fingers through my hair, removing grass and twigs. "That depends on whether they keep thinking we're gods."

Chester grunted. "I don't think that priest is convinced."

"No, I'm afraid not. Somehow we need to get out of this place, and I'd rather do it alive. Any ideas?"

"There are some muskets in the corner." Chester pointed near Pacarina's seat. "The brown devils must have plundered our camp."

I eagerly examined the muskets. As best I could tell, they were in excellent condition, and there were seven leaning against the wall. Loot filled the corner, but I couldn't find any shot pouches.

"Looking for these?" Chester dangled a handful of pouches at me. "I've already loaded the muskets."

"Good. Anything else useful?"

"See that barrel?" He pointed at a familiar barrel half-buried beneath Pacarina's sister's extra dresses. "Powder. Sabas's men used to refill their pouches from that."

"Do you think we can use it in some way?"

"Would be a pretty poor show if we couldn't. Seven muskets and a barrel of powder, all we need is a man Friday and we'll be set."

"Friday?"

He frowned at me. "Haven't you ever read *Robinson Crusoe*?"

I shook my head.

"Read it."

Pacarina spoke. "The natives are becoming restless."

The heads were bobbing more than before and Snake Cheek was fairly dripping with sweat. If only we had an interpreter. Oh well, one can't cry over spilt ink.

"Do you have a plan, Chester?" I asked.

He stroked a musket-barrel. "If we run, they'll catch us. If we stay, they'll get tired of our divine presence and make us into pincushions. We could try blowing them up with the barrel of powder, but I doubt we'd get them all."

"Not to mention that we'd probably die as well, unless you're familiar with pyrotechnics."

"Not a bit. Never heard of them before."

"It's the art of making fireworks and explosives."

"Oh." He shook his head. "I've made a few squibs in my day, but I never tried blowing a village up. I think you'd better take over the thinking part."

I folded my arms and stared at the natives. Beyond them, on the opposite side of the village, was the path leading to the outside world. Even if we created a distraction with the powder and managed to get through them and onto that path, we could never outrun them. A loud whimpering interrupted my thoughts, and I scanned the village, searching for the source. A herd of mules, our mules, was standing disconsolately in the village outskirts on the side closest to the mountain. Once outside Mayamura territory those mules would be invaluable for our journey back to civilization. But they wouldn't outrun the natives.

"Any ideas?" Chester looked at me hopefully.

"Do you think we could cut through the back of this hut and hide in the jungle until night?"

Chester shrugged. "Cutting out would be easy, and we could hide, but we're not used to the jungle. The natives would be sure to find us. It's not like the cave, where it was just as dark and new to them as us, and we could hide away while they fought each other."

I sighed. "Very well. There must be a way. I wonder if—Chester, what did you just say?"

"Mmm?"

"While they fought each other. That's it!"

Chester grinned. "You said fight?" He patted the musket. "I can do that."

"No, not us fight, they must fight, fight each other!"

"How's that?"

I pulled him down and squatted next to Pacarina. "Listen, I have a plan. It's dangerous, slightly irrational, and probably impossible, but I think it's our only chance."

Chapter 42

I knotted the fabric over my Adam's apple. Chester and I stood in our shirtsleeves, exactly alike except for this bit of red cloth, half of Chester's sash. He nodded at me and stuffed the other half into his pocket. Much depended on these makeshift scarves.

"Do you have the lantern ready?" I asked.

"Yes. Lucky they filched it along with the powder."

"Providence, Chester. God has been with us."

"Right. Here they come."

I smoothed my shirt, patted the scarf, and tried to remember how Caesar stood in the Shakespearean plays. I'm not accustomed to bluffing majesty.

Pacarina slipped through the door, Snake Cheek and the chief trailing her. She was acting her part perfectly, her eyes bent to the ground and her shoulders stooped like a year-weary slave's. The chief looked like a little child who has been eating surreptitious chocolate and wants to be defiant but is scared stiff of his parents. Snake Cheek's eyes were cold and impassive. I couldn't read them.

After they entered, Chester draped one of Atalya's extra dresses over the doorway. As the room grew dark both natives sucked air sharply. Chester opened the dark-lantern and a gentle glow lit the room. The natives resumed breathing.

I tilted my nose higher and pointed to Pacarina. She bowed elaborately, holding her arms rigidly before her and touching her forehead to the damp dirt. The chief scanned her for a moment, gurgled, and copied her motions. Snake Cheek, no doubt feeling left out, joined the forehead-rubbing throng. That was the first hurdle.

When they had all resumed an upright position, I nodded to Chester. This was step two. He slowly kicked his right leg backward and placed both hands on the ground, from which position he lowered his forehead to the earth, still keeping his right leg stuck in the air. I hadn't counted on such an elaborate posture. Indeed, he looked very much like a traveling circus performer, but I hoped the natives wouldn't notice the resemblance. I don't suppose that many traveling circuses have toured Mayamura territory.

The two leaders looked at Chester with wrinkled foreheads, evidently surprised that a god would bow to someone. I slapped my chest and tried to pat Chester's head. His boot was actually the only accessible part, but the effect was the same. The natives nodded, and we were established as a hierarchy of divinities, with myself on top. Now for the third step.

I toyed with my scarf until I was certain that both men had noticed it.

"Chester, open the door."

He tore the dress down and tossed it into a corner.

"All right, Dear," I said, "it's your turn again. You're a brave girl."

I pointed at her and tried to indicate that she was to be obeyed. She glided meekly outside, and the two leaders followed. The next five minutes were torturous. Chester fingered his musket, and I pulled at my chin. I found it strangely scratchy and realized that I needed to shave. Strange what the mind thinks of at life-altering times.

Something dark stood in the doorway. "Pacarina!"

She moved aside and let Snake Cheek and his daughter enter. Chester blocked the light from the doorway again, and I folded my arms.

"Frankly, my dear priestly fellow, your figure is revolting." I smiled at him, and he smiled back coldly. "Your daughter vividly reminds me of yourself." He rubbed his hands together and shifted his eyes between me and the girl. "Thankfully, you have no idea what I'm saying, and as I'm smiling at you and your daughter, you think I'm saying nice things. So let it be. Ignorance is bliss, or so they say."

I pointed to his daughter, then laid my hand over my heart, hoping that the uncivilized world operated under the same delusion as we more enlightened men, that the tender emotions emanate from a red blob in the middle of a man's chest. Snake Cheek smiled.

I lifted the lantern, slowly rotated it ninety degrees, and then covered the flame. A moment's darkness and I uncovered it and completed a full revolution. Next, I took the girl's hand—a fat, dumpy affair—and pretended to lead her somewhere. After these maneuvers I returned her hand to Snake Cheek and smiled at them both, hoping that he could interpret my signs. It looked like he did. At least, he smiled, and bowed, and tried to look pleased. That was settled then. Tomorrow morning I was supposed to marry the girl.

"Your turn, Chester, and may God be with you."

I solemnly led the two natives outside and pointed to the nearest hut. I let them precede me to it and took one last glance at Chester. He winked. The other half of the sash was tied conspicuously round his throat. I strutted as quickly as possible in Snake Cheek's trail and paused just inside the hut's doorway until Pacarina reappeared leading the chief and his daughter. They entered the hut I had just left. Our plan was set.

Chapter 43

Something slammed into my shoulder. I rolled over and squinted against the glaring sunlight.

I groaned. "Morning already?"

"Closer to afternoon." Chester leaned on one of the muskets, his figure framed by the doorway. He grinned. "Cheer up old chap, it's your wedding day."

Our plan returned to my consciousness in full force. Our lives depended on these next few hours. *Funny, that fact is becoming a refrain.*

I rose, twisted some of the kinks out of my back, and shaded my eyes so that I could bear the sunlight. The center of the village was crawling with natives, half of them working on a tall arbor-like structure made of sticks and vines.

"I feel sorry, deceiving those girls like this."

Chester grunted. "We didn't say anything about marriage, and it's not our fault if they jump to conclusions. You could have been motioning that you had bad digestion, and expressing your hopes that they wouldn't suffer from the same in the morning."

I inspected our arsenal. "Are these muskets all loaded?"

"Oiled, loaded, primed. Not the latest model, but they'll do."

The barrel of powder was missing. "Where's the powder?"

"Under you."

My legs stiffened of their own accord, and I searched my feet for signs of black powder. The earth looked freshly turned, but that was all. "Buried?"

"Of course." Chester pointed to a cord that lay on the floor and disappeared underground right next to my feet. "Ready for action."

Pacarina slipped through the door and touched my arm. Her cheeks were flushed, her eyes wary, and her chin firm. "The natives are ready."

I scanned the room one last time, then tied the scarf around my neck. "Very well, Dear, you stay here until it's time. You know what to do?"

She nodded.

"I wish you didn't have to be the one, but I don't see any other way."

She laughed, a shade grimly, yes, but at least it was a laugh. "You two have sacrificed so much for me, it's only proper that I do something for you."

Chester coughed. "Yes, well, let's not get into gratitudinal exchanges here. Our brides are waiting."

I lifted my sword-belt and threaded the metal tooth through the last hole in the leather. "Lead on, Brother Brawn."

Chester waved at the door and bowed. "Not at all, Brother Brain. You're the high-god, or something of that sort."

The whole village was gathered to view our exit, making me feel like some traveling freak exhibit. Chester strutted behind with the utmost dignity and composure. He could be an actor.

Snake Cheek and the chief met us. The usual bands of yellow paint on the chief's cheeks were replaced by red bands. So Chester had been able to communicate his message. Snake Cheek was eying the change morosely.

They bowed as we approached the arbor, and over their lowered heads, I saw the two girls. Each was decked in her best, in alpaca fur blouses and cotton skirts. Vine-wreaths twined through their brown hair. The only difference I could see was that one had red streaks on her face, and one had yellow. Each was dressed to the best, and each thought she was the sole bride of the high-god.

We gravely detoured round the arbor and approached the mules, which stood lazily in a group flicking their tails at flies. Snake Cheek sidled over to us and shook his head, gurgling away like a surfacing hippopotamus. I stared at him with my arms folded and my jaw clenched. He stopped talking. He obviously didn't believe in us fully, but he didn't seem eager to test the extent of our powers. He smiled weakly and waved some natives to tie saddles onto two of the mules.

"We need three mules," Chester muttered.

"Then saddle a third."

"That'll make them suspicious. You'll have to ride two."

My jaw dropped, but I remembered that this didn't look majestic and snapped it shut. "Why me?" I asked through clenched teeth.

Chester grinned. "You're high-god, or worst indigestion-sufferer, depending how you look at it."

A native crouched as a footstool next to one of the mules. My boot-heel left a red mark on his naked back, but he didn't complain. I looked at the second saddled mule and gulped.

"I can't straddle them, Chester, my legs aren't wide enough."

"Try a foot on each inside stirrup."

I tried, stabilizing myself with a tense arm round each mule's neck. The arrangement was flawless until they began moving and I realized that they had differing thoughts on pacing. In a moment my left foot was two feet in front of my right and the gap was increasing.

"Pull that fellow in," Chester said.

I pulled at the left one's head, and the other mule profited by the delay to take the lead, thus reversing my foot position. *This is a self-inflicted racking!*

"Now pull on the right one," Chester commanded.

I did so, and the left advanced. I pulled on him and the right advanced. In this zigzag fashion, one foot in front of the other and back again, I managed to reach the arbor. Chester ambled easily behind me and took his position on the left, just under the leafy roof. I no longer regretted that little episode of the *masato*.

If the natives were surprised by this new method of divine transportation they didn't show it, but bowed and chanted one of their awful songs. The two girls had modestly retired to the back of the crowd, but their fathers spotted them and soon had them captive.

"'The best laid plans of mice and men often go awry,'" Chester quoted. "Robert Burns. There's no mice around, so hopefully our plan will succeed."

Snake Cheek and the chief elbowed their way through the crowd and approached, each aiming for me. My heart beat violently. My fingers clutched the coarse mule-hair. *This is it.*

The two leaders banged together about four feet from me. Snake Cheek was on the chief's right, thus closest to Chester, and he glared at his rival and motioned him to go around to Chester. The chief glared back and motioned the same. My insides were whirling, but I kept a calm face. *It's working!*

Each man knew that the greatest of we twins wore a red scarf round his neck. We had shown them that yesterday. Each knew that I half-stood, half-sat in front of them, with the same scarf around my neck. Each knew that the Red-Scarfed One had specifically asked for his daughter. Neither knew that Chester had an identical scarf, and that he had done the asking honors when the chief was admitted to his private audience.

Now I must escalate their anger from the passive to the active state.

The natives dropped their daughters' hands and faced each other. Snake Cheek gurgled and pointed at his daughter. The chief gurgled back, his forehead wrinkled in a half-dozen lines. The red lines on his cheeks rippled. Snake Cheek reached out with his right hand and smeared the lines on the chief's left cheek.

The chief's fists clenched. Much as I despised Snake Cheek, I admired his bravery. The chief stood a head taller than anyone else in the village, and his muscles resembled small tree trunks.

The crowd murmured. Slowly, a gap opened in its midst. The majority, headed by most of the old men, shuffled to Snake Cheek's side, but many of the younger warriors aligned themselves with the chief.

The chief stuck his hand back and a young fellow gave him a knife.

"Now!" Chester whispered.

I sucked a deep breath and balanced on tiptoe in the shifty stirrups. "Now, now, boys, don't fight," I said loudly.

They jolted and swung to face me.

"I'm raising my hand heavenward now, you see, as a signal, and to look majestic. Yes, keep watching carefully, you're about to see something exciting." I flicked my eyes to the left. Pacarina glided out of the hut toward us.

"Are you familiar with gunpowder?" I asked. The leaders shifted nervously, eying each other and me as if deciding which threat was most imminent. "I'll excuse you from answering, since you have no idea what I'm saying, but I would recommend studying it. Gunpowder, I mean. It's a combination of sulfur, charcoal, and—"

A roar blasted my eardrums and a wave of hot air enveloped us. The mules stumbled against each other, pinning my legs. A flurry of sticks, vines, and leaves collapsed over my shoulders. The arbor was down.

Men and women screamed, groaned, yelled. The mules separated and I fell to the ground. My shoulder felt odd. A splinter of bamboo stuck out of my arm. I closed my eyes, clenched my teeth, and plucked it out.

"Here's for the last straw," Chester whispered.

I looked up. Snake Cheek and the chief staggered through the falling debris, their faces stretched by fear and their bodies coated with dust.

Chester darted past me and rammed Snake Cheek in the back. He plunged into the chief. The next moment he lay flat on his back, decked by the chief's mighty fist. Shrill screams filled the air and a hundred forms chopped through the billowing smoke in bloody quest of rival faction members. Battle was joined.

"On your mules," Chester shouted, "we haven't a moment to lose."

I groped through the thick air until my fingers closed on a metal square. I thrust my foot into the stirrup and clambered onto one of the mules. Pacarina was on hers in a moment, and Chester leaped onto his without a glance at the stirrups.

He spoke softly, but tersely. "Pacarina, middle. Law, rear. Forward."

We tried to skirt the fighting and headed for the path to freedom. A fresh breeze was rapidly blowing the smoke away, and already a belt of clear air about thirty feet wide was between us and the path. If the natives saw us leaving they might delay their bloodletting long enough to include us in the fun.

I kicked my mule in the tender spot between its ribs and right rear-leg. He jolted forward, and I found myself hunched over his back, as if that would make me less visible.

Fifteen feet. Ten. I hunched closer. Five. Almost there—trees on our right hand and left, only a square of visibility left to the rear. The path turned slightly, and the jungle blocked us from view—safe! No one had noticed. Everyone not dazed by the explosion was still clawing and knifing each other. Only a few more miles, and freedom.

Chapter 44

"We're being followed."

I stared at Chester. "How would you know? You're leading."

He yanked on his reins and pulled his mule around. "Listen."

A bird chirped. Another wave of buzzing gnats swooped at my head. A monkey hooted in the distance. That was all.

"What is it?" I asked.

"Crunching, there, to the left." He pointed to his left, my right.

Pacarina gasped. "I hear it."

"Law, you take the lead."

This hurt. "Chester, haven't I proved that I'm not a coward? I'm not afraid—well, I am, but I'll not let the fear win."

"Oh, it's not that." He shoved his mule back, grinning as he passed me. "You've had all the fun today, so it's my turn now. I haven't had a proper sword fight for months."

My mule was jaded but I pushed him relentlessly, prodding him whenever he showed signs of fatigue. He could rest once we were out of Mayamura territory.

Twang—thud. My mule jerked forward, nearly toppling me. An arrow protruded from the tough saddle inches from my right leg.

"Yi!" Chester shouted. "Ride for it!"

I grasped Pacarina's bridle and yanked. Both beasts stretched their legs and dashed forward nose-to-flank. Creepers clawed at my legs and I bumped along, scraping trees and branches that stretched into the narrow path. One branch thwacked my sore arm and nearly squeezed tears from my eyes. My mule had lost its head, and his partner followed his lead.

Chester's pistols cracked in quick succession. Two men screamed.

The path in front of us was widening and more light was coming through the jungle-canopy overhead. The trees on each side of the path thinned, both in size and concentration. What was that ahead?

"Lawrence—look!" Pacarina cheered.

The trees ended abruptly. A short swath of undergrowth and then—oh, joy! Green hills splotched by patches of white rock. Freedom!

I wrenched my mule's head to the left until he slid to a halt. "Did you find my pistols?"

She tossed me a saddlebag. I ripped it open and grasped a pistol in each hand. Sounds crunched through the forest, then Chester's mule rounded a corner. Chester was bent low over its head, his hands pinioning the arms of a little native who was perched on his back and trying to wrestle him off. Two more Mayamuras sprinted at the mule's flanks, their knives twinkling in the increasing sunlight. If they caught up with Chester's legs—

I kicked my mule and we dashed forward. I pointed the pistol in my right hand at the closest native and prayed that I wouldn't hit Chester. *Click.* Nothing happened. I pointed the other. *Click.* Nothing. Weren't they loaded?

Chester whizzed by on my left and something smacked into my mule. One of the natives rolled on the ground, leveled by my mule's broad chest.

Someone screamed behind me and a heavy weight thudded in the undergrowth. Chester must have found his knife.

A hand flung my right foot up and out of the stirrup. I grabbed at my mule's neck but the tough hair slipped through my fingers and I fell, slamming into the ground. A knife waved above my head. I kicked—something yielded to my boot and a man fell on me.

"Wait, Law, I'm coming!" Chester shouted, his voice strangely distant. Waiting didn't seem to be an option. My nerves tingled, my side ached, and my blood felt hot, but I forced the panic from my mind. *Pistols useless, sword remains.*

I grasped my sword-hilt with both hands and wrenched it from the scabbard. The man was off me, and the knife waved again. I thrust the sword up and the knife clanged, steel on steel—the fellow lost his balance again and toppled. The second native stood over me, his eyes staring like deep wells above his fiery cheeks. My arms were trapped under the first man's body. I stared at the falling knife.

"Hiyee!"

A shadow flew over me and struck the native. He collapsed, a knife-hilt sticking out of his chest.

"Hiyee!"

The native on my arms stopped struggling. Strong hands plucked the deadweight off and hauled me to my feet by my collar.

Chester let go and mopped his brow with his half of the sash. "And you said I brought too many knives."

I panted, my heart slowly squeezing back into my chest cavity. "Thanks," I gasped.

"My pleasure." Chester pointed at the ground. One of my pistols lay by the dead man's foot. "Why didn't you shoot?"

"They didn't work."

He picked it up. "Didn't work, eh?" He pulled the hammer back. "Next time, try cocking first."

Chapter 45

Crack.

"Anything?"

"You missed the target, Law."

"But did I hit the door?"

Chester took my second pistol with him while he checked the door. He ran his fingers over the scarred wood. "I do believe you did!"

I grinned.

He gave me back my pistol and I prepared for the next shot. I cocked the hammer.

We stood on thick English grass, Stoning estate, Lancashire, England. Home. I leveled my pistol and squinted over the smooth barrel. Some things had changed, but that sparrow wasn't any bigger.

Crack.

"Splendid, Law. You almost hit it that time!"

I felt warm inside as I set the pistol down. A few months ago, Chester would have been gloating over my miss. Now, he cheered when I came close.

Pacarina came down the walk from the house wearing one of her newest English dresses and being remarkably pretty.

"Haven't you boys had enough of pistols for a lifetime?" she asked. Her grin was once again fresh and lively. The sea voyage had refreshed her blooming cheeks and brought back that sparkle of harmless mischievousness. She was a young woman again.

"Not a bit, Sister," Chester said. "This is but the beginning of a long and profitable career. Someday you will hear of my fame as an American circus-man, Gentleman Chest with eyes like a hawk's and a chest of steel, Sharpshooter, Knife-thrower, and all-around splendid chap."

I laughed. "I'll be your manager. I believe you'd *pay* them to let you perform."

"The sign of a true sportsman." Chester flopped on the grass and motioned for us to join him. "Forget about this gentleman business for a moment, will you? Let's pretend we're back in Peru."

I lowered myself full-length beside him. Pacarina sat cross-legged, and toyed with the empty pistols.

"I'm afraid," Chester said, "that Don Carlos will have to fight his war with empty coffers. We turned out helping the Legion far more than had we stayed in its ranks."

"Do you want to go back to the British Legion?" Pacarina asked.

He shook his head decidedly. "No. I've not done with adventure, but I've done with regular army life. There's no space for creativity, particularly with your clothing."

"They do give you a uniform," I offered.

"I'd rather make my own."

"It impresses the girls." Pacarina grinned.

Chester laughed. "Pacarina, when my time comes to marry, you can pick out a good girl and let me know. You've more sense than Law and I added together."

We all laughed.

"At any rate," Chester continued, "here we are at last and 'all's well that ends well,' as Shaky Bill put it so well. Are they still working on Father's study?"

"The carpenters were paneling the walls when I left." Pacarina sighed. "The old study must have been so cozy before the fire. Your father is such a sweet man. He laughs when I mention the fire, and tells me that it was a good thing."

"And it was." I shook my head. "Pacarina, you have no idea how Father has changed. He's a new man. I gave him my report from Peru to add to his records, and he tore it up. 'Lawrence,' he says, 'your files went up in smoke with that fire, and my only regret is that it didn't happen sooner. I'll be *watching* you from now on, not reading about you.'"

Chester laughed. "He likes you, Pacarina. Three months ago he would have greeted you, treated you to a quote of Socrates, and said goodbye. If you made a very strong impression, he might even have started a file to see how you turned out in life."

Father's voice sounded nearby. "What's this?"

I rolled over. "Hello, Father."

His face had lost the lofty, other-worldly stare. He was dressed in a sporting coat and knee-high boots. He smiled down on us. "So this is where my children gather when they desert their old father."

"Not a bit, Dad," Chester said. "Sit down and have a chat."

He sank beside me. "How the laundry-maid will blink when she sees grass-stains on my trousers. Well, what were you discussing, Chester?"

"You, Dad. Isn't it wonderful? I haven't heard a shred of Socrates all week."

"And you will not next week either. Socrates may have had a large brain, but he didn't have children."

They kept talking, but I stopped listening. I just wanted to lay there and soak in the soft grass, the English country smell, the warm sun, the beautiful, peaceful feeling of familial fellowship. Father was a new man. He read a psalm to us every night, sometimes twice if it was an especially joyful one. Dinner no longer resembled a committee-meeting of mummies. We told stories. We laughed. Mother was still the same, spending her days with her blue-blooded friends, but if Father could change from a philosopher to a man, then there was hope for even her. Life was nearly wonderful.

There was only one thing that disturbed my mind. And it was very disturbing.

"Father," I said, "could I ask you a question in your study after lunch?"

"Of course, Lawrence. I'll be there whenever you are ready."

We soon adjourned for lunch, vanquished the meal, and retired to our rooms.

I stood before the mirror in my room adjusting my waistcoat when a click from the doorway notified me of Chester's presence.

"What *are* you doing, Law?"

"Finishing dressing."

I could see him clearly in the mirror without needing to turn. He folded his arms and leaned on the door frame. I didn't meet his eye.

"Where are you going?"

"Nowhere." My cravat looked slightly unbalanced. I tried to tense my trembling fingers enough to pull the corners straight.

"Nowhere, eh? So you're dandying yourself so you can stand in front of the mirror and admire?"

"No, I'm going to Father's study."

He frowned. "Then why the fussy clothes? It's not the old days. Visiting Father isn't like going before a Greek philosopher-king, anymore. What's the occasion?"

"Chester, you're a worse interrogator than Sabas himself."

"You didn't answer my question."

I sighed. "I'm dressing well because it—it somehow seems fitting." I selected a pair of white gloves from my drawer and tucked them into my left hand.

"Fitting?" Chester straightened. His arms unfolded. "Law—you're not—no, it couldn't—yes—could it?" His eyes widened. "It is! You're doing it!"

I swung my gloves nervously.

"Doing what?"

"You're asking for her hand!"

My stomach tightened. I stared at the floor. My cheeks rebelled, trying to mold into some type of silly, almost giddy smile. He was right.

I think that life is a satire of human emotions. My first thoughts of Pacarina had been regarding love—but only how I could stop Chester from loving her so that we could leave Spain. When she began to be like a sister, it felt natural, as if she belonged. Then—maybe it was in the cave, I'm not sure—my feelings started to change. I thought about the kind of man who would deserve her as a wife—and I found myself thinking harsh thoughts of any man who tried to take her. It began to seem, not that she belonged to me, but that we belonged to each other.

I woke to a massive blow on my chest that almost knocked me into the mirror.

"You're a brick, old chap!"

Chester grabbed my shoulders, lifted, and shook me till I was in danger of biting off my tongue. His face glowed with delight.

"How long did it take the idea to penetrate your thick skull?"

He slammed me back to earth. I groped for a chair and collapsed, breathless.

"Eh?"

"I've known for months that this was coming. It was only natural. She's so intelligent, and lively, and cheerful, and good-natured, and you're so—well, you're you." He slapped his thighs and looked like he might pick me up again. "You were bound to marry. And then of course, you read the whole Bible to her and brought her to Christ."

"God brought her."

"Yes, God brought her, and you were His herder. My only fear was that you might never realize that you were in love."

I forced myself out of the chair and tried to salvage at least a few elements of my awry clothing. My hands had been trembling before Chester came, and they still were, but I wasn't sure if I felt worse or better than before Chester's outbreak.

"My being in love and her returning the sentiment are two very different things," I said.

He roared. "You don't know if she loves you?"

My fingers stopped fumbling. I stared at him, every nerve tensed. "Do you think she does?"

"Do I think—oh, Lawrence." He stopped laughing long enough to wipe tears from his eyes. "My brain may not be museum quality, but if you—" he grinned at me. "Just go ask Father for permission to ask her."

In a moment, I settled my thoughts. I held out my hand. "Chester, come with me. We met her together, we fought for her together, we almost died for her together—it's only right that we should do this together too."

Ten minutes later, Father was smiling nearly as wide as Chester.

"As death has taken all of her natural authorities, I have as much right as any to stand in place of a father to Pacarina. As such, you have my permission and blessing to ask her hand in marriage, but you will abide by her decision."

He sighed. "Lawrence, you make me proud. I only wish that your journey to Peru had been successful, and that you had found the gold that would set you for life far better than I can."

Somehow the light, the air, the warmth, all seemed perfect. I looked him in the eye. "We didn't find the gold, father, but we *were* successful. When we left England, we were brothers *at* arms, always fighting, always warring."

Chester gripped my shoulder. "He's right, Father. But we're brothers *at* arms no longer. Now—we're brothers *in* arms."

"And—" I could restrain my lips no longer. I burst into an enormous smile. "I did find treasure. Where is she?"

He pointed to the library door.

I opened it. Pacarina sat in a chair, a book in her hands. She looked up and smiled at me. I smiled back, entered, and closed the door.

And here I close my story.

The End

Epilogue

Chester here. I'm rather a rotten writer, so I left the book-writing to Lawrence, but I do want to clear up a few things. That's why I made Law let me write this epi-thingy.

First, everything in this book is true. I'll be happy to provide satisfaction to any man who says differently. Of course, I can't say that I agree with Law's perspective on everything—there was nothing wrong with my hat—but he got the main facts right.

At first he wanted to write it history-style, like some dry old textbook—probably in Greek, or Latin—but I sat on that. I made him add some color to things, but believe me, all the color in the world wouldn't properly relate what we went through. So, it's all true, and if you found it interesting reading, that's because I made him write with color, but it's not exaggerated.

Tomorrow is a wedding, so I must go try on my top hat. My new sash fits splendidly, though Lawrence won't let me wear pistols during the wedding. The brute. Perhaps I'll wear them anyway. I don't think he'll look at anything I wear tomorrow—unless it's a white dress and veil.

There are just two more things I want to say, so I'll cut to the chase and say them. One, Law made certain that no one could find Mayamura territory just by reading his book. So don't try. That treasure isn't yours. Second, if you ever come across an adventure, let us know. I'm not finished with life—I've just started. And I've a feeling that I won't be leaving Law at home next time, either.

As the Spanish say, *adieu*.

Your obedient servant,

Chester Stoning

To learn more about the author and other books in the Men of Grit series, visit www.johnjhornbooks.com.